BAD
TO THE
BONE

BAD TO THE BONE

BY
JOHN J. LAHM

SEAWORTHY PUBLICATIONS, INC.　•　MELBOURNE, FLORIDA

Published in the USA and distributed worldwide by:
Seaworthy Publications, Inc.
6300 N. Wickham Rd
Unit 130-416
Melbourne, FL 32940
Phone 310-610-3634
Email orders@seaworthy.com
www.seaworthy.com

Library of Congress Cataloging-in-Publication Data

Names: Lahm, John, 1947- author.
Title: Bad to the bone / John Lahm.
Description: Melbourne, Florida : Seaworthy Publications, Inc., [2021] | Summary: "Could this have actually happened? That's the question you will be left to ponder as you read Bad to the Bone, a science fiction novel with historical references about the unexpected arrival of a new species of shark that developed due to human medical waste seeping down through the Florida aquifer and coming out in offshore submarine springs. As such, this new breed of shark uniquely craves human blood and bone marrow due to DNA changes from ingesting medical byproducts over decades. When full-grown a member of this new species is the largest individual predator on earth. The story centers around the Kings Bay Nuclear Submarine Base in St. Marys, Georgia. Under the backdrop of the construction of the base that took place in the late 1970s, sudden brutal shark attacks began occurring. The attacks were so brutal, that the victim's bodies, if located, were stripped of all flesh and blood products down to the pulverizing of the victim's bones to get to the marrow. Meanwhile, many black, tannin-stained teeth are found washing up on nearby beaches. The Navy decides to remove a limestone mound found during a dredging operation and inadvertently releases a school of young predators into Kings Bay from their birthplace where they escape into the coastal waters and start to raise havoc with local fishermen and beachgoers. Later the Navy uses one of the most famous spy ships in the world, the Glomar Explorer, to lift the 100-ton mound and the mystery underneath. Everything is labeled secret by the Navy, so news of the new species is hushed as the Navy tries to avoid a public relations nightmare. Who knows? Maybe they did cover it all up.."-- Provided by publisher.
Identifiers: LCCN 2021009680 (print) | LCCN 2021009681 (ebook) | ISBN 9781948494175 (paperback) | ISBN 9781948494441 (epub)
Subjects: LCSH: Naval Submarine Base (Kings Bay, Ga.)--Fiction. | Glomar Explorer (Ship)--Fiction. | GSAFD: Science fiction.
Classification: LCC PS3612.A394 B33 2021 (print) | LCC PS3612.A394 (ebook) | DDC 813/.6--dc23
LC record available at https://lccn.loc.gov/2021009680
LC ebook record available at https://lccn.loc.gov/2021009681

PREFACE

Kings Bay is a flat, marshy piece of land located on the southeast coast of Georgia. The land is bounded by the Atlantic Ocean to the east, and the Saint Marys River to the south, which separates Georgia and Florida with a western backdrop of Interstate 95.

Shortly after the last ice age 12,000 years ago, a tribe of Indians known as Timucua settled what is now known as Kings Bay. They planted and harvested crops twice a year, including corn, beans, pumpkins, squash, and wild fruits. They made bread from a plant called arrowroot. The Timucua hunted many kinds of animals including alligators, deer, brown bears, wildcats, lizards, and turkeys. They fished for trout, flounder, turbots, and mullet, as well as collecting clams, oysters, crayfish, and crabs. They developed such weapons as bows and arrows, clubs, spears, harpoons, and traps to assist their hunting. The Timucua were blessed by many ground-fed, freshwater springs with origins thousands of feet below the surface of the earth. These upwellings brought forth large deposits of dissolved limestone that strengthened the skeletal development of the tribe. Anthropologists suggest that the combination of mineral-rich spring water and a varied diet produced a population with an average height of seven feet tall.

The Timucua had early contacts with Juan Ponce de León who claimed Florida for Spain. The Spanish established a mission on Kings Bay and blessed the Saint Marys River. Missionaries arrived and taught the Timucua people the Christian religion. The Timucua suffered several epidemics caused by newly introduced European diseases in the years between 1613 to 1617 A.D., as well as 1649 to 1650 A.D. The Spanish surrendered their holdings to the English in 1763. They did, however, gain the territory back in 1783 and held it until 1819, but by this time the Timucua had already died out or had merged with other tribes, making the Timucua tribe extinct.

The town of Saint Marys began to grow during the 1800s and Kings Bay was converted into a rice plantation until the beginning of the Second World War. In 1941, the U.S. Army took control of Kings Bay and established an ammunition loading facility. In July 1978, the Army depot was transferred to the Navy with the intent of establishing a forward refit site for Submarine Squadron 16 operating out of Rota, Spain. The Navy Department, as required by federal law, funded an environmental impact study, which included a public hearing. Hearing dates were placed in the Saint Marys, Amelia Island, and Jacksonville, Florida papers.

CHAPTER ONE

The winter sun began to dip below the Georgia pines as cars bearing Florida and Georgia tags began to fill the parking lot of Saint Marys town hall.

Sheriffs and deputies directed traffic and escorted people to their seats. At the far end of the hall were seated Navy officials, state representatives, and the mayor of Saint Marys. The moderator glanced at his watch, and then tapped on the speaker with his finger; the noise reverberated throughout the hall. Idle chatter acquiesced, and the room slowly grew quiet.

"My name is Captain Vince Stevens," the captain said with a clear of his throat. "The Navy Department dispatched our team here tonight to give the residents of the communities that may be impacted by the construction and operation of the proposed refit facility a chance to voice their concerns." He stared out at the audience who stared back. "If you have a question, please raise your hand..."

A bearded man in the front row raised his hand and was acknowledged. "Sir, my name is Jamey Bull," he began. "I'm the spokesman for the Saint Marys commercial fishing fleet. The Army depot over at Kings Bay has always permitted us to drag the bay. Will the Navy continue to honor the Army's agreement?"

A rustle accompanied by anticipatory nods made the rounds near Mr. Bull.

Captain Stevens replied, "I think our site engineer can answer that question for you."

A man seated at the end of the table stood up and introduced himself to the audience. "My name is Captain Thomas McDowell; I will be responsible for the dredging and pier construction at Kings Bay. Currently, we are honoring the past tenant's non-binding agreement to allow fishing in Kings Bay. Of course, when dredging begins, a restriction may be implemented. Does that answer your question, sir?"

"Yes," replied the fisherman. The frown on his face revealed his disappointment with the answer.

A woman's hand went up in the front row. The Captain acknowledged her. "My name's Cindy Ware," she said. "And I'm here to represent Friends of Manatee. My question is directed to the site engineer. Sir, what effect will this *dredging* have on the endangered manatee and other marine species?"

"Ma'am, unfortunately, the dredging of Kings Bay will destroy some of the plant life that the manatees feed on."

Assorted grumbles bubbled up around Cindy.

"But..." The captain held up a calming hand. "But there's an upside that you may not be aware of," he said, "The missile-carrying submarines, which will be home-ported at Kings Bay, will discharge large amounts of warm water, which incidentally, is safe to drink, and the manatee will be attracted to these warm outflows during the cool winter months. A study conducted at Charleston, South Carolina submarine base bears this out. If you would leave your name and address with me, I will send the report to you."

"Thank you very much," replied the questioner.

At the back of the hall, a man raised his hand with a piece of paper that he waved back and forth. He wore faded blue jeans and a white T-shirt. Red and blue tattoo lines ran down his arms and extended to his fingertips. The same weaving designs emerged from his shirt collar and ran through his face and head, which was shaved. Long lines etched age on his face and his eyes were black as coal. The audience was immediately drawn to this man, not only because of his tattoos but also because of his great height. No one in the hall had ever seen such a tall man.

A heckler in the crowded room yelled, "Y'all some kind of basketball star?"

This sudden off-colored joke caught the people by surprise. They began laughing in unison. The moderator, Captain Stevens, didn't smile, nor did Sheriff Lowellin, seated in front of the heckler. The sheriff slowly craned his neck to look at the heckler, whose smile had quickly disappeared from his face. "Ah, Sheriff, we's juss havin' a little fun, that's all."

The sheriff took his right hand and wrapped it around his left wrist and turned it slowly. "Next time you yell out like that, I'm gonna arrest you for disorderly conduct."

Calm was instantly restored to the hall. Captain Stevens asked the tattooed man about the piece of paper he kept waving back and forth.

"This is for you, sir."

A deputy took the paper from the man and walked swiftly to the front of the hall and handed the paper to the Captain, who glanced at it and placed it on the desk. "May I ask your name, sir?"

He stretched his arms above his head, and with his fingertips, touched the ceiling of the hall. "My name is Caradon. I am the last living member of the Timucua people who inhabited this land long before the white man arrived. The map I gave you, written by the white man, testifies to my people's ownership. I come here today to protect the destruction of Timucua burial sites." The man lowered his arms and sat down.

Captain Stevens responded, "This map indicates that southeastern Georgia and northern Florida were occupied by your tribe. Concerning the upcoming operation at Kings Bay, we have assembled a team of anthropologists and geologists, with the cooperation of the University of Florida, to identify artifacts of past cultures and remove graves when warranted."

Caradon continued staring at Captain Stevens with his intense eyes, then turned and walked briskly out of the meeting without excusing himself.

The floor was given to a man who identified himself as Thomas Lacrass, Camden County, Georgia's redevelopment commissioner. "What economic benefits can Camden County expect from the building of the base?"

Captain Stevens sifted through his paperwork until he came upon a report entitled *Economic Impact-Kings Bay*.

Stevens looked at the numbers then responded to the commissioner. "The initial cost of dredging and building piers and..." he flipped a few more pages, "and the dry dock will be over 250 million dollars. The Navy will employ 2,000 civilian Federal workers and a complement of 1,500 military personnel. The annual payroll will average fifty million dollars. The Navy has decided to build a modern four-lane highway from the main gate of the base to I-95. The federal government will finance the entire project and no funds will be required from the county or the state of Georgia.

"Thank you, sir!" replied the commissioner. "That's the answer the people of Camden County wanted to hear. Jobs for the local people."

The crowd began to clap in agreement.

The Captain tapped his pen on the table and smiled slightly. *This group was won over by the promise of jobs*, he thought. He motioned to the large man at the end of the table. "I would now like to give the floor to Mayor Tubbs of Saint Marys, Georgia."

The mayor pushed his large frame out of his chair. His cheeks resembled a pair of ripe apples, one possibly holding a moist chaw of tobacco.

The mayor cleared his throat. "I would like to thank Captain Vince Stevens and his group for holding this meeting," he began. "The overflowing crowd in this hall shows the interest the community has on this matter."

Some of the people near the doors began to leave, and the mayor raised his voice, like a preacher in a church.

"I have one last announcement to make! The town of Saint Marys has provided a free buffet for your enjoyment."

Servers entered the hall carrying trays of fried and boiled shrimp, oysters, sea trout, hush puppies, and bread.

"Go on, eat..." The mayor motioned to the crowd with his hands. "All you want," he said. "If you finish that, we'll bring more."

The deputy mayor, who was seated next to Tubbs, stood up and surveyed the crowd. "Mayor Tubbs, I don't see anyone leaving the hall."

Mayor Tubbs chuckled slightly. "It's funny, the power good food has on a person's mind," Tubbs said, putting his arm on his friend's shoulder.

The deputy mayor quipped, "Especially if it's free."

Mayor Tubbs belly laughed. "Come on," he said. "Let's get us something to eat."

CHAPTER TWO

Preparations for the construction of the submarine base began in earnest in early spring. The Navy Department awarded a construction contract to a company known as Conway & Martinson Construction, a subsidiary of Warbird Industries. C&M's mission was to build piers and dry-dock facilities. A site was cleared, and temporary construction trailers were put in place. A preliminary conference was held in the Naval Engineer's office. All the contractors involved in the construction would get to know each other and lay the groundwork for the project.

Naval officers from Washington and representatives from C&M introduced the players, including Captain Thomas McDowell, site engineer, and Joe Brantley, superintendent for C&M. The two shook hands across the table. After the meeting ended, the captain asked Brantley if he wanted to tour the site.

"That's fine, sir," Brantley said. "Ready when you are."

They climbed into McDowell's shiny service truck and drove down a dusty service road.

"Mr. Brantley, I'm going to give you a general overview of what this base will look like after construction is completed. The road we are riding on will eventually have support facilities for the atomic submarines that will be berthed to your right in Kings Bay."

The road turned sharply to the left, then McDowell mashed the brake.

The officer and Brantley got out of the truck and climbed a small hill. The engineer pointed to the far end of Kings Bay.

"See that creek coming into the bay?"

"Yes, sir," replied Brantley.

"That's where the dry dock will begin. It'll be three hundred feet deep and over a thousand feet long."

"Why such a large dry dock?" asked Brantley.

"Well, this is unofficial..." the captain began with a skeptical scowl. "But the Navy plans to homeport its new class of submarines here."

"Excuse me, sir, but may I ask a dumb question?"

"What's your question, Mr. Brantley?"

"Well, sir, I've been in this business a pretty long time," Brantley said.

"Sure," said Captain McDowell.

"Long enough to know that you don't build a Navy base on a swamp," Brantley concluded.

"You don't?"

"Not unless you're looking for severe erosion problems."

"That's a good question you asked," the captain said. "About four years ago I was asked to do a feasibility study on building a new submarine base on the East Coast. At that time, Kings Bay was not even on the list."

"Then why do you think they wanted it here?" asked Brantley.

"Politics! pure and simple," McDowell said after he spat. "President Carter's home is the Peach State, and he was a submarine captain in the Navy."

Mr. Brantley cracked a smile. "Well, I guess that's a good reason to build a submarine base at Kings Bay."

"Come on," the captain said, motioning toward the truck. "Let me show you the rest of the layout."

They drove a short distance when suddenly the truck screeched to a halt.

"Mr. Brantley, look at the size of that!"

"What, sir?"

"Alligator," McDowell said, pointing.

"Ah yes," said Brantley. "A near ten-footer, sir"

The sudden commotion spooked the alligator and he crawled into chest-high saw grass. The officer watched the alligator until it disappeared. He then turned to Mr. Brantley, his face full of worry. "My construction marker stakes lie just inside that saw grass."

Brantley's eyes widened. "Sir, do we have a shotgun on board?"

Captain McDowell began to laugh heartily. "Just kidding, my friend." He patted Brantley on the shoulder, and then drove off.

The land gave way to a flat expanse of sand. Construction stakes with multicolored markers could be seen flapping in the breeze. McDowell stopped the truck, picked up a set of blueprints, and got out of the truck.

"Where we headed, sir?"

"The center of the lake."

They walked from stake to stake while the engineer occasionally reviewed the blueprint. His pace suddenly quickened. "There it is!" Before them was a stake driven into the sand. The letters read: C cut 60.

"This, Mr. Brantley, is the center of the lake that will be dredged by your company. The bottom will average sixty feet with depths up to one-twenty, where pilings will be driven."

Brantley bent over and picked up a handful of sand and let it flow through his fingers. "Sir, what lies below this sandy surface?"

"Sandstone," the captain said. "The sub-strata, based on test core samples, are composed of fragmented sandstone. There's a stratum of hardened limestone that may be difficult to excavate, but the added cost was included in your company's contract bid."

"When can we start dredging?" asked Brantley.

"All the engineering and environmental reports are approved, so as soon as tomorrow if you like."

Brantley nodded his head in agreement. They walked back to the truck and returned to the construction trailers.

"I'm going to get something to eat at the officers' mess hall."

"Okay, sir," said Brantley.

"You wanna come along?"

"No, sir," replied Brantley. "I've got some calls to make, but thanks anyway for the offer."

"You bet."

"I'll see you in the morning, sir."

* * *

Brantley went into his office and called the company dredge operations at Galveston, Texas. Tim Achions answered the phone.

"Tim, this is Joe Brantley, up at Kings Bay, Georgia."

"Hey Joe!" said Tim. "How'd the meeting go?"

"Fine. All permits have been approved."

"Good, good."

"Hey, you have a floating dredge available?"

"We got a one-fifty-ton idled in Mobile Bay, Alabama," said Tim.

"I'll put in a rush order to have it delivered to Kings Bay. Anything else?"

"Yeah, I'm gonna need a thousand feet of discharge pipe."

"You got it!" Tim said. "You need anything else?"

"No, not at this time, but I'm sure I'll be calling you again soon."

"Okay, bud."

"Bye," said Brantley.

"Say, Joe," Tim offered up.

"Yeah?"

"You still smoking that cherry-blend pipe tobacco?"

"Yeah, sure, why do you ask?"

"I can smell that sweet scent all the way down here in Galveston."

The two men both had a good laugh and then said their goodbyes.

* * *

The following week, a strange-looking machine entered Kings Bay. A massive rotating boom and suction pipe that was connected to the deckhouse began to engulf the shoreline forming a deep lake as it falump-falump-falumped along. A long exhaust pipe carried sediment to a large sludge lagoon where it discharged and dried, later to be spread by a bulldozer.

Captain McDowell drove out to the exhaust pipe to take some soil samples. He noticed that the bulldozer operator had stopped working. The operator got out of the machine and picked up something from the sand. Curious, the captain walked over to the bulldozer operator to introduce himself to the man.

"Hi there," said the captain.

"Heya," said the operator.

"My name is Captain McDowell, the chief of operations on this project."

The man cleaned his hand off on his pants and shook the engineer's hand. "Pleased to meet ya. Name's Joe Pike. I work for C&M Construction."

"What's that in your hand?"

"Oh nuttin'," the operator said. "Juss an old shark's tooth." He brushed off the palm-sized tooth and handed it to Captain McDowell, who examined it closely. The surface was jet black and highly polished.

McDowell ran his index finger down the serrated sides of the tooth. "Ouch!" he exclaimed. "This shark still bites."

"Yessir. I gotta bucket full on the 'dozer."

"What are you going to do with all these teeth?"

"I'm selling them to Captain Bob," the operator said. "He owns the Ship's Anchor Novelty Shop in Fernandina Beach. Gives me five bucks for the big ones, and a dollar for the smaller ones."

"Fernandina Beach? Isn't that where they have the Shrimp Festival?"

"First of May... every year, sir. That's when the pastor of Saint Michael's Church comes down to the piers and blesses our fishin' fleet."

"Do you live in Fernandina?" asked McDowell.

"Yessir, my kin has lived there more than a hundred years. The festival used to be sort of a quiet affair, but lately it's become much more commercialized. Got pirates fightin' it out on the Amelia River, live bands playin', and of course, lots of fresh shrimp."

"The festival sounds interesting," replied McDowell. He looked at his watch. "Welp, I better get going... it's been nice talking to you."

Pike walked back to his bulldozer, and gently placed the shark's tooth into a bucket. He started the machine and began to spread sand in front of him, ever watchful for blackened relics of the past with dollar signs on them.

* * *

The Kings Bay dredge site was not the only place where blackened teeth were being found. Incoming waves of the Atlantic Ocean began to discharge sharp objects on North Beach, Amelia Island. Residents and tourists had been accustomed to finding an array of multi-colored shells, an occasional conch shell, or some driftwood, but this was different. The beachcombers began to find and target these new arrivals to the beach. The locals soon realized that the best time to hunt for these artifacts was at high tide. They met informally at the water's edge and discussed and displayed their various finds.

Arthur Greiner, a new resident to North Beach, was in the middle of unpacking his furniture when his wife gazed out of the window where she saw surf fishermen moving to the water's edge

Arthur plopped down on the couch in his driveway and wiped his brow. "Honey," he called out. "Why don't we stop unpacking and go for a walk on the beach?"

"Sounds like a good idea," Mrs. Greiner said, grabbing her hat and sunglasses. "This stuff will still be here when we get back."

"If I get my *back* back," mumbled Arthur, hoisting himself back up to his feet with a groan.

The Greiners left their oceanfront home and walked along the shoreline. Gentle waves lapped at their feet.

"Boy, is this water warm," commented Arthur.

"Right?" his wife replied. "Like bathwater, unlike those cold waters in New Jersey." Mrs. Greiner noticed some interesting shell formations that were exposed by the outgoing tide. She bent over and began to collect the most interesting-looking ones.

Arthur walked up to the surf fisherman who was waiting anxiously for the first bite on his line. "Any luck?"

"Nah, not yet," the fisherman replied. "I'm waiting for the tide to start pulling out hard, that's when the fish start biting."

"Why would they bite then, instead of, let's say, low tide?" asked Arthur.

"'Cause now's the time when baitfish hiding in shallow water will be forced to retreat." The fisherman worked his line a few times. "Right into the hungry mouths of predators."

Arthur looked past the fisherman and noticed a small group of people gathered. "What're those people doing over there? I don't see any fishing rods."

The surf fisherman glanced up the beach. "Oh, they's a bunch of local beachcombers," he said dry as the sand. "Call themselves the *Shark Tooth Hunters*."

"Shark Tooth Hunters... is that so," said Greiner.

"I'll tell you... I've caught a lot of sharks in my life," the fisherman continued, "including Mako and the Great White, all of 'em. But I've never seen teeth like the ones been washing up here lately. Sharp as razors but black as night." Suddenly the fisherman felt a vibration run down his fishing rod to his fingertips. "Something's mouthing my bait!" he exclaimed.

"Well, good luck."

The fisherman, fully immersed in his fishing, did not respond to Arthur's goodbye.

Arthur casually walked up to the group of people who stood before him. "How are you all doing today?"

"Fine," replied one of the women in the group, "And yourself?"

"Oh, I'm just happy to get away from the unpacking."

"Newbies, huh?" one of the men said.

Arthur nodded. "Guilty as charged."

"You the people that bought the beach house at the end of Fletcher Ave?"

"Yes," Arthur said. "We got tired of the cold winters in Philadelphia and decided to retire down here."

"Hope you enjoy our island as much as we do."

"Thank you," said Arthur.

"By the way, my name is Lynn Sanders. I'm on the Amelia Island Welcoming Committee. Would you like us to stop by when you're settled in?

"Sure, sounds fine," said Arthur.

"Don't you need to check with the captain?" Lynn said, nodding toward Arthur's wife, still hunting shells.

"Oh," Arthur said with a chuckle. "She delegates housewarming invites to her first mate."

"It's all set then," said Lynn.

"Hey, if you don't mind me being nosy..." Arthur said. "The fisherman down the beach told me that you were shark tooth hunters."

Lynn smiled. "Well, he's right."

A potbellied man with a full beard reached into his blue jeans and retrieved a palm-sized tooth and handed it to Arthur. "Seen anything like this before?"

"No, I must say I've never seen a fossil tooth as large as this one. I'm impressed."

"How old ya figure that this tooth is?" asked the whiskered man.

Arthur fingered the tooth. "I'd estimate that this Carcharodon tooth is about 30 million years old."

"But Captain Bob told us that these teeth were 50 million years old and that the only remains of ancient sharks are their teeth."

"We can resolve the first question by having a specimen analyzed or carbon-dated."

"Sounds expensive... right?" asked the bearded man.

"No, not necessarily," replied Arthur. "I worked as a paleontologist at the Academy of Natural Science in Philadelphia. We performed radiocarbon dating all the time. To answer the second question though... Dr. Gordon Hubbell has discovered a fossilized shark, with its skull, jaw structures, and all its hundreds of teeth intact."

"Well tribe, looks like we got a shark expert among us," said Lynn.

"Would you like to join our group?" asked the bearded fellow.

"Yes, I would," replied Arthur.

"Well we'll need to hold a vote," said Lynn. "All in favor..."

A scattering of "Ayes" peppered up from the group.

"It's official!" said the bearded man. "Now, all you need is a pair of sharp eyes and the willingness to get your feet wet."

The group began to disperse in both directions down the beach. Arthur watched as the Atlantic Ocean expelled shell material on the beach then retreated again. Arthur spread the material with his foot, but no shark teeth appeared. He scanned the beach and watched as the club members began to reach down to retrieve what had washed up.

Suddenly, a black object deposited by a wave lay within his grasp. He reached over to pick it up when a second wave swept the tooth away. Arthur could hear laughter behind him.

"What'd I tell you about sharp eyes? When you spot a tooth washed up on the beach, you gotta grab it right away!"

Arthur thanked the bearded man for his advice and soon began collecting shark teeth.

CHAPTER THREE

Work at the Kings Bay dredge site was going smoothly until one afternoon Captain McDowell received a call from the construction superintendent.

"Sir, we got a problem."

"What is it, Mr. Brantley?"

"The vacuum head," said Brantley.

"What's it doing now?"

"Well, it's come upon a mound of hardened material that can't be sucked into the pipe."

"Okay..."

"You think we can go down into the pit and check it out?"

"Yes, of course," said Captain McDowell.

"I think we need the divers," said Brantley.

"All right," said the captain. "Call the dive team ASAP to meet us at the temporary dock."

McDowell picked up his work bag and headed to meet Brantley.

* * *

The two men arrived at the temporary dock almost at the same moment and got into a waiting workboat. The dive team was already aboard donning their equipment.

"Where to?" asked the pilot.

"Past the dredge to the far end of the lake."

Brantley introduced the head of the dive team who was busy checking his equipment. "Jack, this is Captain McDowell. He's the chief naval engineer on the project."

"Pleased to meet you, sir," Jack said. "Could you give me an idea of what we are looking for?"

"We'll have a better idea when we get there," replied McDowell.

The lead diver leaned over the side of the boat and gazed into the lake waters below. "I'll tell you one thing: the visibility is a hundred percent, and that's fine with me."

The workboat motored past the floating dredge and then began to slow. The diver suddenly stood up. "Damn it, I opened my mouth too soon."

"What do you see?" asked Brantley.

"You see that dirty water mixing with the clean?" the diver asked.

Both Brantley and McDowell nodded.

"My visibility will be cut in half."

Captain McDowell reached into his workbag and retrieved a glass beaker. He removed the cork and then took a sample of the lake water. After he inserted the cork, McDowell flipped the beaker and watched the tiny bits of sediment drift to the bottom.

The diver asked, "What do you see?"

"Tannin," replied McDowell.

"Tannin... is that poisonous or something?"

Captain McDowell smiled. "No, it's perfectly safe to swim in. Tannin is a product of rotted plant material that seeps through the ground, and into the aquifer."

Brantley asked, "What's it doing here?"

"Apparently, the dredge has exposed a spring of some sort."

Brantley noticed that the outboard engine had increased its speed. "Are we going faster?"

"No," replied the pilot. "I'm experiencing turbulence. It seems to be coming from the direction of the mound."

"Make a swing around it and see if the turbulence is the same at the other entry points," Brantley said, raising his voice above the roaring motor.

The workboat circled the mound and from time to time steered directly towards it. Brantley kept a record of the RPM reading of the engine. After making the circle, the pilot allowed the upwelling to push the workboat away from the mound.

"Where to now?" asked the pilot.

"Drive 'er straight into the mound," said Brantley.

"All right..." said the pilot. "Hold on, everybody, it's going to get a little bumpy."

With the engine at full throttle, the workboat cut through the oncoming current.

Brantley crawled to the front of the boat and picked up the end of the landing rope. "When we hit the mound, I'm going to jump off and hold the rope taut until Captain McDowell gets off. You guys can drift away from the strong current and start your survey dives."

Everyone on the boat nodded in agreement.

The boat pushed through the current and landed unceremoniously against the mound. Brantley scrambled off the boat with Captain McDowell in tow. Brantley released the rope and watched as the boat was pushed away.

"We got a lot of water current from under this rock," said Brantley. "A helluva lot."

"I agree with you fully," replied McDowell. He began to walk around the edge of the mound, taking temperature readings as he went. Plumes of darkened water billowed out, bringing with them a variety of sea life. Shrimp and jellyfish retreated to the deep waters of Kings Bay. Fiddler crabs the size of thumbnails struggled through the maelstrom and climbed onto the mound. The scene reminded McDowell of the Normandy Invasion. Allied troops climbed the sheer granite cliffs, and then assembled on the high ground by the tens of thousands.

McDowell reached down and picked up a retreating fiddler. The red and blue claw, larger than the crab's body, slashed at his attacker with abandon. McDowell moved his wrist within range of the pinchers and was attacked. He felt the points of the claws press into his skin, but the irate fiddler was unable to draw blood. McDowell pulled the crab loose and placed it on the ground, where it rejoined the safety of its thousands of fiddler comrades, who protested the intrusion of the men by raising their claws in defiance.

McDowell continued to walk around the mound until he met up with Brantley, who had made radio contact with the workboat. "How's the dive team making out?" asked McDowell.

"Oh, he's getting tired of fighting the strong currents, but he should be finished with his survey shortly."

McDowell noticed an odd-looking rock formation protruding from the surface of the mound. He began to chip away at the base of the formation until it broke off. He handed the stone fragment to Brantley. "See the hole that runs through the center?"

Brantley raised the stone in front of his face. A glint of the midday sun struck Brantley's eye. "I see it, sir. What causes this to happen?"

"Although limestone is very hard, it is susceptible to wear from contact with the water. This process takes millions of years to complete, but the result is a series of tunnels and caverns that weave under the earth's surface."

"That's pretty interesting," replied Brantley.

McDowell marked the limestone fragment, and then put it in a plastic bag. He retrieved a measuring tape and blueprints. "Mr. Brantley, would you be so kind as to help me get a reading on the length and the width of this structure?"

"No problem, sir." He grabbed the spool of tape and walked around the mound. "Thirty feet wide," he yelled into the wind. The two men repositioned themselves lengthwise. "Sixty feet," came the call.

McDowell released the end of the tape.

Brantley reeled in the tape and then radioed the workboat. "You finished with the survey, over?"

"Affirmative," came the reply.

"Well, you boys sit tight!" Brantley said. "I'll give you a call when it's time to pick us up."

"Copy that."

Brantley walked over to McDowell and peeked over his shoulder. "What are you looking at, sir?"

After studying the blueprint carefully, McDowell said, "Mr. Brantley, my print indicates that a pier is to be installed here. This mound must be removed. We may have to pour concrete into the shaft to block the erosion of the pier piling."

"Yes, sir."

McDowell rolled up the blueprint and placed it in his workbag. "Are my eyes going bad, or is that the tide coming in? I swear that my workbag was at least five feet from the waterline, and now it's ready to float away."

Brantley reached into his wallet and pulled out a tide chart. "Yep, you're right," he said, squinting at the chart. "Tide's corning in." He glanced at the moon phases on the chart. "Oh, shit!" he exclaimed.

"What's the matter?" asked McDowell.

"We're going to have a full moon for the next couple of days. That will cause the waters to rise above the mound during the high tide."

"Looks like you will have to work this job around the tides."

Brantley nodded and radioed the workboat to pick them up. The craft responded by pushing through the outflowing current, its bow landing against the mound. Brantley took hold of the bow, allowing the captain to climb aboard. He then rolled into the boat, which immediately drifted away from the mound.

"Where to?" asked the pilot.

"Head on back to the dock," replied Brantley. He then motioned to the head of the dive team with the end of his pipe. "What did you see down there?"

The diver scratched his head. "Well, let's see. Suppose you got a pot of potatoes boiling on the stove, and for some reason, the lid is a little too big and doesn't sit well on the pot. The boiling water gushes out past the edge of the lid. That's the best way to describe what's going on down there."

"Observe anything else?" asked Captain McDowell.

"Yeah, the water coming out of there is as warm as bathwater."

McDowell looked at his notes. "I got a temperature reading averaging eighty-six degrees Fahrenheit."

"Why's the water so warm?" asked Brantley.

"Thermal convection," replied McDowell. "This spring water probably had its origins thousands of feet below the surface. The higher temperature you get at the wellhead, the deeper the source."

"That's interesting, sir, I didn't learn that at school."

"You can learn something new every day," replied McDowell.

The workboat reached the wharf, and the occupants disembarked and walked toward the trailers.

Captain McDowell looked at his watch. "Mr. Brantley, I've got to run. The base commander doesn't like anyone coming late for his briefings."

"See you in the morning, sir."

* * *

Brantley walked into the trailer and called C&M's Jacksonville office. Bob Wells, the yard foreman, answered the phone.

"Hey, Wells this is Brantley, up here in Kings Bay."

"Heya Brantley."

"Say, we got a problem. The dredge is down."

"Broke down?" asked Wells.

"No, no, the dredge is working just fine. We just got some rock to bust up."

"So you need a crew?" asked Wells.

"Yes, and some heavy equipment."

"Alrighty."

"Up here by tomorrow morning."

"Tomorrow?"

"Yeah. Send a crane with a digging bucket and a man basket, a compressor and hose, a jackhammer, and some portable lighting. This job is going to run around the clock till it's finished. I'll need a three-man crew to start the day shift. Tell them to be at the main gate at seven sharp. I'll get them signed up, and get their body passes, and stickers for their cars. I'll tell you, Wells, it takes more time to sign people up and get a pass than to do the job. Do you know that I must pass through three checkpoints just to get to the job site? The first two checkpoints aren't bad. But when you come up to the last checkpoint, there's a big sign that reads, *Attention. When alarm sounds and red lights flash, stop all vehicles, shut off engines.* And so on and so forth."

"Sounds perfectly maddening."

"Right? And you can't start your vehicle until the alarm stops. So last week a whole line of cars got stopped just before we got to the job site. The sirens went off, and flashing lights began to blink up and down the road. Next, a wooden barricade drops down in front of us. I must have been sitting there for what seemed an hour. I guess that the guy behind me got impatient. He pulled out from behind me and went around the barricade. You wouldn't believe what happened next."

"What? What?" asked Wells.

"Out of the side of the ditch lurches a mammoth camouflaged half-track, to block the road. Marines with automatic weapons bailed out of the back of the truck and surrounded the car like bees on honey. They dragged the man out of his car, handcuffed him, and took him away."

"What ultimately happened to him?" asked Wells.

"He must have been fired because I don't see him around here anymore," Brantley said.

The men chuckled and said goodbye. Brantley finished his paperwork.

* * *

McDowell arrived on time at the base headquarters and began to sift through his paperwork. Officers from other commands began to filter into the conference room and take their seats. Captain James Jarvis, base commander, entered the conference room in his dress whites and stood behind his desk. Everyone in the room stood up to show their respect for Jarvis. Jarvis sat down and then motioned everyone in the room to be seated. "Raise your hand if you have any progress reports."

Two hands went up. Jarvis recognized McDowell.

"Sir, the civilian dredge is down," said Captain McDowell.

"Perfect," said Captain Jarvis.

"We expect a construction delay of no more than four days, sir."

Captain Jarvis noted it in his book. He then acknowledged the second officer, Lieutenant Robert Brock, chief security officer for Kings Bay Submarine Base.

"Sir, we arrested a man the other day on federal trespassing charges. He tried to walk through the main gate without a pass."

"Where is this suspect now?" asked Jarvis.

"A holding cell at the federal courthouse in Camden County, Georgia."

Captain Jarvis began to tap the end of his pen on the table, and then he looked at the security officer. "Is that the tattooed man I've seen hanging around the front gate?"

"The same, sir."

"Is he affiliated with an environmental group, such as Greenpeace?"

"I don't think so, sir."

Captain Jarvis' neck began to swell, and the pitch of his voice became loud, "Do you know what that so-called environmental group did to our sister submarine base in Bremerton, Washington? Blocked a Trident Submarine from leaving the base until a federal judge intervened and locked their asses up. I think that group is funded by the Soviets. As for this nut, he may be working alone. When is the hearing to be held?" asked Jarvis.

"Tomorrow at zero nine hundred hours, sir," replied the security officer.

"Make sure that you attend the hearing. Is the public relations officer in the room?" asked Jarvis.

Lieutenant James McPeake raised his hand. "Sir...?"

"You go with Brock to the hearing. If there are reporters at the courthouse, try to gauge their intentions. If they are hostile, don't confront them, but get in contact with Mayor Tubbs. Tell him that the Navy Department would like to avoid bad press which could be detrimental to the further expansion of the base. Are there any other questions? None? Then this meeting is over."

CHAPTER FOUR

The following morning, Lieutenants Brock and McPeake sat in the front row of federal court. Directly across from the public relations officer sat the suspect.

Brock elbowed McPeake. "There's the psycho we arrested. Ain't he freaky looking?"

"He sure is," replied McPeake. "I'll bet that he doesn't weigh more than a hundred and twenty pounds."

"He told me that he was fasting," replied Brock. "We offered him food, but he wouldn't touch it."

"All rise," came the call from the bailiff. "Judge William Cox presiding."

The federal judge took his perch high above the audience. "The first case to be heard will be The United States of America versus Mr. Caradon on federal trespassing charges. How do you plead?"

The judge looked at the defendant and was surprised by his appearance. This ought to be an interesting case, thought the judge.

Caradon raised his arms high above his head. "The president in Washington claims I trespassed on his land," he bellowed. "But how can you buy or sell the sky... the land? The idea speaks strange to me."

The federal prosecutor raised his hand to protest but was brushed off by Judge Cox. "Go on, Mr. Caradon."

Caradon continued: "Strange indeed! If we do not own the freshness of the air and the sparkle of the water, how can you buy them? Sell them? Trespass upon them? Every part of the earth is sacred to my people. Every shining pine needle, every sandy shore, every mist in the dark woods, every deep green meadow, and every humming insect. All are holy in the memory and experience of my people. We know the sap, which courses through the trees, as we know the blood that courses through our veins. We are part of the earth and it is a part of us. The perfumed flowers are our sisters. The bear, the deer, the great eagle... these are our brothers. The rocky crests, the juices in the meadow, the body heat of the pony and man all belong to the same family. The glistening water that moves in the streams and rivers is not just water, but the blood of our ancestors. Each ghostly reflection in the clear waters of the lakes tells of events and memories in the life of my people. The water's murmur is the voice of my father's father. The rivers are our brothers. They quench our thirst. They carry our canoes and feed our children. So, you must give to the rivers the kindness you would give any brother. The air is precious to us because the air shares its spirit with all the life it supports. The wind that gave our grandfather his first breath also receives his last sigh. The wind gives our children the spirit of life. So, if we sell you our land, you must keep it apart and sacred, as a place where a man can go to taste the wind that is sweetened by the meadow flowers. Will you teach your children what we have taught our children? That the earth is our mother? What befalls the earth befalls all the sons of the earth. This we know. The earth does not belong to man. Man belongs to the earth, and all things are connected like the blood that unites us all. Man did not weave the web of life; he is merely a strand in it. Whatever he does to the web, he does to himself. One thing we know: our god is also your god. The earth is precious to him and to harm the earth is to heap contempt upon its creator. Your destiny is a mystery to us. What will happen when the secret corners of the forest are heavy with the scent of many men, and the view of the ripe hills is blotted out by skyscrapers? Where will the thicket be? Gone! Where will the eagle be? Gone! On the day when the last memory of my people has vanished with this wilderness and this memory is only the shadow of a cloud moving across the salt marsh, will these shores and forest still be here? Will there be any of the spirit of my people left? As we are part of the land, you too are part of the land. This earth is precious to you whether you realize it or not. One thing we know: there is only one God. No man can be apart."

Caradon dropped his arms to his sides and said no more. Judge Cox told the defendant to be seated and then ordered a recess. He motioned to the prosecutor and the navy men to join him in his chambers. After the last man entered the room, the bailiff closed the door.

"Gentlemen," said the judge, "it is my opinion that this defendant is passionately committed to his cause, as witnessed by the eloquent speech he gave. I can give him ninety days in detention and request a court-ordered psychiatric examination of Mr. Caradon."

Lieutenant McPeake motioned to the judge, "Your honor, may I at least try to talk some reason into this man?"

"He seemed quite reasonable to me, Lieutenant," replied the judge, "But of course impress upon him, to the extent you can, that spending time in jail won't further his cause."

McPeake walked through the courtroom and pulled up a chair next to the defendant. "Mr. Caradon, my name is Lieutenant McPeake. I am the public relations officer at Kings Bay. Pleased to meet you, sir. Judge Cox is considering sending you to jail for an extended period. It is my hope that if you promise not to trespass on the base again, the judge will give you probation."

Caradon looked down at McPeake and said, "I shall comply with the judge's order."

"Good," replied McPeake. "Can I ask you when you first heard about the construction of the base? We placed an announcement in the Jacksonville, Amelia Island, and Saint Marys newspapers."

"The conch shell informs me of things to come."

"Conch? What the hell is that?"

"Have you never, as a child, picked up a large shell from the beach and cupped it over your ear, and heard the roar of the ocean, and the cry of the gulls? I put the conch to my ear and was told of the evil that is to befall my white brother."

Bearing an awkward grin, McPeake shook Caradon's hand, which enveloped his own. McPeake walked into the conference room. A few minutes later, the judge and prosecutor returned to the courtroom.

The judge sat down and told the defendant to rise. "Mr. Caradon, I am going to sentence you to a suspended sentence of ninety days. If you are arrested again after reentering Kings Bay Sub Base within that time frame, you will serve the full amount of time set forth by this court. You are hereby released. Next case!"

McPeake approached the courthouse parking lot exit and put on his right-hand turn signal. He turned his head to the left looking for oncoming traffic. What he saw was the thin vanishing frame of Caradon.

"Hey Brock, there goes your trespasser."

"Is he headed toward the base?"

"No, he's heading westbound."

"Good," replied the security officer.

McPeake changed his turn signal and made a left-hand turn.

"Where the hell you going, McPeake? You're not going to pick up that madman, are you?"

"Brock, I'm surprised at you. I would think that the security officer would want to know where the defendant lives."

"Well, alright, but if he stinks, he's gonna ride in the bed of the truck."

The truck drove past Caradon then slowed and pulled over.

"Where ya headed, sir?" asked McPeake.

"My home, which is west of Folkston."

"Hop in, we'll drive you there."

The old man raised his hand and blocked the sun's rays. "The position of the sun tells me that Kings Bay is directly the opposite of the way I am traveling."

"Oh, our security officer would like to see where you live."

The old man laughed heartily, then climbed into the back seat of the truck.

"So the security officer would like to see my entire home... Is he willing to do six weeks of hard walking?"

Brock turned and looked the man in the eyes. "Where the hell do you live?"

The man began to laugh again, exposing a mouth full of blackened teeth.

"My home is the Okefenokee Swamp," the old man said proudly. "Which stretches from Waycross, Georgia all the way to Lake City, Florida near the Gulf of Mexico."

"How long have you lived there?" asked Burke.

"I was born and raised there. My people left Kings Bay and settled in the swamp for fear of the plague, which was brought to the land by European settlers."

"How can you stand living in there with all the mosquitoes and gnats?"

"They are repelled by me. My people over time have built up an immunity to their bite."

"Sounds like you got it pretty good back there," said Burke. "How do we get to your paradise on earth?"

"Take Highway 40 west to Folkston. I will guide you from there."

The truck pulled out on the hardtop and headed into a canopy of live oak trees whose arching limbs blocked the heat of the springtime sun and emerged into an expanse of saw grass mixed with ancient white pine trees.

Caradon stuck his arm out the window and pointed to a tree that was being invaded by crows. "You see how the flock of crows continually dive into and around that tree?"

"They're sure making a ruckus," said Burke, swatting at a mosquito.

"Deep within the boughs lies a great horned owl. The crows will harass him until he either flies off, or the sun begins to set. During the night, the great horned owl will enter where the flock of crows has roosted. His talons will be open for the kill. Now, if the flock of crows ceased to harass the owl during the day, maybe he would spend more time pursuing mice and voles at night. The answer to their behavior and other natural events is beyond human reasoning. As the Great One says: 'My ways are not your ways, my thoughts are not your thoughts. As far as the stars are in the skies are my ways above your ways.'"

Lieutenant Brock began to shake his head from side to side. "Where do you come up with these sayings?"

Caradon began to laugh and then patted Burke on the shoulder. "Sir, when you reach my age, you will have gained more knowledge than I."

The truck crossed Route 1 at Folkston, Georgia, and followed the signs to the park office.

When they arrived, a large group of Cub Scouts and a den mother milled around. Caradon opened the door and squeezed out of the truck's confines.

The sight of the tattooed giant sent most of the children scurrying for the protection of the den mother. She, with her flock in tow, approached Burke's window. "Sir, are you part of the search team?"

"Why, no ma'am... I don't think so."

"No one is in the park office. I called 911 and no one has arrived yet. I'm responsible for these children and could never forgive myself if harm came to them." The den mother's apprehension increased when she noticed a little boy walking toward the tattooed man. "Come back here," she yelled, "Stay away from that man!"

"Oh, don't worry about Caradon, he wouldn't hurt a fly."

Just then, a dusty green truck pulled up. A stocky man clad in forest green clothes and a Smokey Bear hat emerged. "I'm Stockton Orvis, Park Ranger. Did anyone make a 911 call regarding a missing person?"

"Yes, yes, I called, did they find him?"

"No, ma'am. I just received the call."

McPeake and Burke got out of the truck and introduced themselves.

The child that had approached the tattooed man was now standing in front of him. "Mister," he said to Caradon. "can you help me find my friend Jessie?"

"Where is your whistle?"

The young Cub looked down at his chest. "Here it is, mister."

"You and your friends must blow on your whistles at the same time and then I will tell you to stop."

Caradon was soon surrounded by Cub Scouts, whistles in hand. "Start blowing," he commanded. Caradon cupped his ears and walked through the crowd to the forest's edge. "Now stop." Caradon brought his hands away from his ears. His mind filtered out the chatter of the squirrels, the splash of fish in the lake, and the cries of the bald eagle above. Caradon turned around and walked over to the man with the Smokey Bear hat.. "Stockton, I hear a call for help. It comes from the cedar thicket that lies south of the wooden boardwalk."

"That's not far," replied the park ranger.

"Can I come along?" asked the den mother.

"Yes, you will be a comfort to the child."

The ranger asked McPeake and Burke to supervise the Cub pack.

"No problem," came their reply.

"One more thing. I need a Scout to lead the way. Where is the boy who first spoke to me?"

"It was me, mister." A blonde-haired boy pushed through the crowd and stood before Caradon.

"You, young Cub, will lead the search party."

The callow boy, full of pride, pushed out his chest and said, "Come, follow me."

The search party returned a short time later. The den mother and the found child, his wrist clamped firmly in her hand, led the way.

When the lead Scout emerged from the woods, his friends immediately surrounded him.

The friends' questions fired off. "Where was he?"

"Was he in an alligator pit?"

"Did you use your compass to find Jessie?"

The young boy had now become a Davy Crockett in the minds of the Cub pack.

McPeake approached Ranger Orvis and asked him what had happened to Caradon.

"Oh, after finding the boy, he said goodbye to me and then headed into the swamp. Say, is Caradon doing work for the Navy? I know I've tried several times to get him to apply for the deputy ranger position, but he wasn't interested."

"We got him to train some of the Navy SEALs on survival skills," said Burke.

The Navy men said goodbye and drove out of the park.

"Where did you get that crap about training Navy SEALs?" asked McPeake.

"Well, I didn't have the nerve to tell the ranger that his hero was a trespasser. And another thing: I just wished that you hadn't picked him up at the courthouse."

"Why? I get the feeling you like him."

"Yeah, sure," said Burke. "But of course I'm the one who'll have to arrest him if he comes on the base again!"

The truck passed the ancient pines just as the sun set. The flock of crows was now roosting within its boughs for the long, perilous night.

CHAPTER FIVE

The following morning, Joe Brantley, the construction superintendent responsible for the dredge work, pulled into the pass and T.D. office parking lot. He glanced at his watch, 6:45. *This will give me a few minutes to smoke my pipe,* he thought. Just then, he felt a tugging on his shirt sleeve.

"Where the hell have you been hiding?" asked a man.

Without turning his head, Brantley said, "Let's see, I must be talking to the greatest skirt chaser, gambler, and boxer south of Waycross, Georgia."

The man released Brantley's shirt and began to laugh. "Ain't you forgetting one thing?" he asked with a chuckle. "I'm also the greatest crane operator."

Brantley turned his head and looked directly into the man's face. His brown eyes were deep-set, with a nose that swept out from the face. "I don't know why they call you the wolf with all those gals. You look more like a coyote to me."

"And I make them howl." The man tilted his head back and made a howling sound.

Brantley shook his head and said, "What a way to start the day." He got out of the truck and shook the man's hand. "Joe Jackson, where you been working? I haven't seen you in a coon's age."

"All over. Just finished a bridge job in Saint Augustine."

"Is that right," said Brantley.

"Yeah yeah..." Jackson said.

"Tell me which one, so I know not to drive across it."

The two old friends chuckled.

"Hey, the yardman at our Jacksonville office told me this job's running twelve hours a day until completed."

"That's right..."

"Do we get a bonus if we finish the job early?"

"Yeah the Navy giving bonuses," replied Brantley. "Now I really don't wanna cross that bridge—as high as you musta been when you built it."

"Worth a shot, right?"

Brantley looked down at Jackson's high-top cowboy boots. "Do you still carry that pistol in your boot?"

"What pistol?" replied Jackson, with a smirk on his face.

"Just a friendly warning. You get caught with a gun on base, you'll be standing before a federal judge."

"Thanks for the warning." Jackson looked over Brantley's shoulder. "Say, here comes our tractor-trailer." Jackson waved his arms back and forth.

The driver noticed Jackson's signal and pulled up next to him. He shut the engine down. "This must be the place."

Brantley looked at his watch. 7:00 a.m. "Come on out of that truck, I'll get you boys signed up. Say, where are the signalman and laborers?"

"They're here," replied Jackson. "I saw them come into the parking lot this morning."

"Will you go round them up," Brantley asked.

Sure thing, boss."

*　*　*

After the workers received temporary passes and stickers for their vehicles, Brantley escorted them to the job site. Brantley parked his truck and walked up a hill to the edge of the lake and lit his pipe. Joe Jackson soon joined him.

Jackson picked up and pitched a clod of dirt, looking down into the pit below. "How come that dredge ain't working?"

Brantley grasped the bowl of the pipe, and pulled the end out of his mouth, and used it as a pointer. "That dredge is idled because of that mound of rock down below us."

"Shit, that rock ain't so big!"

"That's only the visible part," Brantley said. "The incoming tide has most of it covered up."

"That's right, we have a full moon tonight." Jackson began to howl like a wolf.

"Alright, alright, that's enough of that!" said Brantley with anger in his voice. "You get on your crane and get to work and tell those boys to come over here. I want to talk to them."

A few minutes passed.

"You wanna talk to us, boss?"

"Yeah. Which one of you is the signalman?"

"That'd be me, boss," said the man on the right.

"What's your name, boy?"

"Jesse," came the reply.

"Jesse, you go over and help the crane operator and truck driver to attach the boom to the crane. When you're done there, I want you to walk the crane over to the edge of the cliff."

"Sure thing," said Jesse.

"Don't get too close, though, the ground is unstable. Just get the crane close enough to the edge so that the crane operator can see the mound below. Make sure you have enough wire rope on the crane drum to reach the mound. Oh, by the way, the tide is coming in, so there will be no work done near high tide."

"Yes, sir."

Brantley turned to the other man. "What's your name?"

"Jake McClose, sir—"

"Well, Ja—"

"They call me 'One Eye.'"

"Well..." Brantley paused to notice a scar that ran from Jake's hairline to just under his cheekbone. "Where'd that happen... Vietnam?"

"No, sir. Blasting dynamite in a quarry. They tell me the charge went off early. I didn't set it. Someone else did." Jake puffed his chest out a bit.

"Musta hur—"

"Six weeks in the hospital, sir."

"Construction work is a dangerous profession," noted Brantley, to himself as much as anyone. "Say, you ain't afraid of heights, are you? Because we're going to have to lower you to the job site on a work platform."

"No, sir," replied One Eye. "Ain't afraid to fall in the water either."

"That reminds me..." Brantley walked to the back of his pickup and opened a box. "I got life jackets for all of you. They will be worn at all times while working on the job site." "Here you go... one size fits all. Jesse, you take three life jackets and tell those boys to put them on. If that crane operator gives you any shit, tell him to come see me."

"Come see you," said Jesse. "Right sir."

"I am generally the man to come see when shit's being given."

"Yes, sir."

Brantley dutifully put his jacket on, then handed one to One Eye. "Your job is to jackhammer through the center of the mound. Then we'll hook up a wrecking ball to the crane and pound on the center of the mound till she splits in two. Sound like a plan to you?"

"It sure does," replied One Eye.

"Now you go over and check the fuel level and oil in the air compressor. Oh, and make sure they sent us some pointed jackhammer bits and those flat kind—you know, the wide ones they use for cutting through blacktop. I'm gonna go to the trailer and see if those portable phones are charged yet."

"Yes, sir," said One Eye, turning to walk away.

"Oh and Jake..." Brantley added.

One Eye jerked to a stop and turned back. "Sir..."

"You let me know before you go wiring any charges, okay?"

"Copy that, sir."

Brantley returned to the construction trailer. The red light on his answering machine was blinking.

"Uh yeah... this is Wells' yardman in Jacksonville," said the recording. "Your laborer for the second shift has called in sick."

Brantley hit the stop button, then walked over to a large battery-charging machine and took three radios from the charger. He returned to the work site and handed a radio to the crane operator and the signalman.

He then walked over to the laborer who was connecting an air hose. "Here, take this radio, and make damn sure you wear it when you're down in the pit."

"Yes sir, I will," replied One Eye.

"Listen, I'm in a bind. My night shift laborer has called in sick. Would you like to work a double shift tonight?" Brantley noticed the hesitation in the laborer's face. "You will be paid time and a half for twelve hours, and you can take a snooze when that mound is covered by the tide."

"That sounds like a pretty good deal, sir. Yes, I believe I'll work a double."

"Good. Well, that's out of the way. If anyone gives you a hard time about sleeping in your car, you tell them to come see me."

* * *

When the night shift arrived at the work site, the crane towered at the edge of the precipice. The wire cable that extended from the crane drum was secured to the work platform which was loaded with construction material. A portable light plant sat idle waiting for darkness.

Tom Grey walked up to the crane to relieve the first shift operator.

Joe Jackson looked at his watch. "It's seven-thirty, boy. Where ya been?"

Tom looked up into the crane and saw a familiar face. A broad smile came across his face. "Hey, *Wolf*, I thought you were working in Saint Augustine."

"Just finished up." Jackson climbed off the crane and shook the man's hand.

"Joe, the church is having a covered-dish dinner next Sunday. Would you like to come as my guest?"

"Do they invite short-skirted women and serve hard drinks?"

Tom put his arm around Joe Jackson's shoulder in a fatherly way. "You know the Lord don't condone such behavior. We have some fine Christian women coming to dinner, which is what you need."

"Oh yeah?"

"Maybe I can introduce you to one."

"Women! that reminds me," said Jackson. "There's a gal that works at the donut shop in Waycross. She's got legs that run all the way up to her ass."

"How old is she?" asked Tom Grey.

"Almost nineteen," replied Joe Jackson, with a grin on his face.

"Why, you're old enough to be her daddy!"

"That's right... her sugar daddy." Jackson turned and headed for his truck.

"I'll keep praying for you," yelled Tom Grey.

"Well don't pray too much; I'll never have any fun."

"Okay okay..."

Joe Jackson raised his hand and in a loud voice and said, "Praise the Lord!"

* * *

Brantley gathered the night crew together and gave them the same safety instructions that he had given the first shift. He concluded with, "Are there any questions?"

"Who do we contact if we have an emergency?" asked Bill Roan, the new signalman.

"Press 911 on the radios that I gave you. That will put you in contact with base security. They're on call twenty-four hours a day. Any other questions?" He paused and looked around. "None...okay."

The laborer gathered up his safety equipment and then walked over to the equipment platform, where the signalman was waiting. The two men shook hands. "My name is Bill Roan."

"Jake, but they call me One Eye," replied the laborer.

"Pleased to meet you, One Eye," Roan said.

"Pleased to meet you, Bill."

"Remember, all phone transmissions will include our trade name. I am the signalman, you... the laborer, and the man over on the crane... the crane operator."

One Eye nodded his head in agreement. "Got it," he said.

"You ready to go for a ride?"

"Ready as I'll ever be," replied One Eye.

The signalman steadied the suspended equipment platform until One Eye climbed aboard. The signalman then began to gather up a heavy rope with a grappling hook attached to the end of it. He threw the rope and grapple onto the platform. "Now when you get down near the water surface, I'm gonna stop you, and then I'll swing you against the side of that rock mound. You take that grapple and cast it up on the mound and tie it off to the bulkhead on the platform."

"Why can't we just land the platform on the mound?" asked One Eye.

The signalman became agitated. "How in the hell are we supposed to land a flat bottom on a round surface?"

"Alright alright, I'm sorry."

"Okay," said Bill, seeing he'd agitated the kid who was about to be slung and dangled along the side of what was practically a cliff. "Look, everything will shift to one side and flip the platform with you on it!"

"We'd best stick to your plan then," conceded One Eye.

"Okay, where were we? Oh, after you've tied off, just take the equipment with you to do the job when you're done at one site, radio me, and I'll move the platform to your new location." The signalman looked at his watch. "The tide's just starting to come in. We got about four hours of work down there before the incoming tide stops us. You better sit down somewhere. I don't want you to fall out." The signalman pushed the button on the radio. "Signalman to crane operator."

"Crane operator here."

"Hoist up, up, up. Stop! Swing left, swing left. Stop. Coming down slowly, coming down..." When the platform reached the work area, the order was given to stop and lock the brake.

One Eye picked up the grappling hook and cast it onto the mound, then retrieved the rope slowly until a grapple point wedged behind a rock crevice. He gathered up the line, and then tied it off. One Eye opened up the toolbox and picked up a measuring tape and a can of fluorescent paint—actions exuding that of a seasoned pro. He climbed off the platform and began to mark the centerline of the mound. After this was completed, he climbed back on the platform and started up the engine-driven air compressor. The lengths of air hose were connected, then he inserted a pointed bit into the end of the heavy jackhammer. One Eye dragged the jackhammer and adjoined air hose off the platform and onto the mount. He located the centerline at the water's edge, and then righted the jackhammer, the chiseled point centered within the point line.

The laborer steadied himself, and then depressed the hand lever, releasing compressed air into the chamber of the jackhammer. A heavy shaft within began to rise and fall in rapid succession, driving the pointed bit into the surface of the mound. Bits of limestone flew in all directions like shrapnel. The pointed bit broke through the surface crust. Compressed gas from below surged through the opening, causing the heavy jackhammer to rise in One Eye's hands.

Long years as a laborer had taught One Eye one thing: that a heavy jackhammer does not float in the air. He instinctively released the handles and ran onto the equipment platform.

The signalman called the laborer. "What the hell's goin' on down there?"

One Eye returned the call, "You tell me. Do they have any natural gas lines going through here?"

"I don't think so," replied the signalman.

Suddenly, the jackhammer rose out of the ground, followed by a geyser-like gas.

"Get me the hell outta here!" commanded One Eye.

The signalman called the crane operator, "Be prepared to hoist."

"Hang on a sec..." yelled One Eye.

The laborer watched as the gas, which at one point reached the top of the pit, began to dissipate rapidly. He climbed onto the mound and cautiously walked toward the gas spray, which was dissipating. He stopped and got on the radio. "Laborer to signalman."

"Signalman here."

"Hey, look here," said One Eye, breathing heavy. "The spray ain't coming out of the hole no more."

"Well, what the hell happened?"

"Dunno. We may have hit an isolated gas pocket."

"You still good to go?"

"Sure," replied One Eye. "But if I run into another one, I'm gonna call it quits."

One Eye changed bits on the jackhammer. He installed a wide plate, which was used for cutting through blacktop. The jackhammer was placed over the pilot hole, and began to chip its way through the surface rock: One Eye kept his torso away from the jackhammer for fear of another gas release. The blade sliced through the surface without incident. One Eye's confidence began to build. On successive cuts, he leaned on the hammer to speed the cutting process. The splitting of the mound began to weaken its entire structure. Fissure cracks and large pieces of limestone began to fall away at the incision site.

The laborer continued to cut to the rhythm of the charging hammer. *Shit, this is a piece of cake,* thought One Eye. *I'll be back in my car sleeping by midnight.* Dark shadows began to envelop the mound. It was now sunset. One Eye stopped hammering and radioed the signalman. "Hey, it's getting dark down here; turn those lights on."

The signalman walked over to the portable light plant and started the engine's electrical power, which ran up a metal pole to a set of six amplifying bulbs that lit up the night sky. The signalman diverted beams of light in the direction of the mound.

The signalman radioed into the pit, "You got enough light down there?"

"Plenty," came the reply. The laborer resumed splitting the shell open. His goal of reaching the midpoint was now in sight.

An incoming wave rolled over the mound with enough force to knock One Eye to his knees. He quickly stood up and waited for the top of the mound to reappear. It didn't.

Remember to watch the tide, it's always moving. *That's the last thing Mr. Brantley told me,* thought One Eye. "I got to get the hell out of here!" he whispered, spinning around and lunging a step in the direction of the equipment platform. The rising water had concealed the gash and One Eye's right leg slipped into it. A piece of jagged limestone cut through the laborer's pants and embedded itself in his thigh. One Eye tried to pull himself out, but his leg was hopelessly wedged between the limestone. Uncontrollable panic overcame him.

"Help! Help!" One Eye yelled at the top of his lungs.

One Eye began to kick his injured leg violently, further mixing his blood with the nutrient-rich seawater. This co-mingling was to form a bond, a bond with devastating effects. The source of the blood flow was located and pieces of flesh were torn from the open wound. Severe pain rushed through One Eye's body. He began to dream of his mother, holding his hand as they entered the church. There, in front of him, was a stained glass window with the image of the Lord rising into heaven.

One Eye regained consciousness, and then cried out, "Jesus, Jesus, Jesus!" Dark forms began to work their way out of the long gash that One Eye had made, searching for the remainder of their first meal.

CHAPTER SIX

The signalman and operator stood at the edge of the pit, calling to One Eye vainly.

"I see something floating around down there," said Joe Grey. "It looks like a life jacket. I'm gonna call 911."

"Base Security, Corporal Bacon speaking, how may I help you?"

"There's a man down! He won't answer the radio!"

"I need you to calm down, sir," instructed the corporal. "The first things I need are your name and current location."

"Bill with C&M, and I'm near the dredge."

"Okay, Bill, and you say that you're on the dredge."

"No, we're on top of the hill overlooking the lake."

"I am dispatching rescue personnel to you. Are there any reference points at your location to guide them?"

"Bright lights shining on the water."

"Okay, now tell me what happened."

"We heard screaming from below, and the laborer didn't respond to our radio call."

"Stand by, Bill."

"Okay... it's an emergency."

"I understand, sir," Corporal Bacon said with highly skilled serenity. "The dispatcher radioed a marine security boat that was patrolling nearby. Dispatcher to boat number five. Code one, man overboard, north of floating dredge. Look for lights trained on water's surface."

"Aye aye, sir. Boat five we copy," Bill heard in the background.

"Dispatcher to all available units... converge at the north end of the new lake. Reference point is an emergency light plant."

Nearby in Fernandina Beach, Florida a local ham radio operator was listening to the emergency radio traffic and adjusted his headset, and then jotted down the last transmission in shorthand. He reached for a glass on the table and took a sip of its amber liquid. *Ah, you can't beat the taste of good corn liquor,* he thought.

The marine security boat, running at full throttle, began to slow down after it passed the floating dredge. The pilot saw the bright lights at the far end of the lake and steered the boat towards it. Upon arrival at the north end of the lake, the marine security boat gently bumped into the equipment platform and tied off.

"Turn on the searchlights, and play the lights across the water's surface," said the pilot.

The first mate grabbed the handles to the light and began to sweep the surface of the water. The light picked up bits of cloth and foam as it swept the area.

"Sir, I think I have a visual," said the firstmate. "It's a life jacket floating out there."

The pilot revved up the engine and proceeded toward the life jacket. The low water indicator began to blink. The pilot turned the wheel hard to the right.

"What's the matter?" asked the first mate.

"We were in deep water, now we're in less than six feet," replied the pilot. He steered the boat near the underwater structure, taking soundings as he went.

After circling the area, the pilot determined that the security boat could not come in any closer without grounding the boat. "Throw out the grappling hooks, we'll try to snag the life jacket."

A young marine picked up the three-pronged hook, which was tied to a length of curled rope. He picked up the grapple and began to swing it above his head. The release was perfect. The grapple landed just beyond the life jacket and then began to sink. He pulled in the line to keep the grapple on the surface. The sharp points raced through the water and caught the life jacket mid-center.

The marine's shoulder muscles strained as he tried to haul in the catch. The first mate assisted him. Their combined efforts broke the life jacket free from its mooring, and it was then dragged swiftly to the patrol boat.

"Don't pull it aboard yet," said the pilot. He picked up a long pole with a hook on it and began to probe the jacket and the debris that was entwined within. "You wanna know what I think? I think someone fell off their boat last fall and drifted into the marsh where the crabs and alligators fed on him."

"That thing doesn't even look human... why, it looks like a pile of shredded wheat," replied the first mate.

The pilot got on the radio and called the dispatcher. "This is boat number five. We have retrieved a life jacket, and some possible human remains."

Bill, eavesdropping on the radio action while looking down into the lake, cringed.

"The report this office received conflicts with what you've found. Bring back the remains to the dock, I will relieve you with the number two security boat."

The latest report was dutifully noted in the ham operator's logbook. He took another slug of amber hooch while waiting excitedly for further transmissions but was interrupted by a voice calling up the stairs. "Snoop, how long are you gonna stay up there playing with that radio? It's after midnight and you got work tomorrow."

"Yes, dear," came the reply.

From the radio room, Snoop shut off the receiver and placed his ledger in the top desk drawer. He finished off the glass of corn liquor and shut off the desk light.

Boat number five returned to the dock where Lieutenant Brock, chief of base security, was waiting for them. "After you boys tie off, bring that body bag with you," he said. "Put it in the back of my pickup."

Brock jotted down the time of arrival: 0030. A black body bag was laid out gently in the bed of the truck.

"Open 'er up, let's see what we got," said Brock, sliding a pair of bifocals down his nose.

The first mate opened the bag, and then pulled back on the flaps revealing the contents.

Brock, with a cringe, sucked air through his teeth. He pulled out a pocketknife and began to probe the carcass. The knife's edge slid along a protruding rib, slicing off a piece of fat. The knife's point returned to the carcass; Brock gently pushed the point against a piece of exposed life jacket. It would not penetrate the fabric.

"Flip this mess over. I wanna see something."

The crew complied.

Lieutenant Brock's knife's edge flipped back a piece of torn life jacket material. The exposed cloth revealed the letters C&M.

Brock radioed the dispatcher. "This is the chief security officer—I got two questions. What is the description of the missing man, and second, what's the name of the contractor or subcontractor doing the work here?"

After a long pause, the dispatcher responded, "Black male, five feet eight inches, approximately a hundred eighty-five pounds. And the only contractor on that site is Conway & Martinson Construction."

"I can't believe that this carcass is the construction worker we are looking for." Brock gathered the crew behind the truck and gave them a direct order, "Do *not* talk to anyone regarding this incident, not even amongst yourselves. I *will* contact you individually for personal reports."

Lieutenant Brock then got into the truck and drove away.

When the truck was out of earshot, the first mate commented that the corpse they dredged up probably fell into the nuclear reactor.

The pilot chimed in, "I know one thing. You boys better start packing your duffel bags."

"Why?" asked the first mate.

"Because we know too much," another crew member said. "Betcha we'll all be transferred to other duty stations within the month."

"If there's one thing the Navy's good for..." said the first mate.

"It's covering things up," mumbled the pilot.

* * *

Caradon knew instinctively that something unbelievably evil was happening on the base. At close to midnight, he was drawn towards the base by feelings of uneasiness. Nearing the main gate, the traffic light in front of him turned green. He stepped off the curb and proceeded to cross the road. Suddenly he detected a strange smell in the air. A chill ran up his spine causing him to chant in the words of his grandfather; the ancient words.

He turned in the direction of the base, taking deep breaths, suddenly a scream came from behind him, "Get out of the road, you're blocking traffic!" Car horns began to blare. "Move it, buddy!" yelled a sailor. "What are you, a stoner?"

But Caradon was in another place and time. The horns and shouting drivers could not reach him. He could only hear the words of his grandfather describing the smell of evil itself as he slowly walked towards the smell.

Suddenly, a rapid response team from the base descended on Caradon and lifted him off the ground, carrying him hand and foot to their waiting security van. Breathing in deeply as he was being carried, his chest began to fill like a big balloon. He released the air slowly; the strange odor was now gone.

CHAPTER SEVEN

Lieutenant Brock drove to a building adjacent to the base dispensary. He picked up his clipboard and went up to the front door. Locked. He rang the bell and a man wearing white pants and a shirt opened the door.

"I'm Lieutenant Brock, chief of security for Kings Bay. I have a body bag that needs to be stored."

"Fill this form out... I'll go get the gurney."

"I won't need a gurney; this bag is light enough for me to carry."

The orderly looked at his availability list. "Let's see... number seven is open."

"Okay, I'll get the body bag," replied the security officer.

The security officer returned shortly, as the orderly waited, with an arm leaning against the open door to the crypt.

Lieutenant Brock slid the bag into the tube.

The orderly then slammed the door closed. He padlocked the clasp, and then handed Brock a key and kept one for himself.

"I'll take that key!" said Brock, in an authoritative voice.

"Can't, sir, the morgue maintains a duplicate key."

"Look, I'm not gonna argue with you. Either you give the second key to me, or I'll haul your supervisor down here to resolve the matter!"

The orderly meekly handed over the second key.

Lieutenant Brock got into his truck and sat for a few minutes wondering what to do next when his radio transmitter started alerting with transmissions about an arrest at the main gate. Minutes later in the security building he was staring at the tall thin form of Caradon. Obviously in a state of extreme distress, Caradon was rocking back and forth in his cell chanting in an unfamiliar language.

"Caradon! What the hell's the matter?"

Caradon just kept rocking back and forth chanting in the tongue of his ancient tribe.

"Caradon! What is going on here?"

Slowly, Caradon turned and made eye contact with Brock his black eyes, black as coal, seemed to be burning right through Brock's skull.

Soon the chanting and rocking stopped and Caradon turned away. "I tried to bring the warning of the conch shell," he said. "All of life speaks to me as it spoke to all who came before me. The work being done must stop. Nothing more must be disturbed or there will be more death and the evil incarnate will be released upon the world."

Brock listened to this and thought of the body bag in the morgue.

"Do you have information about an accident that occurred tonight?"

Caradon slowly turned back to Brock and made eye contact again. "I can see what is written in the stars and on the water," the elder said. "I listen to the songs of the birds and they tell me their news. The president in Washington must stop his destruction of the land of my people. Otherwise, nothing but evil can result."

With that Caradon resumed his chanting and rocking while holding the gaze of a bewildered Brock.

Just before leaving the security facility Brock picked up the phone and dialed the number to the base commander's private residence. After several rings, the phone was picked up.

"This is Captain Jarvis."

"Sir, this is Lieutenant Brock, chief of security. Sir, we got a situation out here."

"Situation, situation... always a situation," the captain grumbled, propping himself up in bed up. "Can it wait till zero-dawn-thirty?"

"Sir, this matter needs your immediate attention."

"Alright, alright," the captain sighed. "Come on over to my quarters. Just let yourself in."

When Brock arrived, the base commander was waiting for him at the front door.

"Come on in, I'm brewing a pot of coffee."

Brock followed the base commander into his office and sat down. Jarvis walked over to the bookcase and then turned on the tape recorder.

Jarvis turned to Brock. "Now, I don't want any cursing during this conversation. Oh, and remind me to shut it off when we're done."

"Yes, sir..."

"That was Nixon's mistake."

"Cursing, sir?"

"No—well that too—but the tape rolling," the superior office said. "He kept the tape rolling all the time." The commander sat down with a grunt and sigh and crossed his legs. "Now then, Lieutenant, what do you have to report?"

"Well, sir, the security dispatcher received a distress call at zero zero zero five hours. The caller stated that a construction worker had fallen into the lake that's being dredged. Boat number five was dispatched and arrived on location at zero zero fifteen. They recovered human remains entwined in a shredded life jacket. I scraped some gristle from the rib bone and photographed both sides of the remains. There are letters on the life jacket bearing the marking C&M." Brock passed the photos he had taken to the base commander.

Captain Jarvis slowly fed the photos back and forth between his hands. "No skull. No flesh. Shredded life jacket. This couldn't have happened in a fifteen-minute time slot."

"And there is another odd coincidence. The man we arrested last week at the main gate was caught trying to gain access to the base again. We have him in a cell at the security building. He's in there rocking and chanting like a madman and claiming all work must stop."

"These Greenpeace guys, when will they give me some peace?"

"Begging your pardon, sir, but he's not your typical environmentalist."

"No?"

"He seemed to know something happened or was about to happen."

Jarvis dropped the photos and began rubbing his index finger across his forehead. "Let me guess: the man on the highway was arrested at midnight, same time as this possible accident?"

"Yes, sir, the gate guard recorded the time. It seems odd to me that both events happened at the same time."

"The man you're holding... what's his story?"

"He's the trespasser we prosecuted in federal court. He was given probation in that case."

"I guess he didn't learn his lesson," replied Captain Jarvis.

"Well, he wasn't exactly on federal property when we picked him up this time."

"Well, where was he?" asked the base commander.

"He was picked up blocking traffic in front of the main gate. It was like he was in a trance talking in tongues. The gate sentry mobilized a rapid response team and brought him to the security center."

The base commander relaxed slightly and sat back in his chair. "Well, then the Navy department just needs that guy to go away," he said. "Get him off my base and turn him over to the local authorities. Make sure you note in your report that Kings Bay employees assisted the Saint Marys officials with a man needing medical intervention."

"Yes, sir," agreed the lieutenant.

"Now then—"

"There's one other thing I can do."

"What's that, Brock?"

"Well, sir, when this trespasser was released from federal custody, the public relations officer and I escorted him back to his home in the Okefenokee Swamp. We are in contact with the forest ranger. He's sort of a caretaker for the man. I'll call him and let him know what happened."

"Yes, by all means. Now, let's get back to the corpse in the morgue. As I understand it, the first call to dispatch reported a construction worker missing, presumed drowned. Call the rescue teams and see if they have recovered anything."

"Aye, sir."

The commander stood and moved to his desk. "If you give me a minute, Brock," he said. "I have to contact Justin down in legal..."

Lieutenant Brock called the dispatcher while the base commander contacted his legal aide.

"Lieutenant Harkins, this is Commander Jarvis. I need you over at my quarters right away. Bring your book of standard operating procedures with you."

Brock was in contact with the dispatcher. He held his hand over the receiver. "Sir, the security boat has nothing to report."

"Keep a security boat working until zero eight hundred hours, that should give them enough daylight to locate the missing man, should he exist. Did the witnesses leave the base yet?"

"I don't think so, sir."

"Good. Then I suggest you get reports from them and confiscate all the life jackets from the contractors for evidence." Jarvis noticed that the coffee pot was now filled. "Lieutenant Brock, would you like a fresh cup of coffee?"

"No thank you, sir, I better get back into the field. Oh, sir, I almost forgot. Here's the key to the morgue. The remains we found are in slot number seven."

Jarvis clasped the key, and then said, "Number seven, this must be my lucky day."

Lieutenant Brock saluted and left. Jarvis turned to the tape recorder and shut it off. He then poured himself a cup of coffee and waited for his legal assistant to arrive.

* * *

The sound of knocking woke Jarvis from a light sleep.

"Come in!"

Lieutenant Justin Harkins entered the foyer. He pushed the door open with his foot

"Good morning, sir, I'm sorry that I'm late. I had to go to the office to grab the S.O.P.'s... they're in bound books."

"That's alright, take a seat."

The legal officer dropped the heavily laden briefcases on the carpet and sat down.

"Harkins, we have a situation here that may require a little legal maneuvering."

"Job security, I call those..."

Captain Jarvis got out of his chair and then pushed the button for *Record*. He returned to his seat and revealed to his legal assistant all that occurred.

Jarvis concluded with, "My first question to you is, who has authority over the corpse that lies in the base morgue?"

Harkins opened the case to the right of him, and fingered through the files, pulling one out. Jarvis shyly waited for an answer that would dictate his next action.

"Sir, the base commander has authority over all deceased persons whether they die on the base or are brought in by some other means."

"So *possession is nine-tenths* sort of thing?"

"Sort of," replied Harkins. "Civilian, federal employees, and contracted employees, with no assigned quarters, shall be turned over to the closest civilian authority within a reasonable period of time."

"What would a reasonable period be?" asked Captain Jarvis.

"Seventy-two hours would not be unreasonable, sir."

"Harkins, I have control of a pile of remains that, at this time, is unidentified. Would you agree with me that I have jurisdiction until a positive identification can be made?"

"Yes," replied Harkins.

"That's *reasonable* then?"

"Yes, sir."

"My second question is: does the base commander have the authority to shut down a base construction job?"

Harkins looked to the window then back at the commander. "With just cause?" he asked.

The commander nodded in the affirmative.

Without referring to his files, Harkins replied, "The base commander has the authority to suspend all construction work, which may be potentially hazardous to life or limb."

Captain Jarvis scratched his unshaven chin, and then said to Harkins, "I'm going to pass this hot potato up the chain of command."

Captain Jarvis reached into his pocket and then brought out a key chain. He located a circular key that he rarely used. He inserted the key into the base of a phone and turned. A red light went on and Jarvis picked up the receiver and dialed his superior officer at the Pentagon. A dispatcher answered the phone.

"This is Captain Jarvis, base commander at Kings Bay, Georgia. Is Admiral Farragut available?"

"No, sir," came the reply. "Can I take a message?"

"Yes," replied Jarvis. "Inform Admiral Farragut that I have suspended all dredge operations inside Kings Bay until further notice due to safety concerns."

"I'll contact him immediately, sir," replied the dispatcher.

The phone sat silent for just a few minutes. Then it began to ring, and Captain Jarvis picked up the receiver.

"This is Admiral Farragut; I'd like to speak to the base commander."

"This is Captain Jarvis, sir."

"I'm calling to confirm a report to my office that you suspended construction at the base due to safety concerns. Can you apprise me of the situation?"

"Admiral, base security received a report of a missing construction worker in the newly formed lake. Base security was on the scene within fifteen minutes and recovered a headless torso that was stripped of all flesh and blood products."

"Has positive identification of the remains been determined?" asked Admiral Farragut.

"No, sir, our morgue is just a holding facility... we have no coroner or pathologists on board."

"What we must confirm, if possible, is positive identification of the remains in your possession, captain."

"Our goals are aligned, sir."

"I'm going to contact the Navy Surgeon General's Office and make it a priority that the remains be transferred to Bethesda hospital for a complete examination. Their report will dictate what our next action will be.

"I concur with that course, sir."

"I don't have to tell you that the Navy brass are anxious to have this base completed in a timely fashion..."

"I'm aware, sir."

"Delays like these catch their attention, and I'm sure we'll have their support in resolving this situation."

"Of course, sir."

"Do you have any other problems to discuss?" asked Admiral Farragut.

"No, sir, I think I've brought forward enough problems for one night."

"Well, you better get some sleep," replied the admiral.

"Thank you, sir; I'll keep in touch."

Captain Jarvis hung up the phone. He looked at his assistant. "You know, Harkins, you ask your superiors for help and they always throw in a caveat for their support. He didn't have to mention to me that the Navy wanted to complete the base without delays. He's just putting undue pressure on me. Harkins, make sure you get a release for the remains in slot number seven."

* * *

Lieutenant Brock, after leaving the base commander's quarters, proceeded to the job site and stopped next to a group of men, who were talking amongst themselves.

"Where's the security boat driver?" Brock asked.

"I'm here, sir," said a man dressed in Navy blues.

"We are curtailing the recovery effort. You can return to your base unit."

"Aye, sir."

Brock then turned his attention to the life jackets worn by the remaining two men. "Do you boys work for C&M?"

"Yes," they replied.

"My name is Lieutenant Brock. I am the chief security officer for Kings Bay. I'm going to need some information from you for my report.

"Of course, sir."

"Your names?"

"Tom Grey. I'm the crane operator."

"And you?"

"My name is Bill Roan and I'm the signalman. Sir, have they found any sign of One Eye?"

"No, but we have a security boat patrolling the lake," replied Brock.

"We heard reports of a life jacket being found."

"Oh! That! We did find an old life jacket that was hung up in some marsh grass... that reminds me... I need those life jackets you're wearing. If we locate the missing person, we'll be able to match his jacket with yours. Just throw them in the back of my pickup."

Brock grabbed his clipboard and got out of the truck. He watched as the workers dutifully removed their life jackets and threw them in the truck bed. The letters C&M were marked on the jackets.

Brock quickly glanced away and began to talk to the workers. "Either of you recall what time the first distress call was made?" he asked.

"About midnight," said the signalman.

Brock looked at the other man.

"That's right," chimed in the crane operator.

Brock jotted the time down and then asked what time the security boat arrived at the distress site.

"No later than twelve twenty... they got here real fast," said the signalman.

The three men walked to the edge of the cliff.

The signalman pointed to the mound below. "The last time I saw One Eye alive, he was down there working."

"You give the impression that the laborer is dead... why's that?"

"I... I don't know... sir, the screams that came out of that pit were ungodly. One Eye's no longer with us. Sir."

"Well, thank you for your report. We have your personnel files at the security office should we need to interview you further. You may go home now."

The men thanked the officer and shuffled off.

Brock stared out into the dark expanse and noticed the running lights of the security boat slowly moving across the lake. The vibrations from the propeller disturbed the predators below. They formed into a tight school and then swam out of the lake and into the deep waters of the Saint Marys River. Brock's long stare was broken by a call on his radio.

"Dispatcher to Lieutenant Brock, over."

"Brock here, over."

"Sir, we have a man here who would like to talk to you."

"Okay, I'll be there in a few minutes. Brock out."

Brock returned to the truck and headed to the security office.

Chapter Eight

Joe Brantley waited nervously for Brock to arrive. He had received a call from Captain McDowell, chief engineer for the dredging project, who informed him of the site accident, and that the base commander had stopped the project.

Brock entered the security office and walked over to the dispatcher's desk. "It's been a long and busy night, hasn't it?" he said.

"Yes, sir," replied the dispatcher. "Oh, before I forget, you got a message from a Stockton Orvis, forest ranger. I left the number on your desk. Also, this gentleman would like to talk to you."

Brock shook his hand and offered him a seat. "Sir, I'm the superintendent of the dredge site, and I've been informed that the job is shut down."

"That's right," replied Brock. "The base commander has shut down the job as a precaution until we sort out the matter of the missing man."

"Sir, I'd like to have permission to go in and secure the equipment."

"Sure, I have no problem with that. Say, what's your policy on wearing life jackets while on the job site?"

"Very strict, sir," the superintendent said. "I'll fire any man that doesn't adhere to the safety regulations."

"Okay," replied Brock.

"I tell every man, I'll fire 'em flat if—"

"Okay, okay."

"Why? Were those boys not wearing their life jackets?"

"Yes, they had them on when I interviewed them."

"So what's the problem?"

"It's just that I'm trying to figure out why we haven't found any trace of the laborer. I'm wondering if he could have taken his jacket off when he was working, then somehow lost his footing, fell into the water, and drowned."

"I don't know, sir. It could well have happened that way, but I wasn't there, so I wouldn't know for sure. That's a damn shame what happened to One Eye."

"Mr. Brantley, would you do me a favor?"

"Sir?"

"Would you gather up all life jackets under your control and drop them off here."

"Be glad to, sir."

They shook hands then Brantley left and got into his truck. He lit his pipe, drawing the smoke in deeply. If I get blamed for losing this job, then those boys will pay dearly, thought Brantley.

After Brantley left, Lieutenant Brock called the number left by Stockton Orvis. "Park Ranger, can I help you?" Orvis said.

"Yes, Ranger Orvis, this is Lieutenant Brock, chief security officer for Kings Bay. I am returning your call, sir"

"Yes sir, I got word that Caradon is being held at the base. Is that true?"

"Yes, Ranger Orvis," Brock replied. "He was apparently having some sort of episode just outside our main gate, so we picked him up for a health and welfare check. He's currently at our security facility in a holding cell. Look, Ranger, I don't know what this guy's deal is, but we need someone to keep him away from this base."

"Yes sir, I completely understand. I'd like to come by for him personally and I'll do whatever I can, but as you've seen, he's got his own ideas, too."

* * *

Ranger Orvis waited patiently outside the security center for Caradon to be released. Eventually, the tired and dazed man walked out.

"Come on, Caradon, let's get you out of here. Here, I got you something." The ranger handed Caradon a wooden cane. Caradon felt the texture of the cane and said, "This is a fine piece of oak."

Orvis smiled. "I got it up at the flea market yesterday. Cost me fifty bucks. It's supposed to be a replica of William Penn's walking stick. It comes with a genuine certificate from the Salem County New Jersey Historical Commission.

"I know that it's not Penn's original cane..." Orvis went on, "that one would probably fetch thousands of dollars, but it is from the original oak tree. Look they even included a picture of the tree. Here take a look at it." Orvis passed the photo to Caradon. "This is a fine oak tree. I bet it's fifty feet or more. Look how the massive limbs reach out to the sky."

Caradon passed the photo back to Orvis.

"My people traded with the peoples of the Northern coastline, the Delaware and Lenape Nations," Caradon began. "Let me tell you a story..." He held the walking stick above his head then brought it down to the ground. "Under this great oak tree, a treaty was signed between the Lenape Nations and William Penn who by British accounts owned Pennsylvania.

"Now Penn was a good person and kept his oath but not so with his son. A treaty with the Lenape called the Walking Purchase stated that the white man could have all the land he could walk in a day and a half. The land would stretch from the tidal waters of the Delaware River where the sun rises in the east to where the sun sets in the west.

"Penn's son hired woodcutters to clear a path from the Delaware River to a point west at the base of the Appalachian Mountains. The son then sent for the fastest runners he could find in England. He brought them back to Pennsylvania. On the day of the walk, both sides were at the ready. When the sun peeked over the horizon in the east, Penn's son yelled, *Go Forth*, and a survey man mounted on a horse was followed by the runners. Two Lenape warriors brought up the rear.

"As the sun began to set over the Appalachian Mountains a warrior yelled, *Enough*. He then threw a spear into the ground marking the end of the walk. The runners had traveled seventy miles in twelve hours. Once again, the white man had shown their cunning ways. They—"

"Say look here I got 10 lbs. of shrimp..." Orvis wanted to change the subject. "Picked it up down at the docks before I picked you up." He pointed to an ice chest in the back seat.

When they arrived at their destination, Orvis put half the shrimp and some ice in a plastic bag and gave it to Caradon. "Here, you have a good dinner tonight," Orvis said.

Caradon took the bag and thanked the ranger. Caradon pulled his canoe out of a thicket and pushed it into the water climbing and launching the canoe in a single fluid motion of balance and skill. He then glided away up the St. Marys River, under the I-95 Bridge traveling until the voices of men and the whining of their machines could not be heard. He slipped into a narrow channel that ended in front of his shack.

Caradon went in and fetched a large frying pan. He then went outside and started a fire, dumping the shrimp and ice into the pan. The old man sat down on his rocker and watched as the fire flickered at the bottom of the pan. His mind began to drift far back to a time when he was a boy, a time when he was first taught the ways of his tribal ancestors. He remembered helping his grandfather load the longboat with traps, nets, a rifle and two long poles sharpened at one end.

Young Caradon asked his grandfather what the poles were for.

The old man pointed to a piece of rope that lay inside the canoe. "Pick that up and hold it in your hands."

Caradon played with the rope as he waited for his grandfather's story to be told.

"My son, we are going to travel south to hunt and kill an alligator with these pikes."

"Grandfather why don't we just shoot it with father's rifle."

Grandfather turned his body to the south, then raised his arms skyward and said, "Did our Ancestors use rifles? No, of course not." Grandfather continued, "Your father and I will confront the beast, when the alligator opens his jaws wide, we will ram the pointed poles down its throat, piercing its stomach, and pinning it to the ground."

The grandfather, his face like dark worked clay, turned to his grandson. "The rope in your hands will be used by you to control the alligator's tail."

Caradon looked into his grandfather's dark eyes then looked down to the rope in his hands and his heart began to beat hard, his stomach churned but he showed no emotion and then asked, "When do we go?"

The old man turned south again. "Tomorrow when the moon is full and the marshes are filled with water." He turned with his arms raised and said, "Our people were great warriors, they were as tall as two men, their bodies strong as any three, and they carved their fingernails to a fine point. Grandfather began to wave his hands in a slashing motion. "When our people were engaged in war, we would run our nails down the foreheads of our enemies causing blood to flow into their eyes, blinding them for the kill."

Grandfather dropped his arms to his side.

The following day the three men set off into the marshes and Grandfather's prediction came true. A great alligator was slain and skinned. They started a fire then took turns cutting off pieces of snow-white alligator tail.

After they had finished eating Caradon asked his father, "What are we going to do with the carcass?"

"Tomorrow we will travel to what the locals call, the Devil's Millhopper, named this for all the things that fall into it such as cows, pigs, deer, and even some humans. None have ever been recovered or seen again."

Caradon's eyes widened, *never to be seen again*?

The father continued, "It is my opinion that the currents of cedar-stained waters inhale both man and beast, perhaps to please the gods of our Ancestors."

The following morning at the crack of dawn the three were off. They arrived at the Devil's Millhopper at high noon. Caradon's father threw the alligator remains into the water watching it slowly sink. Father told Caradon to stand in place, he then picked up the blood-soaked spears handing one to Grandfather, the two split up walking in opposite directions around the circular pond, and they raised and lowered their spears as they walked. Strange chants and clicking sounds came out of their mouths, words he had never heard before.

When they returned to where he was standing Grandfather thrust the spear into his hand and said, "It is you that will throw the spear into the dark waters because my time on the earth is short."

Caradon and his father threw the spears into the dark waters, a chill ran up Caradon's spine.

Popping noises brought Caradon back to the present, *ah my shrimp is ready.* He poked the pinkish shrimp with his sharpened fingernail.

After Caradon finished dinner he rocked back into his chair and fell into a deep sleep.

CHAPTER NINE

The morning sun was breaking over the Georgia pines when Joe Jackson pulled into Tom Grey's yard. Tom looked through the kitchen window. Mrs. Grey was preparing the morning breakfast. Jackson's stomach began to ping with hunger.

Mrs. Grey heard the tapping on the windowpane. "Come in... the door's open."

Joe Jackson entered the kitchen. His long nose instantly picked up the smell of home-cooked food.

"If I could find a woman who cooked as good as you, Mrs. Grey..."

"Yeah..." she said, a smile twinkling on her face. "What would you do?"

"I would marry her in a minute," said Joe, fibbing.

Mrs. Grey looked at him sternly. "Your problem, Mr. Jackson," she said while wiping her hands on her apron, "is not *getting* married, but *staying* married. Did Tom talk to you about the covered dish dinner our church is having?"

"Yes, ma'am, he did mention it."

"I'll tell you, Mr. Jackson: we have some fine, Christian, God-fearing women attending our services. You marry one of them and your life will be a lot happier."

"Yes, ma'am."

"Sit down, Mr. Jackson. Let me pour you some freshly brewed coffee. Would you like breakfast?"

"Yes, ma'am, if you don't mind."

She picked up a plate and walked over to the stove. Three sausage links were rolled off the skillet. Next came a ladle full of grits, topped off with cornbread. She proceeded to do the same for her husband.

"Tom," she called, "Your breakfast is ready."

"Be there in a second," came the reply.

Joe Jackson was tempted to tear into that steaming plate of food, but he knew what came first, so he sat patiently with his hands folded.

"Mrs. Grey, did Tom tell you about the accident?"

"Yes, isn't it a tragedy?"

Tom Grey walked into the kitchen and sat down. "Bless us, oh Lord, and these thy gifts, which we are about to receive. Amen."

Joe Jackson, unfolded his hands, free to eat.

His hunger pangs subsided shortly after the plate was cleared. He eased back in his chair and began to sip on his coffee. After a while, he put the cup down and stared into Tom's eyes.

"What exactly happened down there last night, Tom?"

"I told you when I phoned you this morning."

"Why did the superintendent tell you that One Eye didn't have his life jacket on?"

"Why, hell, I worked with him all day and he never took it off! And another thing... why would they shut down a multimillion dollar job because of a missing man? All this just doesn't make sense to me."

Mrs. Grey looked at the clock on the wall. "I know one thing. If you boys don't get moving, you'll be late for work."

Tom Grey kissed his wife goodbye and then he headed out the door, followed by Joe Jackson.

"Let's take your truck today... I'm falling asleep from that big breakfast."

Tom Grey pulled out of the driveway and headed eastbound on Route 40. After a few miles of travel, he took the on-ramp southbound on I-95 and headed for Jacksonville. They crossed the Saint Marys River, which separates northeast Florida.

* * *

The incoming tide brought with it crabs, shrimp, and numerous species of baitfish that fed in the marshes and estuaries that lined the river's banks. Far downstream, where the river enters the Atlantic Ocean, a wide school of menhaden was entering the river to feed. The vibrating baitfish activated the predators' taste senses. The oily secretions emitted from the baitfish pushed the predators into a frenzy. They rose up the water column with jaws agape. The baitfish swimming at the river's surface instinctively felt the panic of their kind far below. Large numbers of fish began to jump out of the water.

A lone fisherman, who was fishing the north jetty of Amelia, had spotted the boiling mass of fish within his casting range. He tied on a Hopkin's stainless steel lure to his line, and cast it smack into the center of the fishy mix. The man was not prepared for the strike that nearly pulled the rod from his hand. The battle was short-lived. His line suddenly went slack. *Damn, he bit my lure off,* thought the fisherman. He reeled the line in and watched as the main school broke into smaller pods and swam frantically towards the safety of the marshes upriver. The attack stopped as quickly as it had started. The surfacing body parts and bloodlines attracted seagulls and brown pelicans, who dove into the water packing their gullets with bite-sized body parts. The fisherman considered tying on a new lure but decided to leave. This Blitzkrieg was over.

The fisherman returned to his truck and drove through town to the Sunrise Cafe for breakfast. He entered the restaurant and sat on a stool to the right of a spectacled man who was reading the newspaper.

"Morning, Snoop," said the fisherman.

The fisherman turned his head towards the man. His reading glasses perched on the end of his nose.

"Morning, Doug, ya have any luck today?"

"Naw, but I did have a big fish cut me loose."

"Ah, the big one that got away..." a waitress chimed in, filling their coffees.

"Were you using monofilament line?"

"Yup," replied Doug.

"Musta been a chopper bluefish hit you. The next time you go fishing, tie a length of wire to your lure."

"Yeah sure. Wire?!"

"You'll stand a better chance of bringing him in."

Snoop noticed Sheriff Lowellin's squad car pull into the parking lot. Snoop waited until the sheriff entered the restaurant and hung his hat on the door. Snoop motioned for him to sit next to him.

The sheriff walked over to Snoop, and then put his large right hand on his shoulder.

"You're gonna have to help me sit down."

"Don't ask him why," Snoop said to Doug.

"Why?" asked Doug anyway.

"They don't make stools that fit big muscular guys like me..."

The sheriff plopped down and shifted his weight until he found the center.

"There, I made it."

The sheriff turned his head toward Snoop, his face sullen. "Snoop," the sheriff said. "I'm gonna ask you a very serious question, and I want you to answer truthfully. No ifs, ands, or buts."

Snoop thought for a few moments and then said, "I will."

"You will what?" asked the sheriff, his eyes narrowing.

The ham operator raised his right arm and rotely said, "I, Snoop McClenan, shall answer the sheriff's question truthfully."

The sheriff's eyes widened, and the pall was lifted from his face. "Now then Mr. Snoop, what is a Yankee?"

"I guess that a Yankee is someone who lives up north."

"Wrong!" replied the sheriff. "A Yankee is someone who comes down here and spends their money, then goes home."

"Right, right..."

"Next question! What's a damn Yankee?"

"I don't know."

"A damn Yankee is someone from up north who comes down here to stay." The sheriff's broad face burst full of laughter; tears of joy rolled down his cheeks.

Snoop smiled and said, "You're the only guy I know who laughs at his own jokes."

The sheriff regained his composure, and then said, "You have to admit, that was a good one."

"I'll have to admit that I've never heard that one before. You should tell that one to the tourists when they ask you for directions."

Snoop removed the reading glasses from the end of his nose and put them in his shirt pocket. He then folded the newspaper.

"You leavin' so soon?" asked the sheriff.

"I gotta make money for the paper mill."

"Why don't you quit that place and come to work for me? I could always use a good radio dispatcher on the night shift."

"Five more years to retirement, and then I'll look you up."

"Alright, it's a deal."

"Say, Sheriff, do me a favor, check out the report of a possible drowning at Kings Bay."

"Drowning, eh?"

"I don't know, you have to check it out. Do the damn Yankees have to do everything around here?"

"I don't know anybody at base security, but I do know everybody at the Saint Marys Sheriff's Office. What time did you receive the call?"

"Oh, a little after midnight last night," replied Snoop.

"I'll see what I can find out," said the sheriff.

After finishing his breakfast, Sheriff Lowellin drove back to his office and called the Saint Marys Sheriff's Department.

"Saint Marys police, Corporal Woodworth speaking, how may I help you?"

"This is Lowellin."

"Oh, how are you doing this morning, Sheriff?"

"Fine, fine," replied the sheriff. "Can you do me a favor and check out a report of a drowning at Kings Bay last night?"

"Hold on a second, I'll check the logbook."

After a few minutes, the corporal got back on the phone. "Sheriff, there's no reported death at Kings Bay last night," he said. "But some sort of protester was picked up on a health and welfare check just outside the base."

"Is that so..."

"Right. A sentry spotted a man blocking traffic just outside their gate and dispatched a rapid response team to get him out of the road."

"What'd they do to him?"

"They held him on the base for a few hours then released him into the custody of a local park ranger friend."

Sheriff Lowellin thanked the corporal for the information and then hung up.

CHAPTER TEN

Inside the base, Lieutenant Brock watched as the medical team from Bethesda Hospital unloaded their workbags into the back of his truck.

The team leader stepped out of the Navy helicopter and introduced himself to Brock, "I'm Captain Geran. I have orders signed by Admiral Zolloff, the Navy Surgeon General, to pick up a corpse."

The captain then handed his paperwork to Brock for his signature.

After reading the orders, Brock signed his name and then retained a copy for himself. The medical orderlies finished loading the truck and then climbed into the back seat.

Brock drove to the morgue and secured the release of the corpse. He handed the key to slot number seven to the team leader. Captain Geran requested that the building be evacuated

"Do you want me to stay?" asked Brock.

"No, Lieutenant! My orders are to treat this corpse as being either chemically or biologically contaminated. I can't allow anyone without proper safety gear near the body." Brock wiped his hands on his pants leg.

* * *

Brock cleared the building of personnel and then posted himself outside the door. He watched as the team members put on white one-piece suits. Canisters were then strapped to their backs. A tube extended to a clear headpiece that was secured to the collar of the suit. Team members turned valves on the canisters releasing oxygen. The suits quickly filled. Brock began to smile. *Those boys look like a scene out of the movie Ghostbusters.*

From the back of the truck, the team members began to remove testing equipment and a large black plastic case that resembled a coffin. After the last suited man entered the building, Brock secured the door and then waited for the team to complete their tests.

The rays of the late springtime sun began to heat Brock's body. Perspiration appeared on his forehead, which he wiped away with his hands. The salt-laden sweat entered the pores on his hands, causing a small abrasion to sting. Brock inspected his hands thoroughly but found no open cuts. *Could I have been exposed to radiation from handling that damn corpse?* he thought.

Brock pulled the release form from his shirt and read it slowly until he came to a heading that read: *"Caution! Subject may have been exposed to radiation, biological, or chemical agents."*

Brock slowly folded the paper and placed it back in his shirt pocket. Just then, the door opened. A bubble-headed man appeared carrying one end of the black case. Brock backed up to avoid further contact with the corpse. A second man appeared, holding the other end of the black box. They slid it in the back of the truck, and then went back inside the morgue to get their testing equipment.

The team leader emerged from the morgue and opened the protective suit. He climbed out of it and then walked over to Brock.

"Well, Lieutenant, our mission is complete," said the team leader. He looked at his watch. "We should be in Washington by thirteen hundred hours."

"Sir, did you find any contaminants on the corpse—"

"I can neither con—"

"The reason I ask..." continued Brock, "is that I handled it with my bare hands."

"I'm not at liberty to say. I can say that it's not uncommon for us to detect low levels of radiation at nuclear facilities. If you have a concern, I suggest that you get a full medical workup."

"Thanks for the advice." Brock began to look at his hands with increased anguish.

"Lieutenant, you can tell the morgue personnel that they can return to work."

Brock walked over to a small group of men, who were watching the unfolding events with great curiosity.

"What the hell are bio heads doing in our morgue?" one of the men said.

"Oh, that's just a practice test conducted by the Surgeon General's Office," Brock said. "You boys can return to work."

When Brock returned to the truck, he found the bed loaded and the medical team sitting quietly in the cab. He drove them to the waiting helicopter, and then drove over to the base hospital.

* * *

The following day, base commander Jarvis and dredge site engineer McDowell were summoned to Washington for a conference with Admiral Farragut and Admiral Zolloff, Navy Surgeon General. The Kings Bay officers were escorted into the conference room and seated by an attendant, who took their dress hats and poured water into glasses that sat before them. Captain Jarvis ran his hand across the highly polished mahogany tabletop. He picked up a long-stemmed crystal glass and took a sip of water, then gently placed the glass on its coaster.

"Captain McDowell, is this place going to be your next duty station?" Jarvis turned his head and looked out the picture window behind them. "Look, you'll even have a view of the White House."

"Sir, I would think that you would be stationed at the Pentagon before me."

"I've been passed over for colonel so many times I feel like the ugly girl at prom."

"Well, you look good enough to make captain, Captain."

"I'm afraid that Kings Bay will be my last duty station."

"Any plans after you retire?"

"I'll probably get a consulting job with Lockheed."

"Well if you want to score points in there, compliment Zolloff's beard."

The door at the other end of the conference room opened. Four white-suited officers entered the room. Jarvis and McDowell got out of their chairs and stood at attention. Admiral Farragut and Admiral Zolloff took their seats. Their aides sat on either side of them.

"Sit down," said Admiral Zolloff.

The officers from Kings Bay took their seats.

"Gentlemen, you have been summoned here today to add any information regarding the retrieval of the unidentified human remains found inside Kings Bay Naval Base." A fact sheet was passed to Admiral Zolloff. He read it intently, and then placed the paper on the desk. "Captain McDowell?"

"Yes, sir," he replied.

"As I understand it, you are the chief naval engineer for new construction at Kings Bay?"

"Yes, I am, sir. In a written report, Lieutenant Brock, the chief security officer at Kings Bay, stated that a distress call was made at approximately twenty-four hundred hours, on May 28, 1978. Security boat number five was dispatched. At zero zero ten hours, boat number five retrieved the aforementioned human remains."

"Do you think that there is any connection between the work site and the corpse?" Zolloff leaned back in his chair and began to stroke his scraggy beard with his long delicate fingers.

"Sir, I visited the work site yesterday. I expected to see a strong flow of fresh water coming out of the split in the limestone."

"Could there be an obstruction of some sort?" asked Zolloff.

"That very well could be the case, sir. Another thing that I noticed: there was a strong, pungent odor being emitted from the cut."

"Are you a geologist?"

"No, sir. I've had courses on the subject, but my field is mechanical engineering—"

"Thank you, Captain McDowell. Captain Jarvis, you are the base commander at Kings Bay Submarine Base?"

"Yes, sir, I am."

"On the date in question, you were given photos of an unidentified corpse, and at that time determined that construction be stopped until further notice."

"Yes, that's correct."

Jarvis's blood pressure began to rise. *I guess they will try to attack my credibility*, thought Jarvis.

Admiral Zolloff directed his aide to pass out enlarged photos of the corpse to those attending the meeting. After a few minutes of silence, he began to speak.

"Gentlemen, the dots on the photo represent bite marks, which number approximately two thousand bites. Forensics, with the aid of an electron microscope, determined that the individual tooth marks were made by a shark. The size of the tooth would have come from a predator weighing around twenty pounds. If we divide fifty teeth per predator into 2,000, we come up with a school that numbers forty fish. The question must be asked: did these killers leave Kings Bay or did they enter the spring? Is this an isolated incident, or will more attacks occur? Oh, by the way, Captain Jarvis, you made a wise decision in stopping construction, in light of our finding."

Jarvis felt a release of tension. "Yes, sir. I needed to be sure of what we are dealing—"

"What I can't understand is..." Admiral Zolloff cut Jarivs off while reexamining the photo before him. "The ferocity of the attack." He turned the photo around and held it up before the captains. "The predators not only tore the flesh from the body but also went the extra mile by crushing all the bones open and stripping out the marrow." He laid the photo back down and sighed. "I have performed hundreds of autopsies, and I can tell you that I have never run across anything like this. I have appointed Admiral Farragut director of this inquiry. I will now turn this discussion over to Admiral Farragut."

"Gentlemen, all I have to say is that the Navy Department had determined that Kings Bay shall be the homeport for the next generation of ballistic missile submarine," began Farragut. "Just one of these submarines will have the capacity to destroy the entire Soviet Union. Our mission is to see that the facility is built according to specifications. In the interest of safety, I have stopped all new construction at Kings Bay until this situation is resolved. Are there any questions? No? Good! This meeting is adjourned.

CHAPTER ELEVEN

Dr. Paul Gillon, project manager for the U.S. Geological Survey, Woods Hole, MA, received a call from the Washington office.

"Hey, Paul, how are you doing?"

"Just fine, Sam, how are things down there in Washington?"

"Nothing changes, only paperwork seems to increase all the time."

"Ha! Same here."

"Hey Paul, the reason I called was to have you send a team to Kings Bay Submarine Base to gather information on a submarine spring that may impede their construction program."

"I have a team that's idle right now."

"Perfect!"

"You want me to order a drill for bore samples?"

"No, that won't be necessary, the head of the spring is exposed. All they want are experts in the field of submarine springs to critique them."

"Well, I got just the man for you... Matt Maury."

"I've heard good things about Matt," Paul said.

"Yes, he's done a lot of work in that field. I've contracted with the Marine Fisheries Department to lease a research vessel for the survey. The Sea Quest is being readied at the Charleston Naval Shipyard. Fly your team down there as soon as possible. The Navy Department is sending in an ichthyologist. His area of concern will be a large fish kill that is occurring near a spring."

The project manager, after saying goodbye, got on the loudspeaker and requested that Dr. Matt Maury come to his office. After a few minutes, a tall gray-haired man walked into his office.

"What's up, Paul?"

"I just received a call from Washington. They need someone with your expertise —"

"How to play more than four cards in bingo?"

"Ha! But no, to examine a submarine spring in Saint Marys, Georgia."

"Saint Marys, you say?" Maury mused with a tinge of adventure in his voice. He walked over to the wall map and located the town of Saint Marys. "You sure they're not talking about a land-based spring? Saint Marys lies west of the Intracoastal Waterway. They must be dredging down there."

"BINGO! how did you know that?" asked Paul.

"Well, the closest offshore spring is three miles from Crescent Beach, Florida." Matt pushes a finger on the map. "It lies in fifty feet of water." He draws a circle with his finger.

"I'm impressed, Bingo Boy."

"This sounds like an interesting discovery. When do we go?"

"As soon as you can pack your bags," said the manager.

CHAPTER TWELVE

She awoke to the sound of seagulls. A light breeze from the Pacific Ocean entered the beachfront hotel window, giving the room a scent of the sea. The ocean waves could be heard crashing against the rocks below. The gulls called outside her window. Her smooth hand caressed the man's broad shoulders. He began to feel her hot breath enter his ear. Goosebumps ran up and down his body in anticipation.

She asked, "Why don't you teach me to ride those dolphins of yours?"

"Someday," he murmured.

"I think today would be a good day."

She slipped her left leg over his body and lifted herself on top of him. Her tongue found his ear. It began to flick in and out; all the while streams of hot air entered his brain. The woman's own body became excited. Her spread thighs began to pump against the man's closed cheeks. Beads of sweat began to appear on her forehead.

"Is this the way it's done?" she whispered.

The man only groaned in anticipation. A hard knock on the door broke the moment

"Who is it?" yelled the girl.

"Navy Department Courier. Lieutenant Thomas Chamberlain is listed as living here."

"Can you come back later? He's sleeping."

She felt her boyfriend tense up. She pressed down with her body, holding him in place.

"Sorry, ma'am, I can't do that. Could you please wake him up? I have orders for him to sign."

"I'm up," groaned Chamberlain.

He pushed himself up, flipping his girlfriend on her side. She immediately covered herself with the sheet and began to brood.

Chamberlain got out of bed and grabbed the towel draped over a chair and wrapped it around his waist, tying it in a knot. He then unlocked the door and opened it slightly.

"Lieutenant Chamberlain?"

"Yes," he replied.

"May I see your military ID, sir?"

Chamberlain sighed and reached for his pants.

Through the ajar door, the courier took notice of the woman, who was obviously naked under a tightly clutched sheet. He fought back a smirk.

After checking the ID, the courier slipped a brown manila envelope and release papers through the crack in the door. "Sir, I need you to sign the forms and keep the original for yourself."

"Yeah yeah..."

Chamberlain signed for the envelope, and then returned the copies through the crack. He noticed that the courier was wearing a Marine Uniform.

"Say, are we short of Navy couriers?"

"No, sir. I guess the Navy Department figures that Marines are better at tracking people down." The courier clicked his heels and said, "So long."

Chamberlain closed the door, sat on the edge of the bed, and slowly opened the envelope.

Rebecca's moodiness was set aside by curiosity. She sat up with the sheet covering her body up to her neck. She scooted in close behind her boyfriend, peering over his hairy shoulder, trying to read the printed material that he held in his hands.

"What's it say?" she asked inquisitively.

"My dolphin's sick..." Chamberlain said with a grin.

"Oh yeah," she purred. "What'd he come *down* with?"

"He came down with," he proceeded to read the letter, "Lieutenant Thomas Chamberlain, stationed at Naval Base, San Diego Dolphin Research Facility, return to base by zero nine hundred hours, 5-28-78. T. D. to Kings Bay Naval Base."

"Well, what's that mean?" with sultry concern in her voice.

"It means that I'm being transferred!"

"Great," she got up and stomped to the bathroom, still holding the sheet. "What about us?" she continued while peeing. "When we started living together, you told me that the chances were slim that you would ever be transferred from San Diego."

"But honey!"

He approached the bathroom door and she stuck her head out.

Storm clouds formed in Rebecca's eyes. "Don't touch me!"

He reached for a hug. She threw her arms out in front of her boyfriend as a warning. The sheet that had covered her now lay at Chamberlain's feet. He retreated to the bed and sat. Rebecca's firm, upswept breasts were directly in his line of sight. He looked away as to not anger her any further. She drove her fingers through her crimson hair in frustration. She looked at her hands.

"And what about our future?" she whined. "When are we going to get engaged? Oh, that's right! What's the old Navy saying? 'If the Navy wanted you to have a wife, it would have issued you one?'"

"Honey, now listen, I'm only going away for thirty days."

"Are you sure?" she asked.

"I'll be back before you know it."

To show his unconcern for the orders, he threw them against the wall.

A smile appeared at the corners of Rebecca's lips. Tom faced her and began to stare at her breasts. She cupped them in her hands and asked him if he wanted to taste one.

"Two, if you please," he said.

Tom kissed the left nipple, then the right. She then lay back, drawing him down with her.

He whispered in her ear, "Now I'm going to show you how I ride the dolphins."

"Finallyyyy," she moaned.

* * *

The following morning, Lieutenant Chamberlain boarded a jet at the San Diego base. He met a courier and signed for a briefcase marked *SECRET*. He was also handed a single key. The Navy steward escorted Chamberlain to the front row of the thirty-seat jet.

"Take your pick, sir; they're all yours."

"Where are the other passengers?" asked Chamberlain.

"You're it, sir! The reason I put you up-front was that it's close to the galley. Would you like coffee or tea when we get aloft?"

"Coffee, please," replied the Lieutenant.

The steward opened the door to the cockpit and informed the pilot that all passengers were aboard.

After closing the door, the steward walked over to Chamberlain.

"Sir, you must buckle your seat belt."

Chamberlain was mesmerized by the lettering on the briefcase. *Secret! What the hell could this have to do with me?* he thought.

"Sir, did you hear me? Buckle up!"

The steward's command snapped Chamberlain out of his trance. He found the ends of the belts and clicked the metal clasps together.

The steward noticed the red letters on the briefcase. He sat down at the other end of the aisle, as to not appear nosy. The pilot taxied down the runway, and then throttled the engines. The jet rose into the cloudless California skies, circled the base, and then headed east. Destination: Charleston Naval Base.

* * *

Dr. Maury and his assistant Vince Ekman boarded a commercial airliner at Logan International Airport.

After being seated, Maury leaned back in his chair, reached into his pocket, and brought out a notebook. He began to review the equipment manifest when suddenly his right eyelid began to twitch involuntarily.

"Vince, did you include an abstract of Blake's Plateau?"

"Yeah, Doc, it's packed with the testing equipment. I sent everything directly to King's Bay."

Maury's eyelid ceased twitching.

The young assistant retrieved a similar notebook. He fingered quickly through the book.

"Let's see," he mumbled, "Priority Mail to Captain McDowell, Construction Branch, Kings Bay, Georgia." Vince snapped the notebook closed, and briskly placed it in his coat.

Maury noticed Vince's agitation. He turned to his assistant. "Vince, I know that you have total recall and an IQ of a hundred sixty-whatever, and that is precisely why I selected you. The reason I carry a notebook and urge my assistants to do the same is that an event or important issue can be documented, whereas a recollection of prior events stored by the brain, regardless of the size of the brain, is not as reliable."

Vince looked out the window and watched the landmass below. "Where are we at?" he asked.

"We're hovering over the place where you acknowledge what I've said."

"Okay. Yeah. Yes, sir. I got it."

"Thank you," Dr. Maury said. He paused and relaxed and added, "It looks like coastal North Carolina. There are large patches of green interspersed with several river systems."

"They look like rattlesnakes slithering through the grass," said Vince. "Does all the rainwater that falls on the United States make it back to the sea?" he asked.

"No, of course not. Human consumption, irrigation, and evaporation play a role also. Vince, are you aware that twenty percent of all rainwater that falls on the landmass is unaccounted for?"

"No, I wasn't unaware of that."

"Do you know what that means? If we can find the underground water sources, say near the abandoned anthracite coal mines in Pennsylvania and West Virginia, we could bore into the pure underground water sources and flush out the acid mine wastewaters. Another problem yet to be addressed is the intrusion of saltwater into the freshwater aquifer of southern Florida, whose population has increased tenfold. Captiva Island, which is located on the southwest coast of Florida, is now experiencing a gradual intrusion of salt into their well water, polluting many of them. Residents of the islands are buying bottled spring water from a company in north Florida that draws from the same aquifer as Captiva Island. There will come a time when the entire coast of southern Florida will be lined with desalinization plants. The cost of fresh water will skyrocket."

"How do you propose to resolve the problem?" asked Vince.

Maury sat back in his chair and put his hands up to his chin. "The first thing we must do," he continued, "is to learn to conserve our most precious resource, fresh water. The second is to locate and explore all the offshore submarine springs. There's a broad range of data on land-based springs, one example being Silver Springs located near Disney World, but precious little data about offshore springs."

"Why don't we have more information about these springs? We went to the moon, didn't we?"

"Vince, submarine springs have been in place for millions of years. They bother nobody. They are not a hazard to shipping, thus they're not on our maps. It is only now, when man usurps from the environment, that interest is spawned."

"After I become familiarized with the subject, I may consider making it my thesis."

"That's a great idea, Vince," said Maury, "I will be happy to help you in any way I can."

The steward asked all passengers to fasten their seatbelts. The plane started its descent and landed at Atlanta International Airport.

* * *

Maury and his assistant were greeted by Navy officials and Maury was handed a briefcase identical to the one given to Lieutenant Chamberlain.

They boarded a Navy passenger jet and flew to the Navy base in Charleston.

The *Sea Quest* was having its final shakedown. Ensign Joseph Clark, the designated captain of the ship, stood at the stern and watched as the pilot maneuvered throughout the ship basin. He waved to the pilot and then got the okay sign.

Looks like we passed the sea trials, thought Clark. *We will probably shove off tomorrow if everything goes well.* He walked to the back of the ship and was greeted by a seaman who had just completed the installation of a large wire mesh cage, which was bolted to the stern of the ship.

"Mission completed," said the seaman. "Would you like to try it out?"

"Yes," replied the ensign.

The seaman held out an electrical control box. "It's very simple," he said. "You push the UP button, it goes up. Release your finger, it stops."

"What if I keep my finger on the button, will it jam up?"

"Oh, no sir, that can't happen. I installed an automatic shutoff, sir."

"Outstanding, Seaman."

"If I may ask, sir, what are you going to put in the cage?"

"It will probably be used for holding fish specimens."

"Where we headed, sir?"

"I'm not at liberty to say."

Ensign Clark walked to the bow of the boat, then motioned the pilot to return to the dock.

After a gangplank was lowered, Maury and Ekman climbed the incline with their gear. The two passengers' names were checked against the ship's manifest and then they were escorted to their individual quarters.

Maury dropped his bags on the bed, and then walked over to a small desk and laid the briefcase down. He then opened the latch and began to pore over the documents. On occasions, his eyebrows would rise, indicating that the material before him had tweaked his interest.

* * *

Maury woke up to the call of an intercom.

"Chow time," barked the caller. "All personnel not on duty, it's chow time."

Maury sat back and rubbed his eyes. He looked at the documents scattered on the desk before him. Some had fallen on the floor. *I must be a security risk,* thought Maury. He gathered up the papers and secured them in a briefcase. Maury left the room, and then knocked on the berth adjacent to his.

"Vince Ekman... you in there?"

"Yes, this is he," came the reply from within.

"This is Dr. Maury. You going to get some chow?"

The door opened suddenly. "What's chow?" asked Vince innocently, scratching his head.

"A military term for food. It could apply to breakfast, lunch, dinner, or even a snack."

"I'll take 'em all," Vince said. "I'm starving."

"Okay, I'll meet you in the galley."

Maury walked down the narrow hall and followed the signs and his nose to a stairway and descended into a large dining room. He picked up a tray and waited in line. When it was his turn, he asked the cook what was on the menu.

"Hot dogs or filet mignon."

"Fillet, of course, this must be a five-star restaurant," said Maury to the cook.

"No, sir, it's just that I'm good friends with the chief petty officer of the USS *Jackson.*"

"Is that a destroyer?" asked Maury.

"No, sir, it's a ballistic missile sub."

"I see," said Maury, his stomach growling.

"Boy, those submariners eat like kings. You might have been eating lobster, too, but I didn't want to press my luck."

"Stop bullshitting up there," came a call from the back of the line.

The cook quickly filled Maury's tray.

"Where do I sit?"

"Enlisted men and civilian guests use the common center table. The booths are reserved for commissioned officers."

Maury thanked him and then turned away. He noticed a young officer seated in the restricted area with a briefcase at his side that resembled the one issued to him. Maury found a seat with a view of the officer.

"Hey, Doc," came a call from the bottom of the stairwell. Maury motioned for Vince to get in line.

Ensign Clark climbed down the stairs, with a clipboard in his hands. "Attention, I'd like to have your attention for a minute." He referred to his clipboard. "Are there a Lieutenant Thomas Chamberlain, Dr. Matthew Maury, and Vince Ekman here?"

Chamberlain turned his head and raised his hand.

Ensign Clark walked down the aisle and introduced himself to Chamberlain. "I'm sorry that I missed you when you boarded. Come on down to the Captain's table, you'll have more room to eat."

As the officer passed Maury, the geologist raised his hand. The ensign stopped. "And you are?"

"Matt Maury."

"Come on down and have dinner with us."

Maury followed them to a large circular table and took a seat across from the officer with the briefcase. Vince, having loaded his tray with food, walked down the aisle and sat down next to Maury.

"Gentlemen, this is my assistant, Vince Ekman."

"Pleased to meet you," said Ensign Clark.

The young man's mouth was now full, so he only nodded in agreement.

The galley steward walked up to the table with menus in hand. Ensign Clark accepted one and ordered. "Please bring a pot of coffee over. Young man, do you want something to drink?"

"Yes," replied Vince. "I'll have a glass of milk."

The steward finished writing and then left.

The only object remaining on the table after dinner was a pot of coffee and four cups. The light talk had ended. The men began to talk about more pressing issues.

"My orders are to depart Charleston at twenty-two hundred hours tonight. We should arrive at Kings Bay by zero seven hundred hours. No indication yet when we will depart from Kings Bay."

"Dr. Maury, I'm an ichthyologist and know everything about fish but my training didn't touch on the subject of submarine springs, sir."

"Well Lieutenant Chamberlain," replied Maury. "I have been studying them—"

Chamberlain interrupted, "Just call me Tom."

"Well, Tom, it's a funny thing about scientists. We tend to be deeply knowledgeable about our chosen field of study, but when we step outside that line of work, we tend to stumble. The first written text about submarine springs was by Pausanias 8v11, second century A.D. He describes the phenomenon of submarine springs."

Chamberlain watched as Dr. Maury's facial expressions and tone of voice began to change. It was as if the doctor was speaking before a large audience.

"Not only there in Greece is there unmistakably freshwater rising in the sea. In front of Dicearchia, in western Italy, there is water boiling in the sea and an artificial island has been made around it, so that this water is not wasted, but serves for hot baths."

"How are these offshore springs created?" asked Clark.

"Most submarine springs result from the freshwater drive. A second driving force, geothermal heat, is obvious for submarine springs in areas of active volcanoes. The third source is a geothermally-activated convective upwelling, which occurs in non-volcanic areas."

Dr. Maury perceived that he was losing his audience. "An example of the third source is what is referred to as the mud hole submarine spring located twelve miles off the southwest shore of Florida. The location of the spring was known by local fishermen. As part of research on remote sensing of hydrologic phenomena, an overflight was made by NASA aircraft, which were equipped with a thermal infrared scanner in 1966. A sea surface temperature anomaly was discovered, suggesting that the freshwater discharging from the spring was about twenty degrees warmer than the surrounding seawater. Ground truth investigation showed that the discharging groundwater had a temperature of 96.6 degrees Fahrenheit."

"Dr. Maury, why were the fishermen interested in this spring?" asked Chamberlain.

"It is a well-known fact among fishing captains that if you locate an uncharted submarine spring, you have found a fishing goldmine. Many species retreat to submarine springs during the cold fronts, and there are large varieties of nutrients to be found there. This spring has its origins in the Gulf of Mexico and the Florida Straits. In this flow system, cold dense seawater enters the submarine springs and flows inland through the cavernous dolomite limestone to depths of four thousand feet below the state of Florida, where after being heated by the Earth's core, it flows upward and comes in contact with fresh water, which is then recharged through submarine springs that ring the state of Florida."

"That's very interesting," said Ensign Clark. "Do you happen to know the coordinates of the mud hole?"

"You want to perform convection analysis of cold and warm currents?"

"Actually I'd like to try my luck fishing there."

Chuckles made the rounds around the table.

"If the fish aren't biting," the ensign added, "I could always jump in the ocean and take a sauna."

"Vince, do you recall the precise location?"

"Yes, the exact coordinates are—"

"Wait a minute, let me write them down..." said Ensign Clark grabbing for a pen from his shirt and placing a napkin on the table.

"Are you ready, sir?" asked Vince.

"Yes, go ahead."

"The coordinates of the mud hole are twenty-six degrees, fifteen minutes fifty-nine seconds north latitude by eighty-two degrees one minute zero seconds longitude. The spring is also marked on USC and GS chart twelve fifty-five."

Ensign Clark neatly folded the napkin and placed it in his wallet. He then looked at his watch. "Well, gentlemen, this was a very informative conversation," he said. "Maybe we'll talk more when we get to Kings Bay."

Captain Clark climbed the steps and instructed the chief petty officer to hoist the anchors and cast off the mooring lines. The *Sea Quest* slowly motored out of the Charleston Naval Base and then throttled up when she encountered the rolling waves of the Atlantic Ocean.

CHAPTER THIRTEEN

The sun began to rise as the research ship entered the Saint Marys River channel. Traveling ahead of the *Sea Quest* was a small shrimp boat. The men on board were busy shaking their nets clear of debris and undersized fish. Sea birds dove into the offerings, while brown pelicans skimmed the ocean surface.

The captain of the shrimp boat walked outside the pilothouse and yelled down to the crew, "Wrap up da nets now, boys."

The first mate turned from his work and said, "But Dutch—"

He was interrupted with a pointing finger. "Ya see that boat follerin' us?"

"Yeah, that's one of the environmental resource boats."

"When I'z a kid, they called 'em fish wardens," said the captain. He turned the wheel hard to port and then watched suspiciously as the *Sea Quest* plowed up the river channel.

At a point where the Intracoastal Waterway crosses the Saint Marys River, the ship turned north. The pilot rang the ship's bell and announced over the loudspeaker that they had arrived at Kings Bay.

Ensign Clark stood on the bow, then ordered the pilot to stop. Before them was a large sign that was anchored to the seafloor: *WARNING: DO NOT ENTER! U.S. Government Property*. In the distance was a large boat that had been traversing the mouth of Kings Bay. At the sighting of the *Sea Quest*, it had turned on the siren and warning lights, then headed in the direction of the research ship.

Maury and his assistant walked out on the deck and joined the ensign.

"Sir, have you been speeding again?" asked Maury.

Ensign Clark smiled. "I wouldn't want to try to outrun those guys."

The patrol boat slowed, and then shut off its siren. The bands of red light continued to flash across the *Sea Quest* streaking ribbons of shiny pink up her gray sides.

A tall, thin Marine officer, with a sidearm strapped to his hip, called to Clark, "What is your destination, sir?"

"I have orders to report to Captain McDowell, Chief Engineer, Shore Facilities, Kings Bay."

"May I see your orders?" asked the security officer.

The security officer looked toward the bow. Casting off a line, he commanded a muscular-built marine stationed there who threw the mooring line skyward. Two mates from the *Sea Quest* dutifully grabbed the mooring line and pulled until the two ships gently touched. The security officer reached out and grabbed the orders, then climbed up into the pilot's house and got on the radio.

Vince began to survey the security boat. Two stiff-legged Marines paced the boat with loaded M-16s slung over their shoulders. Centered on the stern of the security boat was a machine gun mounted on a tripod. A belt of evenly spaced brass ammunition stretched from the magazine into a metal box.

Vince elbowed Maury. "Hey Doc, what caliber machine gun do you think that is?"

"Why don't you ask the Marines?"

"I don't think so, they don't look too friendly."

"Good answer, Vince," replied Maury.

"Yeah, I guess it's the unfriendly caliber."

The Marine officer reappeared and passed the paperwork back to Captain Clark. "Sir, everything is in order," the officer said. "Drop anchor here. An escort boat will be dispatched to lead you into Kings Bay." He clicked his heels together and then saluted smartly.

Ensign Clark pointed toward the bow of the *Sea Quest*. "Release the mooring line," he hollered.

The security boat started her powerful engines, then drove off at high speed.

"So, this is Kings Bay?" asked Vince.

"Yes," replied Dr. Maury. "In fact, the area of water we're now floating on was dry land only ten thousand years ago. During the last ice age, water was drawn up in the form of ice to the North and South poles. The coastal states, such as Georgia and Florida, had land that extended another 20 miles eastward."

"Doc, do you think I should cancel my plans for a beachfront house, in light of your revelation?"

Maury smiled broadly. "No, Vince, your beachfront property won't lose value just yet. The next ice age won't occur for another ten thousand years, but don't hold me to it."

"It's a volatile market, I got ya, Doc."

Lieutenant Chamberlain walked out into the sunlight and stretched his arms.

"Where have you been hiding?" asked Dr. Maury.

"I must have jet lag," replied Chamberlain with a half yawn. He walked over to the rail and then looked into the seawater below him. "I know one thing: we're not in the clear, cool waters of the Pacific."

"Hey, Doc, you see that boat corning towards us?"

Dr. Maury looked toward the base, straining his eyes. "I see a fleck of something in the distance."

The workboat slowly made its way to the Sea Quest.

"No sirens, no flashing lights," noted Vince.

The boats slowly drifted together. A seaman at the bow and one at the stern were ready with tie lines in hand, ready to cast them off.

"Permission to board?" asked Captain McDowell as he saluted Ensign Clark.

"Permission granted, sir."

McDowell gave the signal to cast the lines. He also instructed the seamen to begin the transfer of the equipment that would be employed at the dredge site. McDowell climbed aboard and was introduced to Lieutenant Chamberlain, Dr. Maury, and his assistant.

"Gentlemen, I will be your liaison officer during your stay at Kings Bay," McDowell said. "Any equipment or supplies you need will be taken care of by me."

The group of men watched as the equipment was transferred to the *Sea Quest*.

"Where's all this stuff coming from?" exclaimed Vince, pointing to a long stainless-steel table being hauled aboard. "Hey, Doc, that's not ours!"

"That's for me," said Chamberlain, walking up from behind. "I asked for all this equipment, including the fish cage mounted on the stern. Generally, I get only half of what I ask for, but for this operation, I got everything I requested.

"The Navy must be very interested in solving the mystery of the mound," Dr. Maury said.

Captain McDowell looked down at the map in his hands. "Oh, Ensign Clark, we must go over the various depths of the bay, and the potential hazards we may encounter."

Clark thought for a second. "Let's go up to the wheelhouse," he eventually said. "I want my pilot to be included in this."

"Well, Maury, we better start checking our equipment," Vince said. "I want to be ready to go to work when we get to the mound."

When the last piece of equipment was transferred, Ensign Clark gave the signal to release the mooring lines. The *Sea Quest* followed the workboat into Kings Bay, past the idled dredge.

McDowell pointed to a hump on the bay surface. "There she is, Captain Clark. The flow of water generated from within the mound is about five knots."

"Can I moor my ship to the mound?" asked Clark.

"Yes, I believe so," replied McDowell.

"Still, a five-knot flow will rock the ship. I am going to anchor off-site."

McDowell nodded in agreement.

Maury walked out onto the deck. Looking into the bay, he noticed flows of discolored water mixing with the clear water below the ship. His eyebrows began to twitch with anticipation. He walked quickly back into the lab.

"Vince, don't forget to unpack the temperature gauges," Maury said. "We're going to need them right away."

The workboat throttled up, leaving Sea Quest not far from the bubbling mound.

Ensign Clark patted his hand on the pilot's shoulder. "Circle the structure, in an ever-widening circle. Call out the depth sounding and roll on the ship."

"Aye, aye, sir," replied the pilot.

Ensign Clark looked out the window watching the mound intently. The Sea Quest made ever-widening circles around the mound.

"Forty feet, no wake," came the call from the pilot.

"Hold position," said Captain Clark, raising his right hand. "Drop anchors."

The Sea Quest became a beehive of activity. Lifeboats, rope ladders, and a long-poled net were readied. Clark handed the equipment to a seaman who tied them off with a piece of rope, lowering it into the waiting hands of his shipmates stationed aboard a lifeboat.

Chamberlain grabbed the railing then rolled his body over the side. Down the rope ladder, he went.

"You're next," said the seaman on deck.

Maury looked over the side and watched as the rope ladder twisted and turned in the wind. "Getting too old for this," he said.

"Hey, Doc," called Vince, "just swing your body over the side then I'll tell you when the footholds are directly under you."

Maury grabbed the rail and climbed over the side. "I don't feel anything, Vince," he said, with a touch of fear in his voice.

The young scientist assistant looked over the side. "Just wait for a second, the ladder is twisted. Hold on... ready... now! Drop down now!"

Maury felt the footholds and began an unsteady descent.

When Maury finally reached the waiting boat, he looked up. "How did I ever make it down that ladder?"

Chamberlain patted him on the shoulder. "Just think, you're gonna have to go back up there."

Maury turned to Chamberlain. "Thanks, you're a real confidence builder."

Vince climbed on the ladder and descended rapidly. When he touched down, he said, "That was fun."

"Yeah, well, if it was so much fun, you can carry me back up."

The remaining pieces of equipment were lowered into the boat, and then the pilot made way for the mound. Maury's heartbeat began to rise at the sight of the maelstrom before him. Blackened waters from the spring overshadowed the clear bay waters. It reminded Maury of a teabag being dipped into a cup of clear scalding water. Maury was knocked to his seat when the boat began to roll, due to the waves that were created by the upwelling.

The pilot of the boat felt the resistance and gunned the engine. "Hold your hats, we're going straight into it."

The boat rose over a wave and landed hard on the mound. A seaman that was positioned on the bow jumped out of the boat with the anchor. He ran up the mound and secured the point of the anchor inside a crevice. The seaman gave the okay signal to the pilot, who then shut the engine down, leaving the stern of the boat to float aimlessly.

Chamberlain climbed out of the boat and helped to unload the equipment. A horde of fiddler crabs, which had been spooked by the beached lifeboat, began to return from the bay. Thousands of crabs massed around Chamberlain's foot. The scene reminded him of a vast contingent of Roman soldiers, with swords and battle flags raised high in the air. The bravest of the clan crawled out of the horde. His claws rose in defiance of the intruder. Chamberlain shifted his toe slightly and was instantly attacked. The crab's pinchers grabbed onto the rubber sole but couldn't penetrate. Chamberlain retaliated by flicking the fearless leader back into the horde with his toe. He then stomped his foot, sending the entire horde into a panicked retreat.

Chamberlain picked up his net and bag and walked up to the split in the mound. He dropped the net, knelt down, opened the black bag, and then took out a thermometer wrapped in a spool of line and a leather case that was tied in the center. He unwrapped the line, which was measured in feet and inches, and then dropped the temperature gauge into the blackened waters. The line slowly slipped through his hands and touched the bottom. He picked up his clipboard and marked ten feet even. The temperature gauge was raised up and recorded 86 degrees at location one. This he repeated along the length of the split. After completing the experiment, he wrapped the line around the temperature gauge and walked over to Dr. Maury, who was walking at the rim of the mound taking pressure measurements.

Chamberlain tapped the scientist on the shoulder. "Hey, Doc, you gotta minute?"

"Why sure," replied Maury. "What is it?"

"I've just recorded depth readings averaging ten feet and water temperatures averaging ninety. What readings are you getting down here?"

"I'm measuring the water velocity, which is tremendous. I bet the discharge of this spring exceeds the maximum discharge of the Silver Springs in Marion County, Florida."

"Right."

"Say, ask Vince, he's recording the outflow temperatures."

Chamberlain walked over to Vince. "What kind of readings are you getting?"

"Oh, I'm averaging seventy, seventy-two, which is indicative of an aquifer source of two thousand feet below the earth."

"Why am I reading in the high eighties?"

"Blockage. Maybe. Or another flow source."

Chamberlain walked back to his starting point, and then put the spool of line into the black bag and brought out arm's-length rubber gloves and put them on. Next, he pulled the string to the black case, which opened up an array of gleaming surgical instruments. Chamberlain selected a long scalpel and a pair of clamps. Then he reached into the bag and brought out a jar for samples. He proceeded to slowly walk along the cut.

Chamberlain noticed tube-like material floating on the surface that seemed interesting. He placed the tools on the ground and then dipped a rubber glove into the blackened waters and grabbed the slimy material, but it would not pull free. Chamberlain picked up the scalpel and cut the organic material loose. Upon close inspection, he made a startling discovery. The slimy material in his hand was the placenta. He quickly placed the specimen in the jar. He then picked up the scalpel and laid it flat on the rock surface with gloved arms fully immersed. He put his arms underneath the rock shell and began to grope around with his free hand. The underside of the coarse limestone shell was smooth to the touch. He pushed against it with his finger. It was also pliable. Guided by the free hand, the scalpel sliced through the underside. Three more cuts and he might be able to pull the specimen free.

The unexpected jolt of pain that shot through Chamberlain's body caused him to curse loudly. "Son of a bitch!"

All the personnel working on the small island were alerted to the commotion. The two seamen tending the lifeboat were the first to reach the distressed man.

"What's the matter, sir?" asked the pilot.

"That son of a bitch tried to take my hand off."

Chamberlain cupped the gloved hand, which had held the scalpel. Drops of blood began to ooze out of the shredded glove.

"Sir, do you want me to get the medics?" asked the pilot.

"Yes, thank you," Chamberlain said. "And while you're aboard the ship, take the survival kit out of the rubber life raft, and I'm going to need that live well that's sitting on the bow."

The seaman hurried to the boat, and passed the scientists.

"What's going on?" asked Maury.

"The Lieutenant's been bitten. See if you can give him a hand."

Maury walked up. "Chamberlain, can I be of any help?"

"Yes, Doc, you can cut this glove off. There's a pair of scissors in the surgical kit."

Chamberlain opened the cupped hand and felt pain pulse through his body. Maury cut through the opened end of the glove towards the fingertips. Chamberlain watched as the shredded glove fell away from his hand and dropped into the blackened water. Blood began to ooze from a series of small puncture wounds, which extended from the knuckle to the end of his index finger.

"I think my finger's broken."

"What makes you think that?" asked Maury.

"I can move my other fingers freely, but it pains me to move the injured finger. I know why I was bitten on the left hand. I was holding a scalpel and the predator must have been attracted to the glitter of the instrument."

Maury turned and saw men running up the mound. The medic was the first to arrive.

"Who's hurt?" asked the medic.

Chamberlain offered his hand for inspection.

The medic put on surgical gloves and picked up a brown bottle from his bag. He removed the lid and warned Chamberlain that the astringent would sting. Small drops of antiseptic began to fall on the puncture wounds, while bubbles began to emerge from the wounds. The medic moved the finger up and down slightly, with no reaction from Chamberlain. He then tried to move the finger from side to side, but Chamberlain pulled his hand away.

"That hurts, Doc."

"You bet it does. Whatever bit you split the bone. You're gonna need x-rays and a splint for that finger. We'll have to transfer you to the base hospital."

Captain McDowell looked over the medic's shoulder. "I guess that you didn't take those written reports seriously."

Chamberlain brushed off the intended pun and asked for the survival kit.

The safety boat pilot stepped forward with the box and opened it.

"Look for a fishing lure and line," Chamberlain directed.

The pilot rummaged through the cans of rations and located a plastic bag with a glassy lure and spool of heavy line within. The pilot ripped the bag open and then tied a knot on the end of the lure.

"Would you like to try your luck at catching this bastard?" asked Chamberlain.

"No problem, sir," replied the pilot.

The shiny lure was dropped into the murky water. Unbeknownst to the men above, the shredded blood-soaked glove, which had fallen into the water, was now being attacked with a vengeance. All vestiges of human blood and scent were being inhaled by the predator. The large yellow eye watched as the lure bounced on the bottom. The bone-crushing jaws inhaled the object and tried to break it in half. The serrated teeth were no match for the stainless-steel lure. Teeth began to split and break off. The fisherman up above felt the bite. He reared back and set the hook. Line began to peel out of the fisherman's hand.

"Run with him!" yelled Captain McDowell.

Chamberlain picked up the net and then handed it to Vince. Suddenly, the entire group was running along the cut barking orders.

"Don't give him slack..."

"Work him over this way..."

"Watch out for the sharp rock outcropping!"

The line reached the other end of the cut. There was no escape possible. The line began to hoist the predator to the surface. With reserve strength, he dove to the bottom only to be pulled up again. There would be no turning toward the bottom again. The men above joined hands and their combined strength was more than a match for the weakened adversary. He was unceremoniously hauled out of the water, and into the waiting net.

"Take him to the live well," Chamberlain commanded. "We've gotta keep him alive."

Vince and the pilot ran down to the safety boat where the live well was tied off.

"I'll open the lid and you dump him in there," said the pilot.

"Yup..."

"If he jumps out of the box, I'll still have hold of him with the hand line."

The operation went off without a hitch. Chamberlain climbed on board, and the boat raced to the *Sea Quest.* Chamberlain looked at the ladder and his good hand, but the imbalance forced him back to the boat.

The pilot yelled up to the deckhands, "Hook up the painter's chair, we have someone in distress down here."

When Chamberlain arrived topside, he told the crew to hoist the live well up to the deck. He walked to the stern of the ship and pushed the *UP* button for the fish cage.

"Where to with this live well?" asked one of the seamen.

"Oh, place it in here," said Chamberlain.

The live well was gently placed on the screen, and the lid was opened. Chamberlain pushed the *DOWN* button until the live well began to float. Chamberlain noticed that Vince and the pilot had arrived.

"Want me to pull him out of the box?" asked the pilot.

"No, not yet. I want to cut those hooks free. Get me a pair of long-handled bolt cutters."

Chamberlain picked up the fishing line with his good hand and felt vibrations coursing through the line. *He's still alive,* thought Chamberlain.

The pilot returned with bolt cutters in hand.

Chamberlain handed the fishing line to Vince. "Pull up until the line extends from the live well."

Vince began to draw the line through his hands despite some resistance. The shiny lure appeared at the lip of the live well.

"Stop!" Chamberlain commanded. "Cut that hook from his lip."

The open steel jaws probed the predator's lip. The large yellow eye watched its adversary. Suddenly, he leaped out of the water and clamped down on the tips of the bolt cutter. The strike on the steel jaws stunned the onlookers. Everyone drew back. Chamberlain's hand began to throb. *What sort of maniac is this?* he thought.

"Vince, take up the line again," Chamberlain barked. "We'll try again."

The second attempt was successful.

"Vince, why don't you keep that lure for a souvenir?"

The young scientist placed the high-polished lure into the palm of his hand. Scratch marks crisscrossed the lure, permanently marring its surface, grim testimony to the fierce tenacity of this species of fish.

"Now, let's turn the live well on its side," said Chamberlain.

Two seamen came forward with long wooden boat hooks and flipped the live well on its side.

"That should do it," Chamberlain said. "Now our nasty new friend can explore his surroundings."

Ensign Clark and the ship's medic approached.

"I have a chopper coming out to pick you up," Clark said. "The medic will go with you."

"Where are we going?" asked Chamberlain.

"I think you're going down to Jacksonville," Clark said.

"The base doesn't have the facilities to address your condition," added the medic.

Chamberlain replied, "Can you have somebody gather up my gear and take it to the lab?"

"Sure thing."

"Oh, and I left a specimen in a glass jar. Make sure that it's put in the refrigerator."

"It's good as done," replied Ensign Clark.

Chamberlain and the medic walked toward the bow and bumped into McDowell.

"Sir, I have a request for an assistant to help me complete my experiments," Chamberlain said. "Preferably someone who can type."

"That makes sense with that hand of yours," replied McDowell. "Anything else?"

"Yes, I need some live baitfish."

McDowell rocked back in disbelief. "You're gonna feed that thing?"

"Yes," replied Chamberlain. "He's part of the research."

McDowell dutifully wrote down the request, and then walked away.

Everyone on the *Sea Quest* watched as the steel gray helicopter briefly landed on the helipad, received its payload, and then headed south.

The chopper followed I-95, crossed the Saint John's River, and then landed on the roof of the Baptist Hospital. Chamberlain and the medic were met by an attendant and escorted to the emergency room.

The attending physician removed the bloody dressing, then looked at Chamberlain's knuckle. "This looks nasty!" he said. "Was this an alligator bite?"

"No, this was a fish bite," answered Chamberlain.

"Species?" asked the physician.

"Undetermined."

"You remember if you had a tetanus shot in the last year?"

"I'm not sure."

The doctor turned to the nurse, who was standing nearby, preparing a tetanus shot. The doctor put his hand under Chamberlains. He tried to rotate the index finger but Chamberlain grimaced.

"Are you in pain?"

"Yes, I am," replied Chamberlain.

"I'm going to have that hand x-rayed. You seem to have a lateral fracture of the left index finger." The doctor put his hand on Chamberlain's shoulder. "Lieutenant, to avoid future bites, I suggest that you refrain from feeding the alligators." The doctor smirked, then walked away.

The nurse cleaned the wounds, then wrapped a gauze bandage lightly around his hand.

"You're scheduled for an x-ray," the nurse said softly. "Return to the waiting room. The imaging department will call for you."

Chamberlain joined the medic from Kings Bay.

"How'd you make out, sir?"

"I'll live. My hand keeps throbbing. That's annoying."

Chamberlain noticed the lone payphone across from him. The excitement of the project had blotted out all thoughts of Rebecca. He walked over to the phone and dialed his apartment in Santa Barbara. The phone rang a few times, and then a familiar voice answered.

"Rebecca, it's Tom, do you miss me?"

"Tom, where are you? I've been worried about you. You're not involved in any dangerous operation, are you?"

Tom looked down at his swollen hand. "No, of course not," he said. "I'm down here in southern Georgia doing an environmental impact study for a new base. I should be done in a week... give or take a few days. When I get back, we'll go down to the beach and catch some rays."

"Sounds nice, baby. I'll wear that low-cut bikini you bought me."

"Mmm, you're getting me excited."

"Well, I'll try not to wear it till you come back..."

"I might go AWOL and take the first plane out of here."

"Don't get yourself in trouble," said Rebecca.

"Look," said Tom, "I gotta get back to work. I'll call you tomorrow."

"If I'm not at the apartment, call me at the beauty shop."

"Goodbye, I love you."

"And I love you too."

CHAPTER FOURTEEN

The geologists had completed their site work and were now working in the *Sea Quest's* lab compiling data for a written report.

"Vince, your velocity discharge report indicates a flow of fifteen hundred feet per second. Do you know that this submarine spring exceeds the discharge of the largest land-based spring in Florida?

"Which spring is that Doc?"

"Silver Spring," replied Dr. Maury. "That's where they float you around in a glass-bottom boat. The water is so clear that Hollywood did all the *Sea Hunt* shows there."

Vince looked perplexed.

"You've never heard of *Sea Hunt*? Lloyd Bridges was the star."

Vince still had a blank stare on his face. "You mean *Jeff* Bridges?"

"Good lord," said Maury. "Have you ever even seen a James Bond film?"

"Yes, he's cool."

"Well, one of his ocean films was done in Silver Springs."

"Why is the water discharging from this submarine spring so murky?"

"Not sure yet," said Maury. "I suspect, and testing will confirm, that the clear water from the aquifer is mixing with rotted plant matter called tannin. It is commonly referred to as *tea water*." Dr. Maury looked at the chlorinate report. "Our samples show a chloride content of sixteen thousand five sixty PPM. The Atlantic Ocean's count is roughly twenty thousand PPM. This indicates that ocean water is mixing with the freshwater rising out of the aquifer and discharging here."

Vince reached into his pocket. "Does the saltwater mix explain this?" He held out the marred lure and dropped it on the table.

"Sure. Well maybe. What you likely have here is a brackish zone. Fish migrate to such places to feed and lay their eggs. An example is the striped bass. This species leaves the ocean to breed in the brackish zones of river systems."

The whirl of chopper blades caught Vince's attention. "Hey, Doc, do you hear that? I wonder if that's Lieutenant Chamberlain's helicopter."

"Let's go see," replied Maury.

Heading to the deck Maury and Vince see Chamberlain exiting the helicopter.

"I thought your finger was bitten. Why did they fit you with a cast up to your elbow?"

Chamberlain laughed and raised his left arm above his head and said,, "The doctors down at Baptist must have watched too many mummy movies."

"Starring Lloyd Bridges?" Vince asked.

"Huh," said Chamberlain.

"The kid's just trying to be funny."

"Oh. Say, Dr. Maury, how's your work coming along?"

"Oh, just fine. We just about got this one figured out."

"Chow time, chow time!" came the barking over the loudspeaker.

Dr. Maury realized that he hadn't eaten all day.

"Why don't we clean up and go to dinner?"

"Sounds good!"

"Would you join us?"

"Sure," Chamberlain said. "But I have to check on something first."

Chamberlain walked briskly to the fish cage. His sudden appearance startled the gulls and brown pelicans that were feeding on the shredded baitfish that had floated to the surface. With cries of contempt, the birds flew from the fish cage and began to circle the *Sea Quest*, waiting for the opportunity to return and feed.

A seaman, who was leaning over the guardrail, noticed Chamberlain standing there. "Sir, you should have been here," he said. "When the boys dumped the bucket of finger mullet into the tank, all hell broke loose. It was a sight to see. When's the next time you're gonna feed Fang?"

"Fang? Where did you get that name?"

"The boys told me that he nearly took your forearm off."

"Sounds like a character right out of that new writer's book," said Vince.

"Who?" asked Maury.

"King. Something King."

"Right. Stephen, I think it is."

It's funny how a factual account can be distorted so quickly, thought Chamberlain. "I'll post the feeding times for you, but I'll charge for each show."

"It will be worth every penny I've got to pay," replied the seaman.

Chamberlain smiled and then walked toward the bow.

Ensign Clark and his guests were midway through their meal when Chamberlain arrived.

"Here comes our Purple Heart candidate, but where are we going to seat you?"

"I'll tell you what, why don't you sit on the right hand of the table. That will give your left arm plenty of room to maneuver."

Vince scooted over, giving room so that the injured party could sit down.

The attendant approached. "Would you like a menu, sir?"

"No, I'll have whatever your special is today, and start me off with a cup of coffee."

The attendant turned his cup over and filled it. "Would you gentlemen like to see a dessert menu?"

"Not yet," said Ensign Clark, "We'll have coffee until our guest catches up. So, Chamberlain, what was the doctor's prognosis?"

"Six weeks before the cast comes off. He doesn't want any articulation in the wrist." Chamberlain took a sip of coffee and leaned forward on the table. "So, what do you think lies below the rock mound?"

Vince said, "The city of Atlantis."

Chamberlain smiled, and then looked toward Maury and Clark. "What do you think, gentlemen?"

They emitted a blank stare.

"My initial findings," offered Chamberlain, "indicate that a large shark lies below the limestone shell."

"Cool," said Vince.

"How did you determine that?" asked Maury.

"Well my first inkling was the fact that so many fiddler crabs were present... they had to be feeding on something. The temperature reading inside the mound was in the high eighties, opposed to cooler temperatures along the outside rim. The stringy filament I recovered is placenta. When I placed my hands into the water, and under the limestone, I felt a smooth, slimy surface that was pliable to the touch. My scalpel readily cut through it. The odor of rotting fish was also present."

"How big is he?" asked Vince.

"It's a she," said Chamberlain. "The length is approximately forty feet."

Maury's eyebrows twitched. "How do you suppose such a large animal got itself trapped in there?"

"It's conjecture on my part, but I think the female sought a cavity to bear her young. When the roof caved in, she began to spin. Sharks often use this technique to tear flesh from their prey. She became trapped in the belly-up position."

"What kind of shark is it?" asked Vince.

"Subspecies of a Carcharodon shark, but there are no records that this shark exists today."

"Is it prehistoric?" asked Vince.

"This species of shark may date back four hundred million years."

"It's not unheard of," said Maury.

"The doc's right," began Chamberlain. "In the early seventies, a U.S. Geological Survey ship working off Waikiki dredged up a fleshy creature that weighed sixteen hundred pounds. That survey team contacted the major museums and universities around the world regarding their find. The scientists were skeptical. Tests on this shark revealed that it was a megamouth, an extinct species of shark."

"Why haven't we come across this species before?" asked Ensign Clark.

"The megamouth is a filter feeder. It lives at a depth of five hundred feet from the ocean's surface to feed. Most commercial fishermen don't drag that deep."

Chamberlain took a quick drink of water and resumed talking. Maury noticed that the zeal with which his colleague spoke was almost like a Baptist preacher.

"Have you ever heard of Megalodon Peruvian?"

"The species of beaked whale?" Vince asked.

"That's right," Chamberlain continued. "It was thought to have never existed on the earth—that is, until an acquaintance of mine, Dr. James Mead, who works at the Smithsonian Institution, found a whole carcass while he was researching along the coast of Peru. Dr. Mead removed the skull and reported his find. Not until ten more individuals were found did the scientific community name a new species. Their abstract stated that a new species of beaked whale is described based on ten specimens that either were stranded or captured between the provinces of Lima and Ica in South Central Peru."

"You intend to present this as a new species of marine life?" asked Maury.

"The scientific community is very skeptical of all new discoveries," replied Chamberlain. "How much harder will it be for me to present my find? The Navy Department will surely stamp this project secret." Chamberlain picked up his wrapped hand. "Look, I can't even type up a report."

"We can help you there," said Maury. "Our preliminary report is complete. I'm sure Vince would type up the report for you."

"Sure, no problem," said Vince.

* * *

After dinner, Chamberlain returned to the lab with the geologist. Midway through his report, Chamberlain stopped his dictation.

"Vince, is it not true that I was the first to discover this new species of shark?"

"Yes," came the reply.

"Then I have the right to name it."

"I'm not sure, I mean we'd have to talk with Doc--"

"Let's see, maybe I'll call it Chamberlain Carcharodon."

"That would be a little facetious on your part, wouldn't it, sir?"

"I was only kidding."

"Hey, I got a good name. Why don't you call it King, after the naval base in which it was found?"

"Hmmm," Chamberlain said, rubbing his chin. "King Carcharodon, that's got a good ring to it. Let it be known, that from this day forward, the bastard that tried to take my hand off shall be called King Carcharodon."

Chamberlain resumed his dictation until the report was completed.

* * *

The following morning, Chamberlain woke to the sound of the phone ringing in his quarters.

"Chamberlain here."

"Sir, this is the switchboard. Captain McDowell would like to speak to you. May I connect him through?"

"Yes, of course."

A clicking sound followed then: "Hello," said Chamberlain.

"Good morning, this is Captain McDowell."

"Good morning to you."

"Have you completed your report?"

"Yes," replied Lieutenant Chamberlain.

"Good, I'm coming over now to pick it up. Do you know if Dr. Maury's report is complete?"

"Yes, I think it is, but you may want to check with him."

"I will," said Captain McDowell. "Also, there's a base commander meeting at thirteen hundred hours. Admiral Farragut from the Navy Surgeon General's Office is flying in for the meeting. We will all be expected to attend. I'll be out to pick up your reports in about a half-hour."

"Captain McDowell, I will need a daily supply of live baitfish sent out here."

"Will do. Say, you don't want that toothy fish to get too big, do you? Hasn't he caused you enough trouble already?

"I'm going to wear steel mesh gloves," replied Chamberlain.

McDowell laughed and hung up the phone. He shook his head and thought, *That's one crazy biologist.*

Chamberlain dressed, and then hurriedly walked to the stern of the ship and looked into the cage. He could see no sign of King on the surface. Chamberlain pushed the *UP* button until the cage revealed a dark form just below the surface. No baitfish could be seen. Good, he thought, at least he's eating well. Chamberlain lowered the cage and then walked slowly back to his quarters.

CHAPTER FIFTEEN

Lieutenant Brock walked out of Kings Bay Headquarters building then climbed into a waiting helicopter. The pilot flew directly toward *Sea Quest*. McDowell looked out the window as the chopper approached the man-made lake.

Where's the mound? thought Brock. *Am I losing my mind? Oh, that's right, the moon is full and the tide is high.* Brock leaned back in his seat and began to relax. *Boy, that's all we needed—to have the admiral come all the way down here and not have a mound to show him.*

The chopper dropped down onto the helipad, picked up the waiting scientists, then returned to base headquarters.

Everyone in the conference room rose when Admiral Farragut entered the room, and remained standing until the admiral was introduced to the audience by the base commander.

"Gentlemen, I have been directed by Admiral Zolloff to resolve the problems that have arisen at Kings Bay. The Navy Surgeon General's Office has three aims. First and foremost is the safety of the personnel who work at Kings Bay, plus the public at large. The second: the Navy's interest in expanding this base in a timely manner."

Admiral Farragut looked down and took a sip of his water. "The third aim is to support the scientific communities in their quest for knowledge, when possible. Lieutenant Chamberlain, your report indicates that a new species of fish was discovered by you... no, strike that. I meant that a shark carcass is pinned under the collapsed springhead. In your summation, you suggest that the captured specimen should be studied at its birthing location. Do you mean to suggest, sir, that a lab be set up in an area where construction will be in progress?"

"No, sir," replied Chamberlain. "The base has numerous lakes with spring-fed outflows."

"Captain Jarvis, do you have any comments on Lieutenant Chamberlain's suggestion?"

Jarvis' face grimaced slightly. "Sir, this goes to your first priority," he said. "I'm concerned about the safety of our personnel."

"Is the base fenced and patrolled?"

"Yes, sir. We have a series of fenced areas that are high security."

"Would it allay your concerns if I brought in security to patrol the test site? The funds would be administered by the Navy Surgeon General's Office."

Jarvis's brows scrunched. "Sir—"

Farragut added, "No funding would be drawn out from your budget."

Captain Jarvis didn't like the idea but nodded in agreement.

Farragut picked up Dr. Maury's report with a face of appraisal. "Doctor, your report indicates that the spring discovered on base is of the first magnitude. Can you explain to me what that means?"

"Sir, that term applies to the pressure and flow of freshwater being disgorged from the spring. Silver Springs located in central Florida has the distinction of being the number one magnitude spring in the state. The outflow of the Kings Bay discovery far surpasses Silver Springs."

"Dr. Maury," asked the Admiral. "What would be the possible ramifications if we removed the roof of this spring and plugged the shaft tight?"

Maury's eyebrows began to twitch wildly. "Well, it's my opinion that the total closure of the spring could be catastrophic. I say this because of the intense water pressure which could build up in one of the horizontal tunnels connected to the main vertical shaft."

"Please explain to me how these horizontal tunnels work," said the Admiral.

Maury opened his hands spreading his fingers far apart. "The horizontal tunnels connected to this shaft could number as few as one or more than ten. They could travel under towns such as Saint Marys and Fernandina Beach, or, as I suspect, out to sea."

The Admiral raised his finger and asked, "What makes you think that a horizontal tunnel may be heading toward the Atlantic Ocean?"

"Sir, the size of the specimen found wedged under the mound suggests it."

"How far out do you think these tunnels go?"

"Sir, based on the geological survey drilled into Blake's Plateau which is sixty-seven miles east of Fernandina Beach, Florida. The test bores reveal that large volumes of freshwater exist at that location."

"Amazing, simply amazing," said the Admiral, shaking his head in disbelief. "To think that fresh water can extend so far out to sea. Thank you for your report, Dr. Maury."

Admiral Farragut was next handed an engineering report.

"Captain McDowell," Farragut continued, "your report states that the mound cap weight is approximately thirty tons. Does this include the carcass trapped underneath it?"

"No, sir--"

"No?"

"I would add in another twenty tons to that original number," replied McDowell.

"Captain McDowell, if you were to include the carcass for removal, what process would you use?"

"Sir, I would employ a series of belly bands, which would be evenly distributed underneath the material to be hoisted."

"Can you clarify what belly bands are?"

"Sir, belly bands are made of woven steel. They are flexible and can be wrapped around angular objects."

"So a sort of flexible harness?"

"Sort of, sir."

"Thank you, Captain McDowell." Farragut looked around the room. "Gentlemen, I must warn you that everything referenced to this operation is secret. Shred all documents; say nothing to those that don't have a need to know. I now give the floor to Captain Jarvis."

"Thank you, sir," said Jarvis. "Gentlemen, you are all invited to dinner at the officers' club."

* * *

The following morning, the professor received a call from Woods Hole, directing him back to the facility. Before leaving the *Sea Quest*, he said goodbye to Ensign Clark and Chamberlain.

"This has been a very interesting survey," Dr. Maury said. "It's been nice working with you guys. Lieutenant Chamberlain, if I ever get to the National Science Foundation to accept my application to survey the offshore submarine springs of Florida, I'll get in touch with you."

The men shook hands, and then Maury climbed over the rail and down the rope ladder to the waiting boat. Vince waved to the crew as they motored away.

* * *

The tide had just crested in Kings Bay and the surrounding creeks and estuaries. The baitfish and crabs, which came to feed in the forest of marsh grass were relatively safe from the schools of predator fish that lurked in deeper water. Old Jube Early, a long-time resident of Saint Marys, Georgia, sat on his back porch watching the river traffic pass behind his house. His fourteen-foot jon boat began to float freely. Only the tie off rope that was secured to an old stump prevented the boat from drifting into the river. Jube looked at his watch. *Shit, I better get going*, he thought.

The old man pushed himself out of the rocking chair and stretched. Slowly the pain in his arthritis-wracked body began to subside. He slowly walked down to his boat and climbed on board.

The light inland craft entered the Saint Marys River and headed downriver. Jube watched the marsh grass as he went, looking for signs of swirling fish. He came to a point where the Intracoastal Waterway crossed Saint Marys. Jube nosed the boat to the left. His intended destination was a secret outflow of water that lies deep within Kings Bay. Jube noticed a fast-moving craft heading directly for him, lights flashing and sirens wailing.

Jube reduced the throttle and knocked the transmission into neutral. The swift boat slowed, and then stopped off his starboard bow. The resulting waves rocked his jon boat so hard that Jube had to sit down to avoid being thrown overboard.

"Sorry, sir," said the tall marine lieutenant.

"No problem, officer."

"Sir, you're inside a federally restricted area. You must leave immediately."

"Leave?" said Jube. "Why, I fished here all my life, 'cept during the war years."

The lieutenant pointed toward the bank. "Sir, do you see that large sign?"

"Yeah, I see it."

The lieutenant then pointed to a buoy sign floating in the bay. "Anyone passing through these two points will be subject to arrest."

"Well, I guess ya can't make it any clearer than that," said Jube. "Wasn't like that last week though..."

Jube waved goodbye, and then engaged the transmission and turned south.

Jube's second choice of the day was a wide shallow outflow that drained out of the marsh and dropped off into a deep hole that was inhabited by a large oyster colony. Jube figured rightly that red bass drum would be attracted to the oyster bed, and that large quantities of bait entering the hole would be an added incentive to feed—*Get their eat on,* as Jube often put it.

Jube approached the deep hole and then threw his anchor into the shallow aggressive outflow. The anchor sliced into the silt on the first try. Jube shut the engine off, and then picked up his cast net. Large pods of finger mullet, which had been feeding in the marsh grass, were now passing under Jube's boat. The old fisherman slipped his left hand through the looped end of the rope that attached the drawstrings of the casting net. His right hand held the bunched-up net at the ready. Jube glanced at the looped wrist. How many times had he been told: never loop a cast net? *I guess you can't teach an old dog new tricks,* he thought.

Jube spotted a large school of baitfish swimming near his boat. He raised his right arm and then flung it forward. The bunched-up netting was released, and it formed a perfect circle. The lead weights attached to the net raced to the bottom, entrapping a large school of finger mullet. The fast-moving water, combined with the weighted net, snatched old Jube off the boat. Down he went. Down to the bottom of the deep hole.

Panic ensued immediately. He grabbed and clawed at the sharp-edged oyster bed, causing his fingers to bleed profusely. The struggling baitfish in the cast net and the taste of human blood excited the horde of predators.

The attack was swift and furious. Jube's flesh was stripped from his body. Vise-like jaws began clamping down on the remaining skeletal structure, crushing bones until the sweet-tasting marrow was released.

* * *

The marine security boat, which had chased Jube earlier, now had its deck-mounted binoculars trained on the empty boat.

"Sir, I don't see anybody on that boat."

The officer walked up to the petty officer who was viewing the boat. "Scan the shoreline, they sometimes sneak up there to collect bait."

The glasses swept across the saw grass and mudflats.

"Nothing, sir."

The officer waved to the pilot and pointed to the empty boat. The powerful engines revved up and then cut white ribbons the shoreline.

Upon closer investigation, they found the boat to be empty, aside from fishing tackle, sandwiches, and a thermos filled with coffee, which were all found aboard. The U.S. Coast Guard stationed in Fernandina Beach was notified and the coordinates of the unmanned boat were given. The patrol boat then called base security and repeated their find to the dispatcher.

Lieutenant Brock happened to be at his desk when the call came in. He got out of his seat, walked over to the dispatcher, and ripped the microphone from his hand.

"This is Lieutenant Brock, chief of base security. What the hell are you doing calling the Coast Guard? This is an internal matter"

There was a pause on the receiving end, and then Lieutenant Jackson of the patrol boat replied, "Sir, my men and I don't appreciate being cussed at on the radio. That said, my standard operating procedure is to contact the Coast Guard when we find an unattended boat off base, then we call base security."

Brock squeezed the microphone. "Lieutenant, did you say the boat was found off base?"

"That's an affirmative, sir."

"Lieutenant Jackson, I apologize for that outburst."

"Roger that, sir," Jackson said. "No offense taken."

"Have you sighted the Coast Guard yet, Lieutenant?"

"No, sir," replied Lieutenant Jackson.

"What's the position of the tide?"

"Pulling out hard, sir," Jackson said. "If there's a floating body out there, it's probably heading for the ocean."

"Thank you, Lieutenant, for your report. I'll keep your command updated on this situation."

Brock walked back to his desk, and then called the base commander's office.

The secretary answered: "How may I help you?"

"This is Lieutenant Brock. May I speak to Captain Jarvis? It's very important."

"Yes, sir, I'll put you through to him."

"What's up, Lieutenant Brock?"

"Sir, an empty boat has been found just outside the base jurisdiction. The Coast Guard has been notified."

"Coast Guard?"

"Yeah, a Marine patrol found it..."

"Ah..." said the captain. "Any bodies been found?"

"No, sir."

Jarvis began to tap the end of his pen on the desk.

"The fact that this accident occurred outside our jurisdiction is a relief to me," Jarvis finally said. "The last few days have been hectic."

"Yes, sir," said Brock.

"Lieutenant I want you to call the mayor of Saint Marys and explain the situation to him. Extend our help in the recovery process."

"Right away, sir."

Jarvis lowered his voice. "Brock, one thing that I want to make very clear to you is if one of our boats retrieves any human remains that you make damn sure that it wasn't found in our jurisdiction."

"Yes, sir, I understand."

"Oh, Brock, contact the public relations officer... he may be of some help."

"Yes, sir, I will."

Brock returned to his office and called Mayor Tubbs and informed him of the accident.

"That's news to me," said the mayor. "Do you know if it was a local person?"

'No, Sir, you'll have to contact the Coast Guard."

"Yes, I'll do that right away."

"Do you need any help in the search?"

"Why yes, yes. It would take me two days to get enough people to do the job."

"We'll get on it right away."

"If you find a body, Lieutenant, I'd appreciate it if you could bring it to pier one, Saint Marys. That's where my other office is located."

"Will do, Mayor; and I'll keep you updated with any news."

Brock hung up with Mayor Tubbs and contacted all the commands on base requesting volunteers and boats that were idled. He instructed the petty officer on duty to drive over to the supply office and request all the grappling hooks in stock and a spool of one-half inch mooring line.

Brock also made arrangements with the mess officer to serve lunch for the volunteers at the security pier. He then called the public relations office.

Lieutenant McPeake answered the phone.

"Hey, ya wanna go fishing?"

"Not today, Brock. I'm going to attend a Saint Marys Chamber of Commerce meeting today."

"Cancel it!"

"On whose orders?"

"On the base commander's orders, that's who. He directed me to have you on board when we look for the corpse."

"*Corpse?*" asked McPeake.

"Yup," Brock said, knowing that would hook him.

"Do tell..."

"You just drive down to the security pier and I'll fill you in."

* * *

Brock, shirt untucked and forehead glistening, was working the pier when McPeake walked up to him.

"I'll tell you one thing, McPeake, it's days like this that make me proud to be a Navy man. Look at all the volunteers. We got apprentice seamen all the way up to the commanders assembled here."

"I guess I know under whose orders now."

Brock looked into McPeake's eyes and said, "You're the only one I had to draft."

"Why would the captain want me out here?"

Brock put his arm around his friend. "When are you going to realize that you're the smoothest talker on base?" Brock said. "You didn't attend all those journalism and communications schools for nothing."

"I've been accused of having a silver tongue before, Brock," said a grinning McPeake.

"Is that so?"

"But I hope this doesn't turn out between us the way it did between her and me."

Brock chuckled. "You go take a seat in my boat," he said. " I gotta throw this operation into high gear."

Brock issued radios to each boat with instructions to radio him if a body was found. The small armada lined up at the mouth of Kings Bay, and slowly worked its way south. Grappling hooks were cast, thrown, and dropped to the oyster-encrusted bottom. Lieutenant Brock's boat stayed ahead of the drag boats.

"We've hooked onto something, chief," came a radio call from one of the boats.

After a few tense seconds, the boat called again, "We're snagged on the bottom."

Brock got on the bullhorn. "Any boat that gets ensnared," he commanded, "cut the line and re-hook. I repeat, any boat that gets ensnared, cut the line and re-hook."

Brock hadn't noticed the Coast Guard cutter that had drifted next to him.

"Good afternoon, my name is Ensign Parrish, we received a distress call from the base."

"Yes, marine security made the initial call. My name is Lieutenant Brock, I'm in charge of the dragging operation."

"I'm sorry that we couldn't get here earlier," said Ensign Parrish. "We were south of the Nassau River towing in a disabled trawler. Well, it looks like you have this area covered, Lieutenant Brock. Did you recover the empty boat?"

"No, we left it anchored where we found it. The boat is registered in Georgia, so we contacted the mayor of Saint Marys. He requested that the boat be brought to pier one."

"Well, thank you for your assistance, Lieutenant Brock. After I drop the boat off, I'll go down to the jetties at Fernandina and do some dragging."

Ensign Parrish saluted Brock smartly, then ordered the pilot to head north towards Kings Bay.

The Navy search vessels continued to drift with the outgoing tide. Their grappling hooks bounced along the seafloor, looking for something to pierce. All movement seaward slowed, then stopped. It was now ebb tide when all sea life seemed to pause. A looped rope that appeared just below the surface was grabbed by a sailor.

"Hey, I got something here," called out the sailor.

"What ya got?" asked a shipmate.

"Don't know but we'll soon find out."

The sailor started pulling the rope into the boat when suddenly he felt tension on the rope.

"Need a hand?" asked his shipmate.

"Naw, I'll get it," said the sailor, his muscles bulging now as he strained to hoist the rope up. "I can't..." he grunted, "I just can't... break 'er free."

"Here, let me give you a hand."

The two men pulled on the rope that was attached to a heavy load.

Lieutenant Brock picked up a pair of binoculars and began to scan the rescue boats. He noticed something unusual on paint boat number four. The crew hung over the side

"McPeake, call boat number four."

McPeake complied.

"What ya see?"

"It's not what I can see!" Brock bobbed a bit with the binoculars.

"What is it?"

"The crew is hanging over the starboard rail."

"Maybe they're seasick," said McPeake with a smile.

"Very funny! Get on the radio and call boat four. Ask for a radio check."

"Security boat to boat four, come in boat four," McPeake repeatedly called. "Navy boat four you copy?"

No reply.

"Wait a minute..." said Brock. "Somebody's moving away from the rail. Try giving him a call."

"Boat four, boat four, radio check. This is Lieutenant McPeake, security boat one.

"Sir, this is boat four, I copy you."

"What's going on, seaman?"

"You better come over here. We found something."

"Boat four, stand by, we'll be there shortly."

Brock grabbed the radio. "Stay out of the water," he ordered.

The Captain's launch drove over to boat four and tied off. Lieutenant Brock was the first to climb on board. He walked up to the sailor with the radio. The sailor's face was white like chalk.

"What did you recover?"

The sailor pointed to his shipmate, who was leaning over the rail. Brock walked over to the man, putting his hand on the sailor's shoulder.

He glanced up.

"Sir, ain't this something," said the leaning sailor. "Me and my mate are pulling up on this rope when all of a sudden, this bony hand comes popping out of the water.

"Tell you what, sir, it scared the shit right out of us."

The second sailor pulled up on the rope, exposing the hand.

"I can see why you were scared." Brock motioned for McPeake to board.

The two men walked to the bow of the boat. They spoke quietly.

"I think we found that fisherman," Brock said.

"What makes you think that?" asked McPeake.

"He ended up just like the laborer we found on the base, all shredded up!"

"What should we do?

"Call the Coast Guard and inform them that we found something."

"You think that's a good idea? Why don't we contact the mayor of Saint Marys? Let him explain to the Coast Guard what happened."

Brock looked at McPeake. "Goddammit!" he said. "I knew I brought you along for a reason."

"'Ol Silver Tongue aims to please," whispered McPeake.

"Okay, call the mayor, but first, have the crew bring a body bag on board. Quietly."

"Yes, sir."

"I'll stand by."

The security crew boarded the paint boat with grappling hooks and a body bag, which was laid open on the deck.

"Hoist up the rope," commanded Lieutenant Brock.

The fleshless hand and arm appeared, followed by a headless torso. Hundreds of fiddler crabs began jumping off the carcass, but just as many clung tight to it, as it was lifted from the water. Chills ran up Brock's spine as the bones and twisted netting were placed in the body bag, zipped up, and taken away.

Brock got on the radio. "Attention, attention, this search effort has been successfully completed. All craft return to Kings Bay and secure your gear. All volunteers are invited to a noonday luncheon at the NCO club, compliments of the base captain." Brock let go of the radio. Then he got back on and added, "Also, all nonessential personnel who were scheduled to work today are granted leave."

Brock turned to the crew of boat four. "I want to thank you for your efforts men," he said, shaking their hands, saluting, then climbing back aboard the security boat.

"Where to, Lieutenant?" asked McPeake.

Brock pointed his finger in a southerly direction.

"Saint Marys, McPeake."

CHAPTER SIXTEEN

Mayor Tubbs stood patiently at the end of pier one. He wore a butcher's apron that extended down to his shoes. He watched as the security boat sped up the Saint Marys river, then slowed and tied off in front of him.

"Good afternoon, Mayor Tubbs," said McPeake.

"Good day to you also," replied the mayor.

McPeake surveyed the area. "Mr. Mayor, this doesn't look like City Hall."

"No, no, you're right, this is the Saint Marys Morgue," Tubbs replied. "It's located here because most of our clients are drowning victims."

Tubbs motioned to McPeake, then walked off the pier.

McPeake and Brock climbed off the boat and joined the Mayor. He looked at McPeake over his wire rim glasses.

"I checked out the numbers on the boat," said Tubbs.

"What did you get, sir?" asked Brock.

"The owner is Jube Early."

"We should—"

The mayor cut McPeake off. "I went down to his house. His truck was in the driveway, nobody was home, but his boat was missing."

"Is he married?" asked McPeake.

"He's a widower. His wife Mary died about ten years ago."

"Did he have any children or friends who may have borrowed the boat?" asked Brock.

"He didn't have relatives around here, and nobody, but nobody, was allowed to drive that boat but old Jube."

"Very well, sir."

Sweat began to drip down Tubbs' face. "Well, we better get started on that examination," he said. "It's getting hot out here, and I don't want to work on a rotting corpse."

"Trust me, Mayor," said Brock. "There's no flesh to stink."

"Come on, gentlemen, I'd like to show you the Saint Marys Morgue."

The three men began walking.

"Mayor, are you the coroner also? asked McPeake.

"You're damn right," replied the mayor. "I ran a funeral home and served as coroner until the city council backed me for the mayor's position. Only thing is, the city council never bothered to hire a new coroner, so now I have both positions. But things are changing around here, what with the Kings Bay expansion. I'm getting way too busy to do both jobs."

The three men arrived at a cinder block building. The mayor opened the padlock then pushed open the steel door. A blast of cold air met them.

"Isn't that refreshing!" said McPeake.

"I keep the temperature at sixty degrees all the time," said Tubbs.

Brock pretends to shiver.

"Council members," the mayor continued, "complain that the electric bill generated by the morgue is too high and they suggested that the air conditioner be turned off except during autopsies." Then Tubbs turned to McPeake and said, "I don't think so!"

The two men began to laugh.

After their laughter subsided, the mayor ran his hand up and down the wall adjacent to the door. His finger found the light switch. "There she goes."

A bright light centered in the middle of the room lit up a marble slab below. Mayor Tubbs ran his hand across the cold stone. "It seems that whatever cleaner I use, I can't get these bloodstains out."

"Mayor, they're here with the body bag," said McPeake, looking back out the door.

"Show them in," replied the mayor, pulling on a long pair of rubber gloves, then turning toward the body bag which lay flat on the slab. "Open 'er up."

Brock put his hand up in the air. "Wait a second," he ordered the men who carried in the body bag. "You two go outside and stand by. No one is to enter."

"Yes sir," they replied.

Brock waited for the door to close, then he unzipped the bag, pulling the flap back as he went.

Mayor Tubbs was confused by the sight before him.

"Well, at first sight..." Tubbs began, "it looks like these remains have been in the den of one of our local alligators for a few months." He grabbed for some tools. "Ya know how that Thanksgiving turkey got picked on till the only thing left was bones?"

The officers nodded in agreement.

"Are you saying that these bones are not of Jube Early?" asked McPeake.

"Now, now, I'm not saying that. It's just that I've never seen a body in such bad shape."

Tubbs walked around the table, touching different parts of the skeletal structure.

"What do we got here!"

McPeake and Brock leaned forward, trying to get a better view.

Tubbs picked up a frayed rope from which a hand dangled. The mayor shook his head and said, "Ya know, this tragedy could have been avoided!"

"How do you mean?" asked McPeake.

"Well hell's bells, boys, everyone around here knows that you never loop a cast net rope around your wrist." He pulled the bag and body to the side. "Just asking for trouble."

"Do attacks like this occur often?" asked McPeake.

"Hell no," replied the mayor. "If the press got a photo of this, it would cause a lot of uneasiness for everybody. Saint Marys is at the height of the tourist season. I'm going to make sure that the casket is sealed."

McPeake reached into his shirt pocket. "Mr. Mayor," he said. "You mentioned something about photos." He took out a photo, then handed it to the mayor.

"This is Jube," Tubbs exclaimed. "He's casting from his boat. Where'd ya you get this?"

"Well," said McPeake with a slight smile on his face, "the Navy can be very sneaky."

"Is that so?"

"Did you ever see that elevated osprey nest erected in the marsh on base?"

"Yes," Mayor Tubbs said, beginning a smile. "I could use one of those cameras at City Hall."

"Mr. Mayor, can you tell us anything else about Jube Early, such as church affiliation, social clubs, or military organizations?"

The mayor's eyes lit up. "Jube belongs to the American Legion with me."

"Is he an active member?"

"Hell yes, he fought The Battle of the Bulge, so he's a veteran thus eligible to be buried in Arlington cemetery," said Tubbs, beginning to use the saw now. "That would be a great honor." He sawed some more. "I don't know of anybody that's buried there."

* * *

After the autopsy, McPeake said, "Mr. Mayor, it's part of the Navy's mission to work with communities."

"That's admirable, son."

"I'll be in touch."

The officers said goodbye, then walked outside.

Brock turned to McPeake with a smile on his face. "I knew there was a reason I brought you along. You got a line of BS that's smooth as silk. You almost got me believing it."

McPeake smiled. "It must be the training I received at all the journalistic schools the Navy sent me to."

The officers began to laugh as they walked down pier one.

* * *

The first aspect of Admiral Farragut's three-point plan was set in motion. Cinclant Fleet, located at Norfolk Naval Base, received an urgent request for a floating dredge with a hundred-ton lifting capacity. The two expeditors on duty began to check their inventories. The young seaman apprentice's screen kept coming up: *Glomar Explorer.*

"Petty Officer Annsworth, I got a problem with this screen."

"Only time to worry about a seaman is when he doesn't have any problems," Annsworth quipped.

"Aye, sir, but I keep getting *Glomar Explorer* on the availability list, but it doesn't have any Navy identifying numbers."

"The *Glomar Explorer* has recently been transferred from the general services administration," Annsworth said. "What's its current status?"

The seaman shifted the screen. "The ship's available. She pulled into the Atlantic Marine Shipyard yesterday for a propeller inspection."

"What's her lifting capacity?" asked Annsworth.

"Four hundred tons, sir," replied the seaman.

"That's plenty," said Annsworth. "Send orders to the *Glomar Explorer.* Leave Mobile bay out at..." He paused and looked at his watch. "It's now fifteen hundred hours. Leave at twenty-four hundred hours, destination Kings Bay Nuclear Submarine Base, located at the confluence of Saint Marys River and the Intracoastal Waterway—southeast Georgia."

* * *

Captain John Dewey walked up to the bow of the ship and stared out into Mobile Bay. He reached into his pants pocket and brought out a rough piece of wood and his trusty Schrade pocketknife. He looked at the worn handle and thought back to when his father had given it to him. They were on summer vacation walking the beach, looking for shells and things of interest. Dad bent over and picked up a small piece of driftwood. He reached into his pocket and brought out a shiny knife. He opened it, then began to shave the end of the wood.

"What ya doing?" John remembered asking his dad. "I'm making a harpoon for you."

"Wow, I'll be able to kill old Moby Dick."

John's father smiled and handed him the sharpened stick. He closed the blade to the pocketknife then handed it to John.

"I'm giving you this knife because you're a good boy and I can trust you," his dad said. "Put it in your pocket, and when we get home, we'll give it a good oiling."

John spent the rest of the day spearing imaginary sharks and whales.

* * *

Captain Dewey's early outdoor experiences drew him to the sea. He joined the U.S. Navy where he was trained to operate cranes and bulldozers. His construction battalion was transferred to the beaches of Korea where he had his first taste of war. The conflict came to a standstill and he was recalled to the United States. Dewey applied to Officer Candidate School and was accepted. He rose through the ranks to the rank of Captain.

During the Vietnam War, Dewey oversaw a recovery dredge. His skill at recovering vessels and his flawless record, along with his complete loyalty to the Navy, landed him in the Captain's seat of the *Glomar Explorer*. The ship's mission was to recover the Soviet ballistic submarine K-129, which was lost with all hands on board.

On July 4, 1974, the *Glomar Explorer* lowered a clam bucket 16,500 feet to the bottom of the Pacific Ocean. The bucket latched onto the submarine and slowly hoisted it into the bowels of the *Glomar Explorer*. The recovery of the K-129 included eighty-six Soviet submariners, three nuclear-tipped missiles, and secret codebooks that were used to plot Soviet submarine movements.

The Central Intelligence Agency marked this as a great Cold War victory, but it came with a great cost to the crew of the *Glomar Explorer*. Captain Dewey himself was exposed to the silent radiant killer. Under his full beard lay scars of skin cancer that almost took his life.

The communications officer briskly walked up to Captain Dewey and said, "Sir, we got orders to make way at twenty-four hundred hours, destination Kings Bay Nuclear Base, southeast Georgia."

Dewey walked back to the bridge and gave commands. "Cease all repair work, cancel leave of the crew members, and fire the boilers."

At 2330, the *Glomar Explorer* slipped out of Mobile Bay and into the Gulf of Mexico. She steamed all night and was rounding Key West, Florida when a Navy chopper requested permission to land on the *Glomar Explorer*. Permission was granted.

Three officers disembarked and were escorted to Captain Dewey's office. They introduced themselves to Captain Dewey.

McDowell spoke first, "I'm the chief engineer of new construction at Kings Bay Submarine Base."

"Base security," said Brock.

"Naval public affairs, Kings Bay," said McPeake.

"Sit down, gentlemen," Dewey said. "And fill me in on the upcoming operation."

McDowell spoke, "Sir, a large mound of limestone is impeding the installation of pilings and must be removed."

Dewey narrowed his eyes slightly. "You mean to tell me that the Navy Department is sending this ship to hoist up a rock from the bay floor? I thought that one of your submarines was listing or in distress!"

McDowell shrugged his shoulders. "Well, sir, all we did was request a heavy lift ship. They sent us the *Glomar Explorer*."

Captain Dewey looked into McDowell's eyes. *This guy's not telling everything.* Why would the *Glomar Explorer* be pulled from the repair yard on such short notice, then in the middle of the night, a helicopter lands on this ship? This story of theirs doesn't wash with me, thought Captain Dewey.

The captain broke his stare. "Do you have any estimate on the weight to be picked up, Captain McDowell?"

"Sir, the mound of material to be lifted weighs no more than one hundred fifty tons."

"That should not be a problem," said Dewey. "I'll have a weight scale installed on the hoisting hook. If your estimate is too low, I'll go to plan B."

"What's that?" asked McDowell.

"We will hook up a specialized lifting device that has a hoisting capacity of four hundred tons."

McDowell put his hand under his chin, then began to crunch the numbers in his head. He smiled, then said, "Captain Dewey, we won't need anything that extreme. We could probably pick up a couple of submarines with that lifting device!"

"I don't know that we can handle two submarines, but I know that we can handle at least one."

"Sir, what is your estimated time of arrival at Kings Bay?"

Dewey replied, "Twelve hundred hours tomorrow, the tide will be low."

A frown swiped across McDowell's face.

"What's the matter?" asked Dewey. "Is low tide a problem?"

"No, no, it's not the position of the tide. Sir, can you move your time of arrival to twenty-four hundred? It will be night."

"Okay, I'll throttle the engines back to half. Our new arrival time will be twenty-four-hundred hours." Captain Dewey looked at the men. "Are there any other issues to be discussed at this time?"

McDowell looked at Brock and McPeake. They just shrugged their shoulders. "None at this time, sir."

"We will contact you by radio when you reach Fernandina Beach," said Brock.

"Well, then, all is settled," said Captain Dewey, standing up and stretching.

McPeake spoke up, "Sir, I didn't notice any Navy marking on the ship when we first arrived."

Captain Dewey pulled at the end of his beard. "You say no Navy marking, not even on the bow?"

"No, sir," replied McPeake.

"That's strange," said Captain Dewey. "Mighty strange."

He opened the cabin door and took the officers on a tour of the *Glomar Explorer.*

CHAPTER SEVENTEEN

It was near midnight when the *Glomar Explorer* approached the Saint Marys channel. Local fishermen who had been dragging the area were forced to give way to the incoming ship.

"What the hell kind of ship is that?" asked Tommy Lions, first mate of the *Anna Marie*.

Dutch Lahm, the captain, picked up a pair of binoculars and scanned the deck of the passing ship.

"Looks like an Army Corp of Engineers dredge to me," Lahm said. "Holy cow!"

"What is it, Cap?"

"You should see the size of the clam bucket they're carrying."

"Sheesh."

"I bet that they could pick up the *Anna Marie*, and with room to spare."

Dutch radioed Captain Maddox of the *Sandpiper*, which was dragging in tandem with the *Anna Marie* when the shrimpers first encountered the *Glomar Explorer*..

"You still with us?" asked Dutch.

"Hear you loud and clear," replied Lou.

"What you up to?"

"Just looking off my bow, waiting for you to call me."

"You're an old Navy man," said Dutch. "You ever seen anything like this?"

"Can't say as I have," replied Lou, "But I'm sure that it can hold a hell of a lot of fish."

The shrimp captains began to laugh, then signed off.

* * *

The last drop of corn liquor rolled into Snoop's mouth. He placed the glass on the desk, took off his earphones, walked over to the window, and watched as a ship's silhouette passed his view. He hurriedly returned to his desk and began to search for the ship's radio band, but with no success.

Snoop picked up his ledger and scanned through it. *Ah, here we are. Band 102 Navy security. Incident report. Drowning near Kings Bay. They sure did a lot of talking that day,* thought Snoop.

After fine-tuning, the receiver began to pick up radio signals that were generated at the base. Snoop picked up the glass and realized that it was empty. *Ah, it's gonna be a long night,* he thought. Snoop reached under the desk, picked up a glass jar, and poured himself a good measure of the golden brew.

The *Glomar Explorer* crept into Kings Bay. Lieutenant Pine, the ship's chief engineer, stood on the deck, inspecting the rigging.

Captain Dewey walked up to Pine with his guest. "Pine, I would like to introduce you to Capt. McDowell."

"I'm Lieutenant Pine, ship's engineering. I'm in charge of the ship's crane and rigging gang."

The two men shook hands, then walked over to where riggers were assembling steel mesh belly bands.

"Do you think your rigging gear will hold up?" asked McDowell.

"Absolutely," boasted Pine. "If we do approach lifting capacity, the alarm inside the lifting scale will go off."

"That's good to know," replied McDowell.

The two men walked over to the port side railing. McDowell pointed to the nearly submerged mound below.

"That doesn't look too impressive," said Pine.

"Just wait till low tide. You'll see how large it is. The base will provide tugboats to help you hold your position while working. We are currently shocking the waters adjacent to the mound and—"

Lieutenant Pine interrupted him. "Shocking the waters? My dive team hasn't informed me of this."

McDowell snapped back, "Lieutenant, your ship's crew will do only the initial rigging."

"Okay..."

"All crane signals and loading will be done by base personnel."

"What are you going to do with the load once your crew has it out of the water?"

McDowell looked at his watch, "A hundred-foot barge is due to arrive shortly," he said. "When the load is free of the water, the barge will slip under it, then we lower it onto the deck."

"Well, that sounds like a good plan," said Pine.

McDowell turned away from Pine and looked up at the massive crane that loomed overhead. "Lieutenant Pine, I need to document the crane capacities."

"Follow me, the steps are straight ahead."

"You don't have to go all the way up there," said McDowell. "I'll be all right."

Captain Dewey stood on the bridge. He watched as the two men on the deck split up. A few minutes later, the door to the bridge opened.

"Sir, what the hell's going on around here?" said Pine.

Dewey turned toward his subordinate. "Explain yourself, Mr. Pine."

"Sir, the *Glomar's* divers will not be involved in this operation! And what's this shocking operation being conducted?"

Captain Dewey put his hand on Pine's shoulder. "We have been sent here to assist, not to run this operation. The base should have informed us of any shocking operations it was conducting. As to why they're doing it—it's a mystery to me. Remember the old adage—Truth is stranger than fiction."

"Certainly seems so in this case, sir."

"The longer you remain in the Navy, the more you'll come to believe it."

Base tugboats began arriving on the scene. The tide was now receding, revealing an ever-widening mound. The ship's crew connected the belly bands to the crane hook, then gave the signal to hoist. The rigging gear slowly left the deck, until it hung high above the ship.

The signalman standing on the mound rotated his arm in a downward motion. The belly bands slipped under the edges of the structure. The signalman raised his arm and moved it back and forth in front of himself. All crane movements stopped.

McDowell contacted the Navy SEAL tenders permitting them to start their part of the operation. The SEAL teams were issued bang sticks as a precaution against any predators that may have survived the shocking operation. The SEAL team members began to drop into the shallow waters of the submarine spring, swimming against the outflow of fresh water, finally reaching the belly bands. McDowell stood on the deck of the *Glomar Explorer* with a radio in his hand. Dewey and Pine joined him.

"How're things going?" asked Dewey.

"Slow but sure, Captain," replied McDowell.

Dewey pulled the Schrade out of his pocket and began to scrape out the bowl of a pipe. He looked at the bowl, tapped it out clean in his palm, blew off the scrapings, then stowed the pipe in his shirt pocket. He closed the knife.

The radio suddenly screeched alive. "Mayday! Mayday!" came the call from below. "Man down, I repeat, man down!"

McDowell clutched the radio in his hand. "I knew this was going to happen, those motherfucking bastards." McDowell raised the radio to his mouth. "This is Captain McDowell! Begin hoisting."

Pine instinctively grabbed the radio from McDowell's hand. "Attention. This is Lieutenant Pine. Disregard that last transmission."

McDowell menacingly moved toward Pine but stopped short.

"What are you trying to do, kill somebody!" barked Pine.

"I'm just trying to get them out of there," said McDowell.

Pine brushed past McDowell to the base of the crane.

"Pine to crane operator."

"Hear you loud and clear," came the reply from the operator perched high above the deck.

"Did you pull on the hoist lever without a proper signal?" asked Pine.

"I was about to hoist, but your transmission told me to stop."

"Good thinking," replied Pine. "You are to follow the directions of the signalman located on the mound."

"Yes sir," replied the operator.

Pine ran over to the ship's PA system. "This is not a drill. Injured personnel will be arriving on board the *Glomar Explorer*. All rescue personnel report to your posts. This is not a drill."

"Diver Tender to Lieutenant Pine."

"Pine here," came the reply.

"Sir, one of our divers is wedged between the belly band and the rock structure."

Pine thought for a second. Finally, he said, "Have the signalman on the mound lower the bands until your diver is free."

"Aye Aye, Lieutenant," came the reply.

Pine looked up at the crane boom trying to detect movement.

"Tender to Lieutenant Pine. He's free. We're bringing him up."

"Pine to Tender. Bring him over to the *Glomar's* main elevator, which will be lowered. A medical team will be waiting for your arrival."

Captain Dewey and McDowell were standing at midship. McDowell continued to stare at the blackened waters below. Captain Dewey touched McDowell on the arm.

McDowell wheeled around. "Oh, it's you, Captain. Forgive me, I must have been daydreaming."

Captain McDowell, they recovered a body."

"Was it a shark attack?"

"No, it was an industrial accident. Say, why did you shock the bay?"

"It was done for the safety of the divers," said McDowell.

"What kind of predator could cause such a threat here?"

McDowell's eyes widened. "Two men were killed in these waters. Their bodies were stripped of all flesh."

Captain Dewey pulled on the end of his beard, then turned and looked down at the mound, where preparations were being made to hoist the mound from the seafloor.

Pine stood at the rail and watched as the tender traveled from the mound to the *Glomar's* lowered elevator.

"Lieutenant Pine to the signalman, you may proceed with the lifting operation."

The signalman rotated his arm above his head. "Yes sir," he replied.

In turn, the crane operator engaged the hoist lever.

Pine watched with anticipation as the belly bands tightened. The strain of the lift was slowly transferred to the *Glomar Explorer*, which began to list slightly. Things not tied down began to roll toward the port side. Pine grabbed the railing for support. *Come on, baby. Break free,* thought Pine. The suction that had held the mound in position released its hold. The entire mass of material rose up and toward the ship, which in turn began to roll wildly. *Come on, old girl, now, stop that rolling.* The ship's rolling subsided, which in turn brought down Pine's heartbeat.

The lifting of the mound drew the attention of the *Sea Quest* crew. Captain Clark peered through the lens of the deck-mounted binoculars. "That thing is surely impressive. Looks like they tried to cover it with tarps."

"Let me see," said Chamberlain.

The captain moved away, allowing Chamberlain to peer through the binoculars. His eyes became riveted on the tarp flapping in the wind. He felt a tap on his shoulder.

"Sir," said the seaman, "There is a bunch of dead fish floating around here."

Chamberlain adjusted the lens slightly.

"Sir... do you want me to net some and feed them to the chopper?"

"Our specimen likes to prey on fish when their hearts are still beating," Chamberlain concluded that the object was not a tarp.

"Hey, Cap, you were looking at the dorsal fin of a giant shark."

Clark patted Chamberlain on the shoulder. "You're lucky the mother shark didn't get ahold of you instead of one of her babies."

Chamberlain looked at his wrapped hand then smiled. "You're right about that."

The crew aboard the *Sea Quest* watched as the mound disappeared below their view.

Lieutenant Pine watched as the mound gently landed on a pre-positioned barge. The rigging crew unhooked the belly band clips, then gave a signal to hoist. Pine watched the crane hook rise above the ship's deck. He gave a sigh of relief and said, "Well, I'm glad that operation is over with."

"Lieutenant Pine, report to the bridge."

Pine turned away from the rail. He headed toward the steps and noticed that the red bulb above the emergency door was still blinking. *Poor guy. I hope he makes it.*

* * *

The Navy surgeon took the vital signs of the stricken U.S. SEAL, and pronounced him dead, and then covered the man's upper torso with a sheet. He instructed two orderlies standing nearby to wheel the corpse into the ship's morgue. The gurney was pushed through the double doors. The men immediately felt the dampness that permeated the room. Apprentice Seaman Hoffman, who had just recently been assigned to the ship, walked down the center of the dimly lit room and began to count the body slots, which lined both walls. By the time he reached the far wall, a hundred slots had been counted. Perplexed, he walked back to the gurney, trying to figure it out.

The apprentice arrived back at the gurney, just as Lieutenant Johnson walked through the doors. "Sir, was the *Glomar Explorer* used as a hospital ship during the Vietnam War?"

"Why do you ask?"

"Well, there are a hundred body slots in this morgue."

The medical officer smiled slightly, and then said, "Rumor has it that this was a guest house for eighty-six Soviet submariners during the summer of '74. Any more questions, Apprentice Seaman?"

"No. None, sir."

"Then secure the corpse in number one."

The medical officer turned and pushed through the swinging doors.

* * *

Pine walked onto the bridge. "You call me, Cap?"

Dewey extended his arm and shook Pine's hand. "I want to commend you for a tough job well done."

"Well, thank you, sir," replied Pine.

Down below work crews were busy spreading tarps over the mound.

"Where's the barge headed?" asked Pine.

"Up to Norfolk Naval Base," said the captain.

"Sir, how'd that diver make out?"

"He didn't," said Dewey, with a tinge of sadness in his voice. "I requested that the base take charge of him but didn't get an answer yet."

The captain looked at his watch.

* * *

Snoop removed his headset, then shut off the receiver. He slowly walked over to the window and watched as the gray silhouette passed his view.

"Snoop, what the hell you doing up there! I wish you would spend as much time helping me around the house as you do on that radio."

"Yes, dear," replied Snoop, taking a final belt of liquid corn.

Snoop shut off the light, then went to bed.

CHAPTER EIGHTEEN

The *Georgia Peach* was dragging the ocean in front of Fernandina Beach when Captain Doug noticed several boats entering the ocean from the Saint Marys channel. He reduced the speed to half throttle.

The sudden reduction in speed caught the attention of the first mate. "Why we slowing up, Cap?"

Doug pointed to the small flotilla of boats ahead. The first mate nodded his head. "Those boats will stir the shrimp out of the bottom," Doug said. "It should be easy picking for us."

The morning sun was breaking over the horizon when the *Georgia Peach* entered the Saint Marys channel. The net began to swell with shrimp, slowing the boat down. The captain adjusted for the slowdown by pushing the throttle lever forward.

Just as the trawler reached the north wall of Fort Clinch the *Georgia Peach's* trawling net was attacked on all sides. Serrated teeth ripped through the finely-meshed net. Strong jaws continually opening and snapping crushed everything in their path. Captain Doug pulled the throttle lever into neutral, and the winches began to hoist the net onto the deck. The fishermen looked on in horror as the shredded net wrapped on the hoisting drum

"What the hell happened to my net?" exclaimed the captain.

"I ain't never seen anything like this in my life," said the first mate. "You won't be able to mend this net. It's destroyed."

The outgoing tide began to flush the remains of the attack out to sea. The chum slick got the attention of a thirteen-foot hammerhead, which had been foraging offshore. He began to follow the scent trail, engulfing dead and dying fish as he went. The school of predators sensed danger approaching them. In one great sweep, they closed ranks and formed what appeared to be one very large predator. The head of the school remained stationary, while the remainder rolled back and forth in the current, resembling the tail of a great fish. The jaws began to open and snap shut like so many mousetraps. The hammerhead stopped his forward movement, trying to discern what form of creature awaited him. The opponent's immense size and the incessant jaw snapping unnerved the hammerhead. He stopped and allowed the outgoing current to take him out to sea. He then turned seaward into the abyss.

* * *

The sheriff walked into the Sunrise Cafe, then stopped suddenly. *Damn, all the booths are taken,* he thought.

"We have a seat at the counter!" yelled one of the waitresses.

The sheriff sat down between two men. He shifted his large butt back and forth until he found the center. The sheriff's right cheek flopped off the stool, bumping into the man on the right of him.

"Hey, why don't you go on a diet? Your butt needs two stools!"

"Excuse me, but I forgot that my New Year's resolution was to lose weight. I'll try again next year.

"Yeah yeah, Sheriff."

"Say, you don't look so good yourself," said the sheriff. "Where'd you get those bloody eyes? Looks like you got poked with ice picks. Been playing with the firewater?"

Snoop smiled and then leaned towards the sheriff. "There was an accident at Kings Bay last night" he whispered. "Do me a favor... find out what happened."

The sheriff looked at Snoop in disbelief. "You want little old me, with my thirty-eight strapped to my side, to go to the front gate of Kings Bay and demand an incident report?"

"You march right down there like a boss and start throwing your weight around, Sheriff Two Stools," said Snoop.

"Let me tell you something about a military base. It's like a flying saucer that comes out of the sky and lands plumb smack in the middle of your community. First, they put up a fence, then they negotiate with the town fathers. They got their own laws; even the governor of Georgia can't enter without command permission. Then when the spaceship has completed its mission, it flies away."

"Anyone who talks about what actually happened..." Snoop adds, "they called crazy.

"Don't take a genius to know that."

"Why, Sheriff, that was a fine analogy you just used," said Snoop.

Captain Dutch, who sat facing the pair, cleaned the last bit of grits from his plate with a piece of bread and then ate it.

Dutch asked the sheriff a question, "Them flying saucers you're talking about—they gonna clean up the bay the way it was when they leave?"

"Probably not," replied the sheriff. "Say, how come we locals can't get those fat juicy shrimp?" added the sheriff contemptuously. "You boys keep tellin' us that the only thing available is popcorn shrimp."

Snoop watched as the skirmish set in motion by the sheriff unfolded.

Dutch, now flustered and nerve-struck, charged back. "You people don't want to pay the price for first quality shrimp. Those Yankees got pockets full of money and an appetite to boot."

The sheriff spread his arms out like a preacher in the pulpit and declared, "Priorities, priorities, we all got priorities. It seems to me that if we all worked together, we would be a sight better off."

Dutch threw his hand up in protest, paid his bill, and then walked out of the Sunrise Cafe.

"Sheriff, now, why'd ya get that man all riled up?" asked Snoop.

Lowellin pointed to the gold badge pinned to his shirt. "Because I'm the sheriff," he said. "Besides, maybe Dutch will bring up the subject of popcorn shrimp tonight."

* * *

Later that evening, the Fernandina Beach Commercial Fishermen's Association meeting was about to begin.

Dutch pushed through the swinging doors of the Palace Saloon touted to be the oldest bar in Florida. "Where's my beer?" he barked.

"Sorry, but we don't serve people who don't know how to tie their shoes," said Amy the barmaid.

Dutch looked down at the floor. "I don't even see any feet. My belly's in the way."

"I'll excuse you this time, but the next time you come in, make sure somebody ties your shoes."

Amy drew a mug of beer and placed it in front of Dutch. "Anything else, hon?"

Dutch winced in pain and held his stomach. She put her hand on his forearm. "What's the matter?"

With a barely audible voice, he whispered, "Hunger pains."

Amy pulled her hand away. Dutch began to laugh heartily.

The barmaid pointed to a long table that lay behind Dutch. "Go fill your gut with that."

Dutch turned his head. "Lordy, Lordy, now what do we have here? Fried and boiled shrimp, steamed oysters, hot wings, and cornbread." Dutch turned back to Amy. "You think you could carry me over to the table? I feel weak."

Amy smiled curtly and then walked away.

Captain Low pushed through the doors and walked up to Dutch. "Why is it you always get here first?"

"The early bird gets the worm," quipped Dutch.

"But catches the hungry hawk's eye," added Low.

"Besides, delicate people like you and me wouldn't get anything to eat, what with those hungry young bucks gobbling all the food up." Dutch rubbed his hand on his rotund belly. "Hey Low, I think it's time to eat."

The captains walked over to the table and filled their plates. Captain Low sat at the end of the table that was reserved for the Association president. Dutch, as Vice President, sat next to him. They were half full before the captains and mates began to arrive. Dutch took a short breath and asked Captain Low if he had encountered any problems during last night's haul.

"Nope," replied Low. "Why ya ask?"

"I got a call today from the *Georgia Peach*. Doug told me they lost their net last night in the Saint Marys channel."

"How much of it?"

"All of it," said Dutch.

"They get snagged on the rock jetty?"

"No, I don't think so, all he said was that the net was shredded into pieces. I'm gonna make a motion that we donate some money to the *Georgia Peach* for repairs."

"I'll second it," replied Low.

Tommy Lions, Dutch's first mate, pulled up a seat next to the captain.

"Y'all save anything for me?" Tommy asked.

"Fill your plate up. You will never starve at our meeting."

The Fernandina Beach Commercial Fishermen's Association's meetings were informal at best. Discussions would pop up while sucking oysters or drinking beer. Dutch, as vice president and treasurer, would jot down information that he felt was of importance to the association. Often he wrote all the notes on the same page, all garbled and doodled. Dutch had been challenged a few times about his note keeping, but every time he tried to give up the job, there were no takers.

Dutch pulled out his weathered notebook and opened it to the most recent entry. "Attention, I got a motion here."

No response.

Dutch then picked up a soup spoon and began banging it on the table. That got their attention.

"You boys can keep eating and drinking but do it quietly. I got a motion to donate five hundred dollars to the *Georgia Peach* for net repairs."

Dutch raised his hand, Captain Low seconded it, with everybody at the table following suit.

"Motion passed!" Dutch said, clapping his spoon on the table like a gavel.

"How's our lawsuit against the base doing?" asked one of the fishermen.

Dutch fingered through his notebook. "Here we are. I had a discussion with the Environmental Protection specialist on... May 28th."

"He say we're no longer allowed in the water?" someone chimed in.

"Not quite," said Dutch. "He said that the suit would have to work its way through the courts. The good thing about this lawsuit is that we don't have to pay no lawyer's fees."

Timmy Holt raised his hand. "I was dragging in front of the base and ran into a fish kill."

"Did you pick any up?"

"Yeah, I put it in my freezer."

"When you get a chance, drop it off at my house. Make sure you mark it, otherwise my wife might fry it up and kill us."

That remark brought a round of laughter from the Association members.

"The next time I go to the EPA office in Jacksonville, I'll take that nuclear fish with me."

Jimmy Longstreet raised his hand. "You ain't goin' nowhere with that lawsuit! They got the politicians in their pockets, including your brother-in-law, the mayor of Saint Marys."

Dutch's face turned beet red. Yelling ensued that turned to grumbling that soon died down into clanking of mugs and an impromptu chugging contest.

His moment of anger subsided, and with a belly full of beer, Dutch calmly and officially replied, "You can choose your friends, but not your relatives."

"You're right, Dutch," replied Longstreet in an apologetic tone. "Worst of all, our own people turned against us. The sub base dangles jobs under their noses, then they forget where they come from. If the locals in Saint Marys had voted against building that base, we'd be fishing there today."

Captain Low raised his hand and then said, "I'd like to take a moment of silence for Jube Early, who drowned in a boating accident."

The men folded their hands, said a prayer, and then resumed their discussion.

"Where'd they find him?" asked Tommy Lions.

"Just south of the base, where the Intracoastal Waterway flows into the Saint Marys."

"Tell you one thing: that man could throw one hell of a cast net."

The lights went on in Dutch's head. He opened the notebook to a clean page and wrote, *See coroner—cast net—Jube Early.*

Tommy Lions elbowed Dutch and said, "Say, is that gal at the bar smiling at me?" Tommy tipped his hat with his fingertips and smiled back.

"She wants you," hollered Tim Holt.

"Well, she ain't gonna have to wait long. Say, President Low, when's this meeting gonna end?"

"Yeah when we gonna adjourn so they can adjoin?" said Longstreet.

"You're excused," said Low, with a smile on his face.

Tommy high-stepped it away from the table and began to converse with the girl at the bar.

The place began to swell with tourists. Chairs now became a commodity. The manager of the saloon walked up to the shrimpers' table and asked that the meeting be cut short.

"We gotta band coming in at nine."

"Country western?" asked Dutch.

"No, we got George Thorogood and the Destroyers booked for the next three days."

"Destroy what?" asked Dutch.

"Haven't you ever heard the song, 'Bad to the Bone'?" a waitress said.

"That's his greatest hit," said the manager.

Dutch pushed himself out of his chair. "I know what I'm gonna do," he growled. "I'm gonna go home and watch some Lawrence Welk reruns."

* * *

The following morning, Dutch drove the *Anna Marie* to Saint Marys and pulled in next to the *Georgia Peach.* Captain Doug, who was standing on the deck, waved to Dutch, then tied the *Anna Marie* off to a nearby bulkhead. Dutch emerged from the pilot's house then slowly descended the steps.

"I remember when you would slide down those steps," said Doug.

"It's that damn arthritis," said Dutch. "There must be a storm headin' this way." Dutch put his arm out. "Doug, give me a hand." He climbed up on the rail, then jumped onto the dock. "See, nothin' to it."

"What brings the vice president of the Fernandina Beach Fisherman's Association here?"

"Oh, I just stopped by to talk to an old friend."

The two men shook hands.

Captain Doug felt a wad of paper transferred to his hand and his arm jerked back.

"What's this?" asked Doug.

"This ain't no charity, before you even get started," said Dutch sternly. "You boys would do the same for us."

After looking off at the horizon, Doug put the money in his pocket. "You tell the boys I'm really thankful."

"Do you still got some of that net?"

Doug hung his head. "Over in the dumpster," he said with a jerk of his head.

"Come on, let's drag it out, and maybe we'll make some sense of this."

The net was spread out and Dutch began to count the holes. "You had a large school of predator fish run through here at the same time."

"Don't make no sense," said Doug.

"Right. King mackerel and bluefish only attack the stragglers and wounded fish. They never directly attack a net."

"I hear ya talking. I can't figure it out myself, but I know one thing. If this turns to a trend, we'll be outta business."

The men gathered up the net and threw it in the dumpster. Dutch started toward his truck.

"Where ya headed?"

"I'm gonna walk up to the courthouse and chew the fat with my brother-in-law."

* * *

Dutch walked past the back of the morgue and up the back steps of Town Hall, into the Mayor's office, which was being remodeled

"Where's the mayor of this town?" he yelled.

"I'm here. Watch your step."

Dutch walked into a small cluttered room. Mayor Tubbs stood up and shook his hand.

"What brings you to Saint Marys?"

"I came here to return your sister."

"Sorry. All sales final."

"She didn't do the dishes this morning, so I hogtied her, and then brought her back to you."

Mayor Tubbs smiled. "If I know my sister, she won't be tied down long."

"How's Margaret doing?"

"She has a hard time getting out of bed, what with that arthritis and all."

"Yeah, getting old is tough."

"We really should get together some time," said the mayor. "Come on, let me show you my office. It's gonna look like the White House. See here, this old window's coming out and being replaced with a big picture window. I'll be able to look out on the Saint Marys River and watch the sun go down." He tapped on the old floorboards. "Rugs are gonna be installed, and new office furniture. Best of all, I talked the town fathers into hiring a coroner full time. Yep, things are looking up around here."

"Speaking of coroners, I heard that old Jube Early got drowned."

The mayor's demeanor changed from a jovial mood to that of a witness in a murder trial. "Yeah, it's a shame about old Jube. He was found with his cast net rope looped around his wrist. He just plain drowned himself."

"Did you save the net?" asked Dutch.

The mayor looked at him inquisitively. "Now, why the hell would I save a chewed-up net?"

"Chewed-up net, you say? The *Georgia Peach* lost a commercial net the night before last. It too was shredded. Do you think there's a connection?"

Mayor Tubbs shrugged his shoulders. "Your guess is as good as mine."

Dutch began to pace the room. "Are you aware that somebody was killed on the base the other day?"

"That's news to me," replied the mayor.

"Yeah, they only tell you what they want you to know."

"Now wait a minute!"

Dutch saw the mayor's anger begin to build. "Alright, alright, don't get your bowels in an uproar. The story will come out in the wash. It always does."

Anxious to change the subject, Mayor Tubbs began to talk about the changes in Saint Marys. "Did you see all the heavy equipment in front of the base main gate?"

"What they building, some fancy housing for the Navy brass?"

"No, the federal government is building a six-lane highway from I-95 to Saint Marys, at no cost to Saint Marys. That new road will be a boon to this one-horse town. The base is now accepting job applications, you know. You can't beat the federal benefits."

Dutch surveyed the mayor's office. "You're right," said Dutch. "You can't beat the benefits. Well, I better be getting back to Fernandina. Why don't you and the wife come on over for Sunday dinner?"

"That's a good idea. What time you want us over?" asked the mayor.

"Any time after noon. I'll have Margaret bake your favorite dessert, key lime pie."

The men said goodbye.

Dutch walked down to the *Georgia Peach* and chatted with Captain Doug for a few minutes, then he headed home. He slowed the *Anna Marie* to watch as a Navy barge entered the North River.

CHAPTER NINETEEN

McDowell and Chamberlain stood on the bow as the barge maneuvered its way up the twisting river. Chamberlain scratched at his bandage and winced.

A bank fisherman yelled at them, "You can't get into the lake anymore, they gated the entrance."

The officers just smiled and waved back to the man.

"What are you going to do with the submarine spring?" asked Chamberlain.

"I'm gonna fill it with concrete."

"Didn't Dr. Maury say that filling this shaft could divert the water pressure to an offshore spring that has not yet breached the ocean floor?"

McDowell shrugged his shoulders. "Big deal. That wouldn't be a concern for the Navy Department. It would just be a natural occurrence. Oh, before I forget, I got you an assistant to help you with your experiments."

"Good," said Chamberlain. "Now I can confirm my girlfriend's flight to Jacksonville, Florida."

"Where's she coming from?"

"San Diego," replied Chamberlain.

"That's got to be the most pleasant place to live in the whole world. Do you think she will like it here? It might be a little too laid back here for a SoCal city girl."

"She's only coming here for the weekend," replied Chamberlain. "I told her that I would be back in San Diego in two weeks. Now I got to explain this extended tour to her."

"I'd advise you not to tell her until after she arrives. I have an even better idea. Kill that creature, and then there won't be anything for you to do. You'll probably get transferred back to San Diego."

"Thanks for the offhand advice," said Chamberlain.

The barge slowed down and then stopped in front of the Peter's Point Bridge.

The pilot yelled down to the mates below. "Come up here and watch my antennas. I don't want to break any off against this low-lying bridge."

The deckhands positioned themselves near the top of the pilot's house and motioned with their hands to move forward. Darkness enveloped the barge momentarily, and then the bright midday sun bathed it in light. The barge moved slowly through an open gate.

A security boat then passed.

"Make sure you lock the gate, we won't be back this way for a couple of months."

The lake before the barge was clear and deep. Schools of finger mullet dashed from place to place. Their bodies shone like many silver spoons. White pines, oaks, and wild roses grew along the banks of the lake. Some of the older trees that had fallen over, lay partially exposed on the lake's surface. Turtles lay on the exposed branches sunning themselves. Further up the lake, a pair of eyes rose above the lake's surface. The vibrations attracted Old Charlie's attention. The resident alligator that had escaped the poachers' guns and spears was now protected inside the fences of the submarine base. Measuring over twelve feet in length, he was the alpha predator of North River Lake. At the north end stood an expanse of chest-high sea oats. The marsh was split in two by a meandering tidal creek.

Captain McDowell raised his arm and motioned for the pilot to stop. The barge drifted into the marsh's bank.

"That'll be alright for now." He motioned to the deckhands to lower the anchors. "Well, Chamberlain, what do you think of your new home?"

"Perfect," replied Chamberlain. "We'll be in perfect isolation."

McDowell pointed to the trail that ended at the lake's edge. "I'm gonna have that area bulldozed and a parking lot installed. Because of the marsh floods, a wooden boardwalk will be constructed. Your list includes a well to be drilled into the aquifer. What's the matter with all the water from the lake?"

"I want to replicate the environmental conditions under which King Carcharodon was born."

"Where did you get that name?"

Chamberlain puffed out his chest slightly. "I named the new species because I discovered it."

McDowell smiled, then pointed to Chamberlain's wrapping. "Looks like you've had firsthand knowledge of this species."

Chamberlain brushed off the remark. "Did you know that a new species of whale was discovered in 1973?"

"A whale! I would think that such a large animal would have been identified before '73."

"The oceans are largely hidden from the scientific community," said Chamberlain. "New species are out there just waiting to be discovered."

"That's a pretty cool concept. I'll probably be reading about you in *National Geographic* or *Smithsonian Magazine* someday."

"Also, I want a fish tank with a viewing window facing the lake. The other window would face the researchers. I'll call San Diego and get some blueprints on the fish tanks that we used."

* * *

Dutch stood on the deck of the *Anna Marie* early the next morning. He sipped a coffee, having completed his haul of shrimp, which were being transferred to the cooler onshore.

"Hey, Cap, want me to wash down the boat?"

"Yeah, go ahead. Hey whatever happened to that gal that you met at the Palace Saloon?"

"Oh, her! All I can say is I never went to bed with an ugly woman, but I woke up with a few."

Dutch laughed at the remark. "I should have never asked you that question."

Dutch leaned against the railing and waved at the shrimpers who were returning to the dock. He waved at the *Wahoo* but got no response from Captain Maddox, who stood like a statue behind the wheel. The stern of the shrimp boat slowly passed his view.

"Holy shit," Dutch yelled. "They must have hit the *Wahoo*."

Tommy dropped the water hose, then ran over to Dutch.

"What's the matter, Cap?"

Dutch pointed his finger at the *Wahoo*. Strips of tattered net blew in the wind like so many flags.

"Damn, would you look at that?" said Tommy.

"Come on, let's go," said Dutch.

They joined the other crews, who were heading for the *Wahoo*. When Dutch arrived, the boat was already filled with concerned onlookers.

"Hey Mad Boy," yelled Dutch. "Lower that net, it don't look too good."

The command snapped Captain Maddox out of his stupor. The net was lowered to the deck, where curious hands examined the remains of the net. Dutch climbed to the top of a piling, which made him the tallest man in the group. The others still groped at the net.

"Hey gents, give me your attention!" Dutch began. "We got a serious situation here that is destroying our livelihood. I want you all to come over to my house now, and we'll figure out what's to be done."

Grumbles of concurrence bubbled up from the men.

"You boys disconnect that net and throw it in the back of my pickup."

Dutch was helped down from the piling and was immediately surrounded by his fellow shrimpers asking questions.

Dutch saw the black and white car slowly drive down the dock street. He put his finger to his closed lips. "Quiet, here comes the sheriff."

Dutch walked through the knot of men and knelt down in front of Lowellin's open window.

"What are you boys up to?" the sheriff asked.

"We're celebrating a fine catch. We hauled in all number one shrimp. I've invited the boys to the house for coffee and cornbread."

"You mean corn liquor."

"My wife don't allow no tobacco or alcohol in the house, you know that sheriff."

"You're right. Margaret's a good churchwoman. I suspect that if I drive past your house, the porch will be loaded with men smoking and drinking corn."

"Ain't no law against sitting on my porch, is there Sheriff?"

"No, none at all. Say, what are you getting for those number ones up in New York."

"Three dollars a pound," said Dutch, with a twinkle in his eye. "Why, would you like to buy some?"

"Hell naw," replied the sheriff. "Not at that price."

"I'll tell you what I'm gonna do. The price for you is seventy-five cents a pound."

"Why so cheap?"

"Why," said Dutch, "because we're like a big family here." Dutch patted the sheriff on the forearm. "Hey Tommy, you go with the sheriff to the cooler and measure out ten pounds of large shrimp..."

"Right, boss."

"Give 'im the Dutch discount."

"Come on, Tommy!" yelled the sheriff. "I'm gonna put you under my protective custody until I get those shrimp."

Dutch watched as the sheriff drove away. He then got into his truck and headed home.

Margaret was making breakfast when Dutch entered the kitchen.

"What's cooking?"

"Breakfast sausage, grits, and cornbread."

"Well, honey, you're gonna have to whip up a larger batch, 'cause we're gonna have an emergency meeting."

"What's happened now?" she asked, with concern in her voice.

"Lou lost a net this morning."

"Maybe it's a sign from God. I could ask Father McClure to re-bless the fleet."

"No! I don't want no priest involved in this."

Margaret nodded in agreement.

"Besides, doesn't it say in the bible that God takes care of those who help themselves?"

The smell of fish began to fill the kitchen and dining room as men wearing worn clothes and heavy boots entered the house.

"Sit down anywhere. Margaret's whipping up some grits and sausage."

Dutch looked out the porch door and saw Tommy Lions getting out of his truck. He went out and met the first mate.

Tommy reached into his pocket and brought out a handful of dollar bills. "Here's your change, Captain."

"Keep that, and here's ten dollars and my truck keys. Go down to Krispy Kreme. Get three boxes. Get some of them twisty kind with sugar sprinkled on them. Margaret loves them with her tea."

Tommy took a glance at Dutch's belly then left.

* * *

Having fetched the doughnuts, Timmy Holt approached the captain as he walked back to the house.

"Say, Cap, where you hiding the corn?"

"Did you say cornbread? Margaret's baking up a couple of trays."

"Naw, you know what I mean."

Dutch smiled broadly. "Go down to the shed. It's sittin' on the workbench. I left some paper cups down there too."

Dutch returned to the porch and began to chew the fat with the other fishermen.

"Ya think that we should notify the Environmental Protection Agency?" asked one of the men.

"Naw," said Dutch. "These government agencies all work together, like hand in glove. If they determined that these net-shredders were contaminated with nuclear waste from Kings Bay, they would slap the Navy on the wrist. Then they'd shut down commercial fishing in the area."

"You're right, Dutch, we'd starve," said Captain Maddox, who was sitting in a rocking chair. "Nobody helped us in the past. We'll take care of ourselves."

"Alright, boys, let's go in and eat something," offered Dutch. "We'll talk about this afterward."

Dutch stood at the screen door and welcomed the fishermen inside. "If you can't find a seat in here, come on back out on the porch. Did you get those twisties for Margaret?" Dutch inquired of Tommy Lions.

"Got a whole box, Cap."

Dutch opened the door and let him inside with the others.

After everyone had finished eating, Dutch called for the meeting to begin. He stood at the far end of the dining room. "Captain Low, you're the president, would you like to say anything?"

"Naw, only that my net was shredded too. You got a better handle on this, Dutch. Go ahead and begin."

Dutch pulled out his notebook. "Let's look at the facts. The Georgia Peach was attacked a few days ago. I went over to Saint Marys and examined what was left of the net. I also talked to the mayor of Saint Marys. He told me that the cast net looped on Jube Early's wrist was shredded as well."

A fisherman who was hard of hearing raised his hand. "What did you say about Jube Early?" he said in a loud voice.

"To anyone that hasn't heard," Dutch replied. "Jube Early was found drowned in the Saint Marys River. The most recent attack occurred on the Wahoo. Gentlemen, we have a pattern developing here that if not stopped will end the fishing in north Florida. Any suggestions from you boys?"

A young mate shouted out, "Blow 'em up with dynamite!"

"Not an option," shot back Dutch. "Next."

Captain Maddox, an old weather-beaten seaman, stood up slowly. "Why don't we beat 'em at dar own game?" He swung his arm through the air, then closed his fist as if catching a fly.

"How's that," said Tommy.

"Place a boat in da lead position," the old captain began. "As a lure. Load 'is net with fresh baitfish, then slowly drag da net through da ocean. Spread a long net between two boats that we have followin' behind. If those critters attack da lead boat's net, da two boats layin' behind will speed up and trap everything in da larger net."

"Hmm, that sounds like a plan," said Dutch.

"Yeah, but how are we gonna keep those bastards in the net?" asked Lions.

"With a steel-mesh net," answered Captain Maddox. "Atlantic Marine down in Jacksonville gotta bunch of 'em. Dutch, what ya doin' today?" he asked.

"Why, going down to get a steel-mesh net."

After the meeting ended, Dutch helped his wife clean up.

Then Dutch walked out of the house with a box tucked under his arm. He headed down to the backyard shed, stepped inside, and in a moment came out cussing.

"Those damnable boys drank every last drop of my corn liquor."

Margaret heard the commotion and ran into the backyard. "What's the matter, Dutch? Are you alright?"

"I'm alright, just stubbed my big toe's all."

"You be careful going down to Jacksonville, hear?"

"Okay, don't worry, I'll be alright. I'll be home for supper."

Dutch drove out of the driveway.

He began fumbling with the box next to him. He opened the lid and picked up a sugar twisty, which he bit in half. Sugar crystals clung to his lips, which he dutifully licked off.

"Margaret loves these Krispy Kreme donuts."

Dutch returned home late that afternoon, his truck laden with the new fishing net. He called the captain of the Georgia Peach and told him of the details of the plan. He also requested the Saint Marys fleet remain in port for the next two nights. All agreed.

CHAPTER TWENTY

The ravenous predators waited at the mouth of the Saint Marys channel for their evening meal of netted shrimp, but none appeared that night. The following morning, a huge school of finger mullet worked its way south. Periodic attacks from marauding king mackerel forced the school into the shallows. They followed the shoreline until their advance was blocked by rocks that extended from the beach to deep water. Death waited within the crevices of the rock pile. Crabs, sea bass, and toadfish lurched out into the school, causing momentary panic, but the urge to migrate instinctively drove the school east, out of the Saint Marys channel, then south towards Fernandina Beach. The predators, sensing an oncoming meal, formed a line of jaws from the edge of the beach seaward. The oncoming mullet panicked. When they heard the incessant snapping and grinding the school swam toward the beach. The blue-green Atlantic Ocean turned pink then crimson red. Shredded mullet began to appear on the ocean surface, alerting seagulls that had been resting on the jetty. They rose into the air and began to circle the maelstrom below.

Young Tom McKnight, the lighthouse keeper's son, was fishing the surf nearby. He watched as the gulls began diving in the ocean. "God'am, the bluefish must be in a feeding frenzy!"

Tom worked his way through breaking waves until the water was waist high. Tom reared back, casting the glittering lure amongst the diving birds.

The strike was instantaneous. Tom's ten-foot rod bent in half; the line began to peel off the reel. Tom held the rod tightly preparing himself for a long battle, but it was not to be. His line suddenly went slack.

Tom shook his head in disbelief. "Son of a bitch cut my line loose."

He scratched his head. "I'm gonna get my wired lure! See if they can cut through that."

He turned toward the beach and began walking. Something latched onto Tom's heel bone as his foot rose out of the sand, causing him to fall forward into the rolling surf. Tom's leg began to shake like a rag doll. Pain and panic ran through him like a freight train.

"Jesus Christ, what the hell's going on?"

Blood from the wound began to mix with the ocean waters. An entire horde ceased feeding on the mullet, allowing them to escape. Their senses directed them to the beach to the taste of their first meal. Early arrivals maneuvered for position, slashing off pieces of flesh from Tom's leg, causing the man to howl with pain. The blood loss weakened him to the point that he could not move forward. The outgoing tide pulled hard on the waves, exposing the victim and his antagonists. The predators released their grip and returned to the shallows.

Tom drifted in and out of consciousness. He awoke to feel the warm sun drying his body. He knew he was now safe. "Thank you, Lord, for saving my life," he yelled.

Tom managed to push his elbow into the soft sand, then turned his head seaward. Panic returned: blackened fish with large yellow eyes seemed to be watching him.

"Those eyes, those yellow eyes. What the hell are they staring at?"

The pounding in his head began to subside. He laid his head on the cool sand, drifting into unconsciousness.

Professor Greiner was standing on his deck facing the ocean.

"Do you hear that?" the professor asked his wife.

"No," she replied.

"Sounds like screaming."

"Maybe it's the seagulls. They sound like screaming babies sometimes."

The professor picked up his binoculars and scanned the beach. The diving gulls and the ocean-hugging pelicans caught his attention.

"Helen, someone's laying at the edge of the water."

"Maybe just getting a suntan, dear," she said.

Unconvinced, he told her that he was going to investigate. "If you see me wave my arms back and forth, call the police," he said, hurrying down to the beach.

Professor Greiner walked briskly down the shore. Upon reaching the stricken man, he knelt down and watched for vital signs. The man's eyes were closed; his face showed no sign of emotion; his breathing was shallow.

The professor stood and began waving his arms back and forth until his wife disappeared inside the house. Turning back, he noticed the puncture wounds and missing flesh on the boy's leg. A chill ran up his back unnerving him. The professor began to rub his forehead with his fingers. I wish I could do more for you, thought the professor. He watched over the boy until the wail of sirens in the distance caught his attention. He turned and waved his arms back and forth frantically until the rescue vehicles arrived.

Sheriff Lowellen pulled in behind the ambulance, got on the radio, and gave his location. He picked up his clipboard and joined the paramedics who were slowly transferring the fisherman to a stretcher.

"How's he doing?" asked the sheriff.

"Still breathing, that's all I can tell you."

The sheriff pulled the brim of his hat down to protect his eyes from the blinding sun. He pulled out a pen from his shirt pocket and began to write on the clipboard. Time: 7:35 a.m. Incident... The sheriff glanced at the victim's bloodied leg and wrote down: Possible shark attack. He put his pen away, then looked at the man who was staring at the victim.

"This your son?"

The man looked up at the sheriff.

"Who me?" asked the professor. "No, I live in the first house on the beach."

"Oh, you moved into the Jenkins house."

"Yes, I believe that was their name. Sheriff, do attacks like this occur often?"

"No, not often, but I don't recommend jumping into a school of baitfish when they're being pursued by hungry predators."

"I think lifeguards should be posted along the beach," said the professor abruptly.

The sheriff smiled. "Lifeguards in this town! They don't have enough money for law enforcement, let alone lifeguards."

The paramedics picked up the stretcher, then began to walk towards the ambulance.

"Where you boys taking him," asked the sheriff.

"Nassau General," they replied.

The sheriff shook Dr. Greiner's hand, thanking him for his help.

The professor watched as the patrol car wheeled around with sirens blaring. He turned toward the ocean. The outgoing tide had leveled the beach sand. The only exception was a fishing rod that lay half-buried.

That must be the boy's rod.

The professor walked down to the water's edge and knelt down. He carefully began to dig the sand away, then extracted the rod from its impending burial site. The professor stood up, shook the loose sand free, then slowly walked back to the house with his find.

Helen waited for him at the back door.

"What do you have there?"

"Oh, I found it on the beach, probably belongs to that boy."

"Leave it outside, it's full of sand. I saw the ambulance go by. Was anyone hurt badly?"

"Yeah, I think he's in a coma."

"That's a shame. What happened?"

"Shark attack they think."

"I didn't think they came so close to shore."

"Let's hope it's an exception," said the professor. "Let's go in the house. I want to call the sheriff's office and inform them about the rod."

* * *

The sheriff sat at the counter of the Huddle House sipping on a hot cup of coffee. Tom McKnight, the lighthouse keeper, walked up to the sheriff then patted him on the back.

"If it wasn't for you, my son wouldn't have made it."

Lowellin turned his thick neck toward McKnight. "Me! I was just doin' my job. The one to thank is that bone doctor who's living at the Jenkins house. He found Tommy laying on the beach."

"Sit down, let me buy you a coffee."

McKnight sat down and began to rub his hands together.

"How's your boy doing?" asked the sheriff.

"Oh, he's gonna make it. They gave him a couple of pints of blood and the doctors worked on his foot a bit."

The sheriff touched him on his knotted hands. "Ya know, I didn't recognize your boy on the beach, what with the blood and sand covering him. It was only after they cleaned him up that I made the connection."

McKnight's hands began to relax.

"Oh, before I forget. Dr. Greiner, that fella that lives at the Jenkins house, he called the office. Said he found a fishing rod near where Tommy was found."

"That must be Tommy's. He was asking about it. You know, my daddy made that special for him."

McKnight stood up suddenly.

"Where ya goin'? You didn't touch your coffee."

"I gotta get to the fish market," replied McKnight.

Sheriff Lowellin finished his coffee.

* * *

The sheriff drove down Dock Street, waving at the shrimpers as he went.

Tommy Lions waved back.

"Hey, cap, why don't we invite the sheriff on our fishing trip? I hear he's a pretty good shot."

"Yeah, and he's got a big mouth," said Dutch.

The two fishermen shook the stainless steel to get the kinks out.

"Do you think this net will hold 'em?" asked Tommy.

"If it don't then we're in big trouble. Say, Tommy, go help those boys on the *Wahoo*."

"What are they doing over there?"

"Loading their hemp net with a bloody brew, I'll tell ya," said Dutch.

"Fresh mullet and shrimp with buckets of fish blood poured in for good measure," said Tommy. "That surely will draw them into our trap,"

* * *

Mr. Lee was busy cleaning flounder when McKnight walked into the store. The fishmonger stopped what he was doing.

"How's your boy doing?"

"Oh, he's coming along just fine."

"Ya know, you can never be too careful," said Mr. Lee. "I remember when I was a boy fishing the southern point of the island, I walked into the ocean and the water came up to my chest. The water was so clear I could see my feet. Out of nowhere, a hammerhead shark slips in behind me. It must have been twelve feet long. He began circling me, closing in for the kill."

"Wha'd ya do?" asked McKnight.

"Don't know, all I know is I made it up the beach. From then on, I only went in up to my ankles. Well, enough of my stories, what can I get you today?"

"Got any local shrimp?"

"Not local," replied Mr. Lee. "The boys didn't go out last night, but I got shrimp from Jacksonville."

McKnight looked skeptical. "Let's see 'em."

The fishmonger slid open the glass case and brought out an ice-filled tray loaded with plump shrimp. Mr. Lee set the tray on the counter and watched as Tom examined a single shrimp.

"They sure are fresh," said Tom. "Look at them pretty colors, and the eyes are black as coal."

Mr. Lee chuckled. "By the time these shrimp get up to the Yankees, the eyes will be dull gray and their bodies will have lost their luster. Guess them Northerners think that's what these shrimp are supposed to look like."

The men began to laugh.

"Mr. Lee, give me five pounds."

Lee grabbed and slid the tray.

"No, make it ten."

The fishmonger began to transfer the fattest shrimp from the tray onto the scale.

"A touch over ten pounds. I won't charge you extra."

The shrimp were slipped into plastic bags mixed with ice. Mr. Lee wrapped the bags in damp newspapers.

"Doesn't the News Leader get offended when you wrap fish with their news articles?"

"Shucks, no..." said Mr. Lee, smiling, "that's the only way anyone will read their paper."

* * *

Helen Greiner heard a knock on the door. "Arthur..."

"I'll get it, hon."

The professor opened the door.

"Afternoon, sir."

"Good afternoon."

"Name's Tom McKnight. I'm lookin' for the fella that saved my son's life."

The professor blushed slightly. "Well, yes, I did help."

McKnight thrust out his arm and shook Arthur's hand. "I'd like to thank you from the bottom of my heart."

Tears began to well up, obscuring his vision. He wiped away the tears with his free hand while handing the package to the professor with the other hand.

"What's this?"

"Fresh shrimp," replied McKnight. "Ya better put them in the refrigerator."

"Well thanks, Tom." Arthur handed the package to his wife.

"Fresh shrimp. Maybe I'll make scampi tonight."

"Come on in. Would you like a cup of coffee or iced tea?"

"Iced tea would be fine, sir."

The three sat down and began to converse.

"Sheriff said that you're a bone doctor."

Before Arthur could answer, McKnight reached into his pocket and brought out a small plastic bag with a shiny black object within. McKnight handed it to the professor.

"Here, see if you can figure it out," McKnight said. "The x-rays showed that this tooth was embedded in his heel bone. The doctors explained it by saying that the tooth was sitting on edge in the sand. When Tommy pushed down the tooth got lodged in his bone."

The professor shook his head in disbelief. "May I see the tooth?"

"Shucks, you can have it." McKnight passed the tooth to the professor.

He held the plastic bag up to the light. "This one is similar to the teeth we have been finding on the beach," said Greiner. "Mr. McKnight. Has this type of tooth washed up on the beach in the past?"

"Not sure," replied McKnight. "You may want to talk to the ranger at Fort Clinch. They got records going back to 1850. You can even take a guided tour over there."

"That sounds like a good place to visit. Maybe I'll get some answers there."

"Well, I gotta get back to the hospital."

"Oh, wait a minute," said the professor ."I want to show you something."

They walked out onto the porch. Arthur pointed to the fishing rod sitting in the corner.

"Does this look familiar?"

McKnight's eyes lit up. "That's Tommy's, alright."

He picked it up and tried to turn the reel handle. "Can't move it," said McKnight. "She's loaded with sand. I'll clean it up when I get home."

* * *

At dusk, three shrimp trawlers left the Fernandina docks, entered the Saint Marys channel, and headed east out into the Atlantic. The *Wahoo* took the lead position with Captain Maddox at the wheel. The *Sandpiper* and the *Anna Marie* drifted apart and began to lower the steel-mesh net Dutch had bought in Jacksonville. The mates on the *Wahoo* lowered the bait-laden net into the dark waters. Removing the lids of the fifty-gallon drums, the mates dipped soup ladles into the foul-smelling brew.

Old Captain Maddox walked out of the pilot's house and called down to them, "Start slingin' that chum overboard, boys. If that bloody mess doesn't attract 'em, nuttin will."

Maddox returned to the wheelhouse and set the rpm to 1200, then radioed the trailing boats that he would travel south along the beach. At the mouth of the Nassau River, off the end of the island, the *Wahoo* planned to make a wide arc towards the open ocean heading north.

All the shrimpers were edgy that night.

Expecting an immediate attack, Tommy Lions stood on the stern of the *Anna Marie*, fingering the cool steel of his double-barreled shotgun.

"Hey Cap," he yelled, "would you like a beer?"

"I don't drink and drive," said Dutch with conviction.

"Since when don't you drink on the job?"

"Since tonight," replied Dutch. "I gotta keep my wits about me. So should you."

"It's kind of chilly out here tonight's all," muttered Tommy.

"Hell no!" Dutch said, raising his voice. "That must be the goosebumps running up your neck. Maybe you're just a little bit scared?"

Hearing the sea captain chuckle, Tommy replied, "Scared?" He spit overboard. "Hell, I ain't afraid of nothin'. Hell, if them bastards come within ten yards of this boat, I'm gonna blast the shit out of them. You won't need a net." Tommy gripped the shotgun tight.

The small armada motored slowly to the mouth of the Nassau, where the *Wahoo* then turned for the open ocean. The other trawlers followed in like fashion. Captain Maddox looked at his watch: it was 3:00 a.m.

Suddenly the *Wahoo* began to pick up speed, prompting Maddox to the radio: "We're being attacked! Tell me when to cut my line loose."

The *Anna Marie* and the *Sandpiper* swept in behind the *Wahoo*. Dutch radioed back, "Cut 'er loose!"

Maddox walked out on the landing and made a chopping signal to the mates. A few strong blows with the ax sent the net's hold-down rope racing up over the ship's mast.

Captain Maddox pushed the throttle to full speed, then radioed the other trawlers. "The net's all yours," he said.

The larger net engulfed everything in its path, and the hoist winches began to raise the net to the ocean's surface. The experienced captains walked out of their respective pilots' houses and watched the hoist rope inch to the top of the masts.

"She's comin' up!" yelled the excited mate operating the winch on the *Sandpiper*.

Captain Maddox repeatedly glanced from the tops of the masts to the rising net. The shackle securing the net was now dangerously close to the top of the mast.

"Stop hoisting!" Maddox screamed to the mate. Getting on the radio, he told the *Anna Marie* to discontinue hoisting as well.

Dutch got on the radio. "What'll we do now? We didn't figure on the net being this long."

Tommy Lions, who was taking a sip of beer, began to hear strange clicking sounds. He peered into the bloody encirclement that was the net, not prepared for the sight before him. Torpedo-like heads with large yellowy eyes were watching him. Their blackened teeth chattered incessantly.

"Jesus Christ!" Tommy yelled as the adrenaline began to surge through his body. He raised the shotgun, cocking both hammers.

"Tommy, NO!" screamed Dutch appearing from nowhere, pushing the end of the gun away.

Tommy pulled both triggers at once, missing his target completely, and was slammed against the deckhouse by the recoil.

"You all right, Tommy?" asked Dutch.

Tommy stood up, feeling the pain of his fall.

"Why'd you do that Dutch?"

"No more shooting, Tommy," he ordered. "Ya coulda blowed a three-foot hole in that stainless-steel net and they'd all be loose again."

The two men looked over the side into the murky water. The staring yellow eyes and clicking teeth continued unabated.

"I ain't never seen anything like this in all my years of fishing" said Dutch. "Those damn things are mutations or loaded with nuclear waste," he concluded, climbing back up the ladder to the pilot's house. "Boys, we got ourselves a problem," explained Dutch to the other captains over the radio. "We can't hoist them out of the ocean and we sure as hellfire can't leave them here. We might pollute our own fishing grounds."

"This is Cap'n Maddox. Why don't I hook dat net with muh winch and see if I kin pull 'em on deck?"

With this new plan, Maddox circled behind the net and came alongside of it cautiously.

"When we get close enough..." instructed Maddox, "hook dat net and walk the line 'round to da stern drum winch."

Expertly, Maddox crabbed the stern of his boat towards the net between the two other boats. Meanwhile, his men readied one of the outriggers and ran the winch line through it then sent it out sideways. His mate stood on the stern platform with the hook and line. Holding a hand up for Maddox he directed him towards the net closure on the starboard side. Then at just the right moment, he signaled Maddox to stop, expertly clipping the hook onto the net closure. He signaled Maddox and instantly the boat pulled away from the net just as smoothly as it had approached. Both men ran the heavy line to the stern drum winch and secured it.

Slowly the large net was pulled up by the winch and outrigger and dragged across the side rail. As it came across, bait blood and guts spilled everywhere along the starboard side and ran out through the scuppers. The clicking teeth never stopped but the fierce eyes now showed signs of panic as the men used their heavy fishing boots to crush the skulls of the creatures right through the stainless-steel net.

After several minutes, all movement in the net had stopped.

"Now stay clear of 'em, till we know what we got here," commanded Maddox.

"What we do wit 'em now," radioed Maddox.

"We can't dump them here if they're nuclear," radioed Dutch. "We might contaminate our own fishing grounds. I say we haul them out to the Gulf Stream, just to be safe, and sink them to the bottom, net and all. They're dead now, so they'll just rot away, and any contaminants will be widely scattered and diluted."

"I second that motion," added Captain Maddox over his radio.

Dutch referred to his map. "Let's head to 30 minutes 50 seconds and 79 minutes 50 seconds west."

The three trawlers steered east and began the long haul out to the Gulf Stream arriving at the given coordinates just as the sun began to peek over the horizon. Once there, several old anchors were attached to the steel net. The net was then raised over the deck and dragged over the side like a sack of dirty laundry. The signal was given to cut the net loose. The fishermen watched and then cheered as the bad omen sank into the blue-green waters.

"Cap, do you think we got 'em all?" asked Tommy Lions.

Dutch rubbed his whiskers. "Can't say for sure, but based on what I observed, I think we got most at least. Ya see, their strength is sticking together, just like us, but it looks as though we beat 'em.

CHAPTER TWENTY-ONE

Helen Greiner said "Arthur... it's getting late," . "Do you want to visit Fort Clinch today or not?"

"Yes, dear. We'd better get going before it gets too hot."

The couple stopped at the front entrance of the park to pay their fee.

"Is this a self-guided tour?" asked the professor.

"No, sir," said the park ranger. "We give a narrated tour of the fort every half hour. Just take this road through the *Enchanted Forest* and you'll see it down below."

"The what forest?" asked Helen.

"A nickname we gave this road that leads to the fort. Giant live oaks line both sides of the drive. The limbs are so long, they block out the sunlight."

"That sounds interesting," said Helen.

After the Greiners entered the *Enchanted Forest*, the air temperature began to cool.

Arthur looked at the Spanish moss draped from the limbs. "It's so serene in here," he said.

"Like driving through heaven," Helen said.

The professor exited the tunnel of oaks and parked in front of an impressive stone structure. They got out of the car and walked up to a set of massive wooden doors.

"Welcome to Fort Clinch," said a tour guide. "My name is Langley; I will be your narrator today."

He directed Helen and Arthur Greiner to a small group of waiting tourists. Langley then proceeded with the group tour.

"Ladies and gentlemen, I would like to begin this tour of Fort Clinch by touching upon the ancient past of the area. About 12,000 years ago, Florida and coastal Georgia's landmass extended out to sea about twenty-five additional miles. As far as the eye can see eastward would have been dry land.

"During this period, a tribe of Paleo Indians occupied the coastal islands, including Cumberland Island to the north, as well as Amelia and Talbot Islands to the south. These people attained an average height of seven feet. They were called the Timucuas, meaning *Lord* or *Ruler*. Mummified remains from this era can be seen at The Fountain of Youth in St Augustine, Florida."

"You know, you can learn something new every day," Arthur whispered into his wife's ear.

"Later, the Spanish supplanted the Timucuas," continued Ranger Langley. "In turn, the Spanish were forced out of the area by the English. King George II named this island in honor of his daughter, Amelia, who never visited the island. In 1850, Congress appropriated funds to construct forts along the east coast of the United States to protect the interior of this new nation from marauding pirates and, more importantly, the British Fleet. Fort Clinch was completed in 1848 and staffed with a militia unit from Ohio. We know these facts because a diary was found during a recent excavation. The men of the Ohio militia refused to swim in the ocean and they also would not eat anything taken from the waters here, fearing the devilfish that was said to have lurked out in the ocean along this coast."

Dr. Greiner's mind began to spin like a slot machine. "Mr. Langley," Arthur began, his arm shooting up in schoolboy fashion. "You mentioned that the militia was afraid of a devilfish?"

"Yes, you have a question?"

The professor reached into his pocket for the shark tooth given to him by John McKnight and offered it to the ranger.

"Ah, what we have here," explained the ranger, "is a prehistoric shark tooth." He held it up for all to see. "Teeth like these wash up on the beaches surrounding the fort. It may be a good idea to take a look along the beach after the tour is completed."

"Does the diary contain any references to this sort of tooth being found?"

"None," replied Langley. "Now back to the question of the devilfish recorded in the diary. The creature was described as being flat, with both eyes on the top of a brown body, with the underside being pure white."

"Sounds like they were describing a flounder," added a woman from the audience.

"What an astute observation," said Langley. "You see, the first defenders of this fort were from the state of Ohio. Many of them had never seen the ocean; therefore, these men feared the strange fish that were rumored to have lurked in these waters. They feared the unknown and made up wild tales about the sea. Some of these myths were based on actual occurrences. Of course, that is why these tales are still so intriguing today.

"Does anyone know the name of Robert E. Lee's father?" asked Ranger Langley moving the group along. No reply came from the audience. "General Light Horse Harry Lee is the answer. He was one of Washington's generals during the fight for independence. Light Horse abandoned his family after the revolution and traveled to the Caribbean. He returned to the United States in 1816 and died while visiting Nathaniel Greene. Light Horse Harry Lee's gravesite is located nearby on the south end of Cumberland Island. His son, Robert E. Lee, visited the site in 1862. It is said that he placed a wildflower on the grave and never returned. Later, Robert E. Lee's son, Curtis, served here at Fort Clinch at the end of the Civil War.

"Well, that concludes the narration, ladies and gentlemen," said Langley, clapping his hands together. "Feel free to walk around the fort and be sure to visit our gift shop. Have a pleasant day."

Helen tugged lightly on Arthur's shirt, "I'm gonna browse around the shop."

"Fine," replied the professor. "I'm gonna stretch my legs around the fort."

Professor Greiner went to the north wall of the old fort and climbed the observation tower overlooking the Saint Marys River. His eyes became fixed on three trawlers entering the channel below, making their way for the Intracoastal Waterway that intersected the Saint Marys River. Two of the trawlers turned left making for Fernandina. The trailing boat continued upriver toward the town of Saint Marys.

* * *

When the *Wahoo* approached the North River, a mate yelled up to the captain, "Captain Maddox, why don't we fish this river anymore?"

"Can't get up to the lake anymore," yelled back Maddox. "Dang Navy's run a gate across the river and blocked us from fishin' up in dar."

* * *

Lieutenant Chamberlain reviewed the orders before him. "So, Ensign Strunk, you came into the Navy through the ROTC. Where did you attend college?"

"Temple University in Philadelphia, sir."

"Do you have typing skills?"

"Yes, sir. Average about forty words per minute."

"Good, but your primary duty will be to feed and care for a particular fish species located at this site. All mail addressed to this department will be picked up at the base post office by you. Our address here is Squadron 16, Kings Bay Submarine Base, Attention North River Holding Facility, Kings Bay, Georgia, 31547.

"I'm going to issue you a truck so that you may acquire baitfish and other supplies that will be needed. When you exit the base, a trip ticket must be filled out."

Chamberlain got out of his chair and shook the ensign's hand.

"Would you want me to call you by your first name? It should be pretty informal out here in the boondocks."

"That would be fine, sir."

"Okay, Albert, let me show you your quarters, then we'll tour the facility."

The two men walked to the newly installed concrete holding tank. Albert peered into the gymnasium-sized tank but could see nothing.

"Come on down here and I'll show you where the action is," said Chamberlain, descending the metal stairway to the observation area which was separated from the pool by a sheet of glass. Chamberlain pointed toward the tank. "Albert, can you see our specimen?"

The young man peered into the mass of swaying seaweed and coral rock. "No, sir, can't say that I can see anything in there."

"Not yet Albert! Not yet! Pull up a seat. I want you to observe my next experiment."

Chamberlain then climbed back up the stairway.

Albert could see and hear the splash from above. A multicolored sea trout darted to the bottom, burrowing itself into the thick seagrass. The attack occurred as a lightning strike.

Holy shit, he sliced that trout in half, thought Albert. The scene reminded him of the frenzied bluefish attacks he and his father encountered while fishing off the Jersey coast.

Suddenly a splash came from above; a second fish had been placed in the pool. The trout, sensing danger, remained near the surface. Albert watched a dark form rise to the surface. Mayhem ensued. Red blood began to cloud the pool, obscuring Albert's view.

Chamberlain rushed down the steps. "What'd ya see?"

"I've seen it all, sir," replied the ensign.

Chamberlain turned toward the viewing window. "The filters will clear the tank shortly, he said. "Albert, what happened to the first trout I sent down?"

"Something came out of the coral rock and split it in half."

"Was it eaten?"

"No, sir."

"The attack on that first fish was territorial," said Chamberlain. "I had fed K earlier in the day. The second fish I dropped into the tank was literally pulverized, then eaten. Why did that occur?"

"I don't know, sir."

"The second fish was injected with my blood plasma," said Chamberlain. "It is a well-known fact that sharks aren't particularly fond of human flesh and blood products. This species is different. The second attack wasn't motivated by hunger or territory, but to satisfy some other desire."

"Sir, the strike was just a blur, but I could have sworn that the attacker's jaws were lined with black teeth."

"Great observation. This species of fish lives in an environment that is permeated with tannin."

"Could you clarify, sir?"

"Yes, I'll give you an example: it's as with heavy smokers' hands when they become stained from the tar in the cigarettes. Tannic acid is the result of decaying plant matter that breaks down and settles in the aquifer. This species of fish is indigenous to these areas, hence the tannin-stained black teeth. Any other questions?"

"No, sir, not right at this moment," replied Albert, still distressed by the savage brutality of the attack.

"Well, then, let's go back to the office. I have the feeding schedules for you to go over. Now I'll be away this weekend. A friend of mine is flying in from San Diego this evening, and so you will be in charge. I'll leave my pager number just in case you run into any problems."

* * *

Lieutenant Chamberlain watched as a summer thunderstorm raged above the Jacksonville airport. He walked over to the attendant and inquired about the arrival time of Flight 309.

"E.T.A. is 8:30 p.m.," informed the attendant.

"Will the storm affect the arrival time?" asked Chamberlain.

"The radar report indicates that the storm will be northeast of the area shortly. The sun should be shining again soon."

"Great, that's a relief, thank you."

Chamberlain walked into the gift shop and began to browse through the magazines. He realized he had neglected to get a welcoming gift for his girlfriend. After making a special purchase, Chamberlain waited at the exit as the passengers of Flight 309 began to disembark.

Rebecca spotted Chamberlain first. His tall frame and his dress white uniform made him stand out in the crowd.

"Tom, Tom!" She waved as she ran.

They embraced, crushing the bouquet and the gift box between them, their faces inches apart. He kissed her hard on the lips.

"Oh, I've ruined these beautiful flowers," she said, looking deeply into his eyes.

The couple sat down in the lounge.

"What happened to your hand?" Rebecca asked. "And what else have you got there for me?"

Chamberlain handed her the package wrapped with a green bow.

"Just a little fishing injury," he said, straining a smile.

"Can I open it now?"

"No," he said softly. "Wait until we get to the hotel room."

"Oh, please can I open it now?" she begged. "You know how I love to open your presents."

"Wellll..."

"I'd do anything if you let me open it now."

"Anything?" he asked sheepishly.

"An.y.thing!" Rebecca replied with a wink.

Gently removing the bow and wrapping paper, Rebecca said, "Isn't that lovely, a seashell candle. You know, I don't recall seeing anything quite like this before. Oh, thank you, Tom."

The couple kissed once more and then left the airport and headed for the Holiday Inn.

The following morning, Tom awoke in Rebecca's loving arms. He attempted to get out of bed, but she tightened her loving embrace.

"Where are you going, said the spider to the fly," quipped Rebecca.

"Don't you want to go down for breakfast?"

"Let's call room service later and have breakfast in bed."

* * *

Thirty miles north, Dutch was just finishing breakfast. He noticed that Snoop and the sheriff were whispering and looking in his direction.

In an obnoxiously loud voice, Dutch said, "Don't it seem kinda strange that those boys down the end are settin' so close together?"

The remark brought laughter from the patrons inside the Huddle House diner.

Dutch paid his bill and headed for his truck. The sheriff followed closely.

"Hey... Dutch."

"What ya want, Sheriff?" Dutch said without turning around..

"I'd like to show you something. Got a minute?"

Dutch turned and faced the sheriff. Their bellies resembled cannons facing off in battle.

"For you, Sheriff Lowellin, I got just two minutes."

The sheriff opened the trunk of his cruiser and picked out a net.

"New type of handcuffs, Lowellin?"

Spreading the mangled mess out on the ground, the sheriff asked, "What do you make of it?"

"Looks as if something has chewed the shit out of it."

"Right."

"So?"

"Do you know what sort of fish could do this?" pressed the sheriff.

"No, I can't say as I do," Dutch said, shaking his head.

"You know, I was talking with Snoop in there," said the sheriff. "He says there were some pretty strange communications picked up over the marine band radio last night."

Dutch tapped the net with his foot. "Well, I can guarantee you, the town, and the tourists that there will be no more attacks.

Dutch walked over to the diner's front window and rapped on the glass. He pointed his index finger at Snoop. His face had disapproval written all over it.

* * *

That afternoon, Dutch drove out to Snoop's house and knocked on the door.

"Come on in, Dutch," said Mrs. Forte. "How's your wife?"

"She's doing okay, though her arthritis acts up once in a while. But aside from that, she's doing fine."

"I suppose you're looking for Snoop? Well, you won't find him working around the house, I'll tell you that." She walked over to the bottom of the upstairs steps. "Hey, Snoop," she yelled. "You got a visitor."

"Send him up," Snoop hollered through a closed door. "Unless it's that loser Dutch."

Mrs. Forte smiled. "You are now going to enter the twilight zone."

Dutch ascended the staircase leading to Snoop's workshop.

"Hey, your wife says you're looking for aliens up here," said Dutch as he entered the cluttered room.

"Don't pay attention to her. I suspect she's working for them. Here, take a seat."

Dutch sat down and looked Snoop dead in the eye.

"The Sheriff told me everything."

"What's the matter?" asked Snoop knowingly.

"He's got a big mouth."

"He promised not to say anything."

"What's done is done. But I'm gonna have to ask you to erase those transmissions you picked up the other night."

Snoop's face hardened. "You're asking a lot," he said. "Dutch, I..."

"No. All I'm asking is that you erase a couple of reports. My concern is that some reporter, or worse, some federal agent from the EPA, should get a hold of this story. Don't think for a minute that they're not already in the area keeping track of the acid discharges from the paper mill."

"Well hell, you can smell the damn thing halfway to Daytona."

"You got as much at stake in this as us fishermen."

Snoop thought for a moment, then relented. "Okay, I'll delete it," he said, opening the drawer and removing the ledger. "Here, you'll find the transmissions you want deleted on those pages. Happy?"

Snoop smiled as Dutch paged through the ledger, trying to decipher the entries. Dutch turned the log upside down.

His frustration increasing, Dutch finally said, "Hey, Snoop, what kind of chicken scratch you got written here?"

"It's shorthand. Didn't you ever have a business course in school?"

"The only business I tended to was the fishing business. Now, I'll trust you to scratch those private remarks."

"No problem," replied Snoop.

* * *

Tom and Rebecca sat talking in the airport lounge.

"Well, what do you think of Saint Augustine?"

"Oh, that was a great place to visit," Rebecca said. "I especially like that Spanish Fort. Imagine a fortress-like that held together by seashells."

The airport loudspeaker announced a list of departures.

"Boooo... that's my flight."

The couple stood up. Rebecca placed her hands on his chest. Their eyes met.

"What is it, honey?"

Tears began to well up in Rebecca's eyes. "I want you to come home." Tears began to drip down her cheeks.

"Oh, honey, don't cry."

"Please..."

The couple embraced.

Tom whispered into her ear. "I'm going to submit my retirement papers, will that make you feel better?"

"Yes, it does."

They held each other until the last call for San Diego forced them to part.

Tom continued to wave, as Rebecca's plane rolled down the runway. Chamberlain returned to the North River holding facility.

CHAPTER TWENTY-TWO

Chamberlain opened the office door. Albert was staring out the window that faced the lake.

"Albert, did K escape?" said Chamberlain, with a smile on his face.

"No, sir, but you should see this alligator. He must be fifteen feet long."

Chamberlain walked up to his assistant. Albert pointed to the spiked silhouette floating near the holding facility's discharge pipe.

"That's old Charlie," said Chamberlain. "He hangs around the end of the pipe waiting for fish scraps from K's tank to enter the river. Funny thing, he never ventures any closer. I suspect he's afraid of the newcomer."

"Sir, that alligator is ten times bigger than K!"

"Charlie doesn't know that. All he knows is that a predator shares the lake with him. With regards to size, K will be nearly as large as Charlie by Christmas."

"Sir, I noticed a tag crimped on K's dorsal fin."

"Oh, yes, that's his identification tag. It reads: King Carcharodon, date of the find, and Navy serial number."

"So, K joined the Navy," said Albert.

Chamberlain smiled, "Not voluntarily, but yes, I guess you could say that."

The phone rang. Chamberlain picked up the receiver. His body stiffened slightly. "Good afternoon, Admiral."

"Chamberlain, my office has received inquiries regarding shark attacks in and around the Kings Bay watershed. My office is to conduct an ecological survey that will include all base tributaries extending to the Saint Marys River and beaches fronting Cumberland Island and Fernandina Beach. I have appointed you acting Naval EPA representative for the South East Region."

"Sir, what authority do I have outside the base?"

"Good question," replied Farragut. "We have permission from the Interior Department to do shocking operations in the area. I want you to be present when these surveys occur. You have the authority to keep any species of fish that you deem detrimental to the common good. The USNS Mizar will be your operations platform. She is now steaming south from Norfolk Naval Base. Any questions?" asked the Admiral.

"None at this time, sir."

Chamberlain hung up the phone, then gently rocked back and forth in his chair.

"Albert, do you know who that was? No of course you don't. The man on the other end of the line was Admiral Farragut. He was one of my biology professors at Annapolis. He funds this entire operation and has just appointed me EPA representative for the Southeast Region. Pretty cool, don't you think?"

"Yes, sir," replied Albert. "That appointment will look good in your career jacket. Oh, Sir, before I forget, Lieutenant McPeake, the public relations officer, called on Saturday."

"Did he leave a message?"

"No, sir," replied Albert.

Chamberlain picked up the phone and called the public relations office.

"McPeake here," came the reply.

"This is Lieutenant Chamberlain."

"Oh, yes. My office was contacted by a man from Fernandina Beach requesting information on the blackened shark teeth that keep washing up on North Beach. I told him that the Navy had completed the dredging at Kings Bay."

"What about the shark attacks on North Beach?" he asked.

"I told him that my area of responsibility was Kings Bay, but that someone will contact him who may be able to answer his question."

"This guy sounds like trouble," said Chamberlain. "Give me his number. I'm going to see what he's up to."

After finishing with McPeake, Chamberlain phoned Dr. Greiner.

"Hello, my name is Lieutenant Chamberlain, the EPA representative at Kings Bay Submarine Base. I am returning Dr. Greiner's call."

"Oh, that would be my husband, please hold."

Helen Greiner cupped her hand over the receiver. "Arthur, come in the house. There's a military person on the phone."

Arthur hurried into the house and motioned for the phone and privacy. Helen clutched it against her breast. "Why in heaven are you calling submarine bases? I don't want any trouble."

"Helen, please give me the phone and a little privacy. I'll explain later."

She reluctantly handed him the phone and left the room.

"Yes, this is Dr. Greiner."

"This is Lieutenant Chamberlain over at Kings Bay sub base, how can I help you?"

"I live on the north end of Amelia Island, Florida," began Greiner. "I collect fossilized shark teeth that wash up on our beach. I was wondering if there is a connection between the dredging at Kings Bay and the increase of teeth washing up lately?"

"The base has discontinued dredging operations; moreover, the likelihood of artifacts washing out of Kings Bay, down the Saint Marys River, out around the Fernandina jetty, and ending up on your beach down at Amelia is slight."

"I agree," said the professor. "These relics must be washing in from the ocean."

"Are these finds localized?" asked Chamberlain.

"Yes, I've walked these beaches from one end of the island to the other. The shark teeth wash up exclusively on the north end."

"That is interesting, but have I answered your initial question sufficiently?"

"Yes, you have been very helpful, thanks."

Chamberlain hung up the phone and began to tap his pen on the top of his desk, pondering the conversation with Dr. Greiner.

"You know, there is something not right here."

"Excuse me, sir," asked Albert offhandedly, concentrating on his daily log.

"Oh, don't pay any attention to me, I was just thinking out loud."

Chamberlain dialed up the engineering department and asked for the chief of operations.

"Captain McDowell here, how can I help you?"

"This is Chamberlain. I—"

"Ah, the shark man," interrupted Captain McDowell. "How is your hand healing?"

"It's coming along fine. Say, have you been doing any work on the base submarine spring?"

"Shit, that job's done. We poured enough concrete down that shaft to reach Miami. Why do you ask?"

"Well, I got a report that debris is washing up on Amelia Island. I'm concerned that there may be a connection."

"Well, Mr. Shark Man, if you find any more holes, give me a call and I'll be sure and fill them up. How's your specimen doing?" asked McDowell.

"He's doing fine. Why don't you stop on over and I'll let you pet him?"

"Excellent offer, but is it okay if I send my ex-wife instead?."

* * *

The following morning, Chamberlain awoke to a banging on his bedroom door. "What is it?" he yelled.

"Sir, you got a call from Dr. Clark," Albert said.

"Clark Clark..."

"He's with the survey team."

"Ah, the survey..."

Chamberlain looked at his watch. Already ten. *How could I have slept so late?*

"Tell him I'll be right there."

Rushing into the office with only his pants on, Chamberlain picked up the phone.

"Lieutenant Chamberlain here."

"My name is Dr. James Clark, team leader of the Kings Bay survey project. I was given your name as a contact person."

"Yes, I'm the Navy EPA representative for the Southeast Region."

"Captain, our survey ship is presently ten miles northeast of the Saint Marys River. We have permission to land at the base. What time should we arrive to pick you up?"

Chamberlain looked at his watch again. "Make it twelve hundred hours."

"Will do. See you in a little bit."

"Albert, get my instruments and put them in a workbag. I'm headed to sea."

"Sir, you also have received a call from Rebecca."

"Oh yes, Rebecca. When she calls back, tell her I'll be out to sea and that I'll call her as soon as I get back."

Albert drove the captain to the helipad where he was whisked away. The chopper landed on the *USNS Mizar*. Chamberlain disembarked and was greeted by Dr. Clark and the ship's captain, Tom Reade.

"Why don't we go up to the conference room and review this operation?" suggested Dr. Clark.

The men walked into a room with a large map pinned to a table.

Dr. Clark picked up a pointer. "Gentlemen, this set of U.S.G.S. coordinates contain every feeder creek, tributary pond, and large body of water in the area."

They began to discuss various strategies for conducting the survey. After a few hours, they came to a consensus: All waters within Kings Bay would be shocked and species identified by the EPA coordinator,

Lieutenant Chamberlain. Additionally, indigenous fish stocks of Amelia and Cumberland islands would be netted, examined, cataloged, and released; the *Glomar Explorer* would drag a surveillance camera along the seafloor from the north end of Cumberland Island south to the south end of Amelia Island where it met the Nassau River. The viewing grid would be spaced five feet apart. The operation would continue around the clock. All seafloor features including hot water outflows and depressions in the seafloor would be noted. All such features would be immediately reported to Lieutenant Chamberlain.

After the meeting broke up, Dr. Clark walked up to Chamberlain. "If I may ask, Captain, why is the Navy interested in hot outflows and sinkholes?"

"Dr. Clark, our concern is security! If we locate a submarine spring with an opening in the seafloor and capable of carrying saboteurs through its tunnel system, think of the devastation that would occur. One-fifth of the U.S. nuclear arsenal lies less than a mile from here."

Dr. Clark's eyes opened slightly. "I would say that this hole is cause for concern. I hope we can find it."

Reade excused himself, and then set the *Mizar* on a course that would cover every square foot of the ocean floor within the survey grid.

* * *

The shocking of the lakes and river systems radiating out from the naval base began the following day. Chamberlain collected samples of the diverse sea life that floated on the surface but found no remnants of the suspected horde of predators. The survey team moved its operations to the mouth of Christmas Creek, which had its source on Cumberland Island, Georgia.

Dr. Clark received a transmission from the *Glomar Explorer*. It was Captain Dewey.

"Is the EPA rep still there with you?"

"Yes," replied Clark, handing the radio mike to Chamberlain.

"What can I do for you, Captain?"

"I found a hole in the ocean floor that may be of interest to you."

"What are the coordinates?" inquired Chamberlain calmly.

"The *Mizar* is over top of it right now. We're approximately eight miles due east of Cumberland Island."

"At what depth?" asked Chamberlain.

"From the ocean surface," began Reade, "to the seafloor is twenty fathoms."

"Twenty?"

"But our sonar isn't recording any bottom depth for the submarine spring. We're checking our instrumentation, but there seems to be no technical problems."

"Thank you for the information," said Chamberlain, handing back the radio mike to Dr. Clark. "They found the submarine spring I was looking for."

"Interesting. Is this a local phenomenon?"

"No, there are at least fifteen springs that ring the Florida peninsula; most have not been explored."

"Do you have any scientific text on the subject?" queried Clark with one raised eyebrow.

"Sure, though not very much."

"I'd like to get a look at—"

"Stop by my office, or I can send copies to you. Can you give me a lift back to the ship? I'm interested in that sonar report and may wish to survey the shaft myself."

"You're a certified diver then?"

"Yes," replied Chamberlain. "I've done a lot of reef diving off the coast of Santa

Barbara."

Dr. Clark engaged the engine. "Really? Well, let's check it out."

* * *

Upon arrival, Dr. Clark, Lieutenant Chamberlain, and two other experienced divers suited up.

Clark gave a general warning advising the diving team not to exceed one hundred feet deep. "I don't want anyone to get the bends. Any questions or comments?"

"Doctor, what's known of these submarine springs is that that they often harbor aggressive predators," said Chamberlain. "I suggest we take along a couple of spear guns and a bang stick with us, *semper paratus*."

"Okay," said Clark. "We'll also need a camera; I would like to document this dive."

When all was ready, the divers stepped into the elevator that was fixed to the davit at the stem of the ship. The speed of the shaky descent caused Chamberlain's stomach muscles to knot up, and his injured finger began to throb. Fear began to creep into his psyche, and he clenched the spear gun tightly as the elevator slowed to a stop. The divers checked their equipment then donned their face masks.

One by one, they dropped into the Atlantic Ocean. The upwelling from below the hull of the *Mizar* forced the divers to swim away from the ship before they could make a safe descent. Visibility was fair, enabling the team to spread out, yet remain within view of each other. They formed a loose circle around the upwardly flowing surge and slowly floated down to the source.

As Chamberlain neared the ocean floor, he stopped. The black hole before him was now surrounded by gigantic pieces of rock. *Must be the effect of filling in the other hole near the base—pressure is being released here*, thought Chamberlain.

Dr. Clark swam past and began to take photos of the shaft and the huge boulders. Chamberlain watched as a diver entered the torrent flowing out of the spring. His diving experience allowed him to escape being twisted out of control. Chamberlain drifted to the lip of the spring and laid down looking into the darkness. *What is it that fascinates mankind about such forbidding places?* Chamberlain wondered. He perceived a glitter of light far below. The light grew in intensity, illuminating the walls of the shaft. Chamberlain watched in awe as the mirror-like images passed him. He watched as the small fish rose in the column of water, and then separated in all directions.

Chamberlain's attention returned to the hole. "Jesus Christ!" he gurgled aloud inside his diver's mask, panicking at the sight of dozens of yellow, hungry eyes that were now watching him from inside the shaft.

Chamberlain rolled away from the lip of the spring and swam erratically along the ocean floor. His sudden movements drew the attention of Dr. Clark, who intercepted him. Chamberlain motioned toward the hole and waved Dr. Clark and the other divers to the spring. He opened and closed his hands repeatedly, indicating the presence of predators. The divers checked their weapons, and then slowly moved to the lip of the spring.

As they neared the edge, a dark figure with yellow eyes lunged forward. The concussion of the bang stick landing on the snout of the predator by one of the divers could be felt by Chamberlain. Streams of crimson blood began to rise in the column as the diver with the spear gun released his dart, striking the predator in the head. The diver then pulled in the line fastened to the dart, and the struggling fish was reeled out of the spring and displayed before the diving team. What Chamberlain had thought was a King Carcharodon had turned out to be a king barracuda. He ran his gloved hand along a nasty, tooth-encrusted jaw and touched the now dead yellow eye.

Dr. Clark checked his watch and then motioned for the team to begin their ascent. The group rose slowly to the ocean surface pausing occasionally to prevent nitrogen poisoning. Small schools of baitfish, attracted by the fresh blood of the barracuda, began to pick at the carcass. The team finally reached the surface without further incident and climbed onto the elevator.

After removing their dive masks, the men began to talk excitedly about their singular observation.

"I've never seen any natural structure like that," remarked Dr. Clark.

"Yeah, and did you see that school of 'cuda in there?" asked one of the divers.

"Say, where's your speargun, Cap?"

"I don't know. I must have dropped it during the excitement."

"Did you get off a shot?" the diver asked Chamberlain.

"Yes, but I missed it."

Dr. Clark put his hand over the head of the barracuda and placed his thumb in one eye socket and his index finger into the other socket.

"This is the only way to handle these toothy devils, dead or alive."

Clark hoisted the fish from the floor of the elevator and held it upright.

"This 'cuda is as long as I am tall."

"I've heard that barracudas are an inedible fish."

"Usually, but in these waters, they can be safely eaten," said Chamberlain. "You do run into problems around the Florida Keys. The baitfish there eat poisonous coral and these fish, in turn, are eaten by the barracudas, which are indirectly tainted by the coral's poison?"

"What say we have the mess cook bake him up then?" suggested Dr. Clark. He added, "My only request is that Chamberlain takes the first bite."

The men began to laugh and retell tales of their ocean adventures as the elevator slowly climbed to the deck of the *Mizar*.

CHAPTER TWENTY-THREE

At the tail end of a briefing, Admiral Farragut paged through the survey report, as Chamberlain looked on.

"So, Tom, you found no remnants of King Carcharodon?"

"No, sir."

"That's good news," replied the Admiral. "Captain Jarvis, the base commander, has been under tremendous pressure from squadron ten to resume construction operations at Kings Bay." The admiral tapped his pen on the table, like a drumstick. "What are we going to do with that new submarine spring?"

"Sir, if I may suggest, we could secure the opening with stainless steel bars, allowing enough water to flow through the shaft, without creating undue pressure."

The Admiral smiled. "That's what I like about you, Tom," he said. "You have quick and efficient answers to thorny problems."

"Thank you, sir."

"Let's see how you handle the next assignment. I'm shipping you to Woods Hole to confer with the geologists up there. They will help you determine if there are any submarine springs adjacent to any other Navy shoreline facilities. Any questions?"

"No, sir!"

"Good! Your orders reside with my secretary. Have a nice trip."

"Thank you, sir." Chamberlain looked at his lieutenant's bar. First EPA Director, now this assignment. Surely a raise in rank can't be far behind, he thought.

* * *

Chamberlain, after registering at the motel, walked down to the Woods Hole, Martha's Vineyard ferry slip. The cool air chilled by the

Atlantic Ocean reminded him of the long walks he and Rebecca had taken together on the West Coast.

He returned to the lobby and called his girlfriend. After a few rings, the answering machine came on.

"I'm sorry that no one can come to the phone at this time. If you would leave your name, phone number, and a brief message, we will get back to you as soon as possible."

The machine beeped.

"Rebecca, this is Tom. Sorry I missed your calls. I was out to sea. I love you."

* * *

The following morning, the alarm woke him. Thoughts of Rebecca filled his mind. He grabbed the phone receiver then gently replaced it. No sense calling California; it was still the middle of the night out on the West Coast. He picked up the receiver again and dialed.

"Ensign Shrunk, how may I help you?"

"Albert, this is Chamberlain. Is everything running smoothly down there?"

"Yes, sir," replied Albert.

"Did I get any calls from my girlfriend?"

"No, sir."

"Albert, I'm on temporary duty assigned to Woods Hole on—"

Albert interrupted, "Sir, that's where the Alvin Submersible is berthed."

"I don't recall the name," said Chamberlain.

"Bob Ballard was on board the Alvin when the Titanic was discovered."

"Oh, yes, that's right."

"I'll see if I can get any information or maybe some photos of the Alvin."

"That would be great."

"Thank you, sir."

* * *

Chamberlain arrived at Woods Hole and was escorted to the director's office where he met Dr. William McConnell.

"Glad to meet you. I've been reading over Admiral Farragut's request. I have the most qualified man to help you with the research." The director tapped on the antiquated speaker, then turned the switch on. "Maury, Dr. Matt Maury, please come to the director's office."

Chamberlain began to smile broadly.

"Do you know Maury?" asked McConnell.

"If that's the same Maury that surveyed Kings Bay."

McConnell thought for a second. "Oh yes, we did send him down there," he said. "He's quite a character."

"Yes, sir."

"When we surveyed the Red Snapper submarine spring, Maury wrote up a real snazzy abstract. Let's see how it read: *Fishermen, get your rods ready, a hole has been discovered in the ocean floor filled with Red Snapper fish.*' Maury in his reports tries to introduce the non-scientist to these submarine springs. Oh, here he comes."

Maury walked into the office. His eyebrows began to twitch.

"Lieutenant Chamberlain, it's nice to see you again."

Maury turned his attention to the director.

"Matt, put your projects on hold. I want you to assist Lieutenant Chamberlain. He's researching submarine springs."

"I'm sure we'll be of some assistance," replied Maury.

Chamberlain spent his day poring over U.S. Coastal maps. His evenings were spent thinking about Rebecca. All his attempts to talk to her were met by an answering machine. He returned to Kings Bay and stopped at the Base post office. In his mail slot sat one pink letter. He opened it. The smell of Rebecca's perfume wafted into his senses.

Dear Tom,

I am writing this letter with hope and sadness. Our relationship can either strengthen or wither. It's up to you.

Quit the Navy and come back to me. You can manage my hair salon or find work with one of the universities.

Please don't call or try to contact me. The only response I will accept is you in my arms. I will always cherish the times we had together.

Love, Rebecca

Chamberlain stood speechless. His mind began to fill with thoughts of anger and resentment, sprinkled with sweet memories of Rebecca.

Love, Rebecca? What kind of love is this? Does she think that I can just walk into the Captain's office and say I quit?

He dropped the letter.

I need a drink, he thought.

Chamberlain called the holding facility. "Albert, please come up to the post office and pick up my bags."

* * *

The bartender poured another beer and placed it on a coaster. "That will be one dollar, sir."

Chamberlain pointed to the bills lying on the bar. "Take a dollar for yourself."

"Thank you, sir."

Lieutenant Brock walked into the officers club and noticed Chamberlain sitting at the bar.

"Shark Man! I never seen you here before."

Chamberlain turned his head. "Oh, if it isn't Lieutenant Brock, chief of all security in Kings Bay. Can I do you the honor of buying you a beer?"

"Sure, why not."

Brock sat down and ordered a beer. He then looked at Chamberlain.

Brock slowly shook his head back and forth. "You're a poor excuse for an officer and a gentleman."

"What's the matter with me?" asked Chamberlain.

"Well, for one thing, you're slurring your words a bit. "What's that in your shirt pocket? A *Dear John* letter?"

Chamberlain reared his head back, "What, are you reading my mail?"

"No, it's my job as Security Chief of the World to read people."

"You are absolutely right. I don't drink often and must have had one too many beers. You're right about the *Dear John* letter. Where the hell does she get off making an ultimatum like that?"

Brock leaned back in his chair. "Let's see. She wants you to resign your commission."

Chamberlain looked astonished. "Right, again, how did you know that?"

Brock began to laugh. "I know because it happened to me. The only thing that reminds me of that ugly bus-in-ESS is the monthly alimony."

"Sound like heaven to look forward to."

"Got any kids?" asked Brock.

"Not even married," replied Chamberlain.

Brock took a sip of his beer, then began to laugh. "Hey, man, you don't know how lucky you are. You're a single man."

"Yeah, but Rebecca and I were together for a long time," said Chamberlain.

"Where is she now?" asked Brock.

"Out in San Diego."

"And you, my friend, are sitting on a barstool in Saint Marys, Georgia! Let me see, how does that song go? If you can't be with the one you love, love the one you're with.

"Sorry, Brock, you're not my type."

"I can get you fixed up in a heartbeat," bragged Brock. "I know all the girls that come in here. And half of them owe me favors."

"How so?" asked Chamberlain.

Brock puffed out his chest. "Because I'm the bouncer in this club. If the girls are not nice to me, they don't get in!"

"Hooked up with a party girl by a bouncer calling in a favor..." Chamberlain said.

"The whole world turns on called-in favors, my friend."

"Sounds romantic."

Brock looked at his watch. "Look the band will be coming in a few minutes. This club will fill with girls who like to dance, drink, and at closing time, like to get laid." Brock patted him on the back. "Trust me, you're gonna have a good time tonight."

* * *

The following morning Albert received a call from his boss.

"Albert, can you pick me up at the Huddle House in Saint Marys?" Chamberlain groaned."

"Yes, sir."

"Do you know where that is?

"I'll be over shortly."

Chamberlain was standing outside the restaurant when Albert arrived. He got in the truck and began to rub his forehead.

"Rough night?" the assistant asked.

"Albert, I have a roaring headache. Do you think we have any aspirins back at the lab?"

"I'm sure we do, sir."

"I'll know next time I go to the club. There will be a little bit of beer, and a lot more dancing."

CHAPTER TWENTY-FOUR

The long hot days of summer, with their often-violent thunderstorms, gave way to the threat of hurricanes in the fall months. This season, in turn, was displaced by the nor'easters and the cooling of the Atlantic Ocean that accompanied winter.

The baitfish began to migrate south as the northern ocean waters began to cool; these large schools were followed closely by larger species that fed on them. Schools of speckled trout began to enter the estuaries and sheltered bays to avoid the dropping ocean temperature offshore.

Old Charlie sensed the arrival of the trout moving upstream with the new tide. The ancient alligator slipped out of his hole and took a position along the base security fence and waited for the trout to wiggle through the mesh fence. Large numbers of trout began to move into the lake, and as if by some primal command, the school broke formation and darted through the fence. The dense concentration of fish gave Old Charlie the opportunity to fill his belly.

The alligator would swim along the fence line, crushing then swallowing whole trout. When the action slowed, Charlie returned to his lair beneath the practically submerged tree trunk. He would wait for the next influx of speckled trout.

Lieutenant Chamberlain sat in his chair gazing into the lake. Albert entered the lab with a clipboard in his hand.

Tom turned toward his assistant. "Sir, K's length has remained constant for the last week. K now measures ten feet, two inches."

Chamberlain began to tap his pencil on the tabletop. "I must have fed him too well. Did he eat anything today?"

"No, sir, he just lets the bait swim around the tank. It seems like he is in a daze."

"A daze!"

"Well, it's just a figure of—"

"No no... I agree with you, Albert," said Chamberlain. "K is in a daze. Besides that, he's outgrown the tank. I've decided to release K into the lake."

"Sounds impossible."

"The hard part will be to convince the Base Commander of my plan. That will be a hard nut to crack. Captain Jarvis doesn't even like us being here. Still, I must secure his permission for the release."

Albert watched as Chamberlain picked up the receiver and dialed.

"Yes, my name is Lieutenant Chamberlain, is Captain Jarvis there? Good afternoon, sir. The reason I called was to request your permission to release our specimen into the North River."

Chamberlain held the receiver away from his head to avoid the outpouring of profanities. After things had quieted down, Chamberlain moved the receiver back to his ear.

"Sir, I feel confident that our specimen can be contained within the lake. I intend to fit the shark with a radio transmitter. All his movements will be monitored from this command center."

Jarvis began to tap on the table. "I want you to sign a waiver absolving base command for your decision to release the shark into the North River."

Chamberlain shook his head in disbelief. "Yeah, okay, I'll sign your waiver."

"Good," said Jarvis. "I'll send my secretary down there with the paperwork." Jarvis hung up the phone.

Chamberlain looked at the receiver and shook his head.

"Well, Albert, we did get the permission for the release. Prepare to tag K with a radio probe."

* * *

The following morning Chamberlain stood before the Security Unit provided by the Base Commander.

"Gentlemen, your mission here will be to patrol the perimeter of North River Lake against trespassers. You will also be required to sign a nondisclosure form that forbids you from talking about what you may see or hear while at this facility." Chamberlain motioned to his assistant. "Albert, please pass out the security forms."

After the documents were read and signed, Albert collected them. Chamberlain then took the squad on a short tour of the holding facility ending at the holding tank.

"Gentlemen, what do you see in the tank?"

The squad leader raised his hand. "Sir, that looks like a bull shark."

Chamberlain replied, "You are partly correct." He turned and faced the men. "The bull shark does live in brackish waters, in fact, a 12-footer was once found swimming around St. Louis."

"Also sharks found in the Mississippi, sir."

"That's right. But no, the shark in that tank is King Carcharodon. This species of shark is very tenacious and may attack humans without provocation. I have installed markers that encircle the lake warning security personnel not to go within ten feet of the lake edge."

A young seaman standing in the back smiled, then whispered into his buddy's ear, catching Chamberlain's attention.

"Hey you, yes, you in the back. Front and center!"

The offending Marine broke ranks, then walked briskly forward. Chamberlain looked at him.

"If you have a funny story to tell, please inform the rest of the group."

The man shuffled his feet slightly. "Well, sir, I said to my buddy, you'd think that shark had feet and could run out of the water and chase after us."

Chamberlain stretched his hand out in front of the man, revealing raised scars on his left hand. "What do you think caused these scars?"

"I don't know, sir."

Chamberlain pointed to the tank.

In a loud voice so that all could hear the captain said, "The shark in that tank attacked me when it weighed only twenty pounds. He crushed my thumb bone. I wonder what damage he would inflict on me today."

Chamberlain let the Marine rejoin his ranks, then fielded questions.

The squad leader raised his hand. "Sir, if this shark is so dangerous, why even keep him alive."

"Research is why we have kept him alive. If the Navy can find out why this species is attracted to human blood products, maybe we can produce an antigen that will repel his species, and possibly all sharks."

"Thank you, sir," replied the squad leader.

"Any other questions? None? Then this meeting is adjourned."

* * *

The following morning Chamberlain and his assistant removed the glass retaining barrier.

Prodding K with poles, the shark reluctantly swam into the depths of the lake. Old Charlie felt the unfamiliar vibrations and the taste of an ancient adversary then made a quick exit from his mud hole. He swam across the lake then climbed up the opposite bank to safety. K slowly moved along the lake bottom, investigating every aspect of the lake topography. His senses were aroused by an ancient food source; the neurons in his primitive brain instinctively activated his lethal, snapping jaws. With a thrust of his powerful tail, the shark rushed the gator hole but found only remnants of the creature he sought. Fish parts littered the bottom of Old Charlie's lair, and K remained there, lying in wait, for the creature's return.

The faint aroma of trout next entered K's taste buds and the vibration of the water confirmed the baitfish presence. The shark rose out of the gator hole, propelling himself into the school of surprised fish. K's entire nervous system was now completely energized. He was doing what his species did best: becoming an efficient predator; crushing and swallowing trout.

Lines of blood began to cloud the clear water as fish parts rose to the lake's surface and drifted in the outgoing tide. Old Charlie, taking advantage of the confusion and carnage, crept to the water's edge and picked at the flotsam of fish parts that had become snagged in the saw grass.

Downstream from the lake, the attack also caught the attention of Gary Wright, a longtime resident of Saint Marys and an avid fisherman.

Gary elbowed his partner. "Hey, Loni, what do you see out there in the middle of the channel?"

"I don't see nothin', I forgot my glasses."

Gary removed the shrimp bait from his hook and began to cast his hooks beyond the floating object. He reeled the line in slowly until the sharp hooks lay just beyond the target. Gary pulled back on the rod, snagging the object. He began to reel furiously.

"Hey, Gary, you snagged a big ass trout," Loni said. "I can see it now."

Loni dipped the landing net under the fish and hoisted it out of the water.

"Hey, Gary, this is the biggest speckled trout I ever seen."

Gary reached into the net and grabbed the trout behind the gills and removed the dying fish.

"Damn, Gary, I do believe we got a state record here."

"Yeah, but there's only one problem. Its head's been sheared off."

Loni reached into his pocket and took out a small scale. He hooked the fish through one of its gills. "Holy cow, it weighs over fifteen pounds."

"Loni, I've been fishing all my life, hoping to catch a fish like this. I tell you, it's a damn shame I snagged a dead trophy."

Gary and Loni remained on the North River counting dead and dying sea trout until the outgoing tide slowed.

"How many did you count?" asked Loni.

Gary stared into the water. "This makes me sick to my stomach. I'm gonna have to see someone about this."

* * *

Gary banged on the mayor's door.

"Come in, come in, the door's open."

Mayor Tubbs didn't expect to see a dead fish dripping blood and water onto his new carpet.

"Gary, put him in the wastebasket, he's dripping blood all over my new carpet."

"Will do, Mr. Mayor," replied Gary.

Tubbs pushed himself out of his chair, then walked over to Gary and knelt down before the massive, speckled trout.

"I know what I'd do if he was mine," Tubbs said. "I'd stick him in the oven until crispy, a little lemon and fried rice—man, you got a meal there."

"I reckon, Mayor."

The mayor slowly stood up and faced Gary. "Where'd you get him?"

"He came floating down the North River from inside the Navy Base. We counted fifteen others besides this one. I tell you, it's not right what goes on around here. And they are blaming us <u>for the environmental problems!</u> The first thing they did was to put up a fence, then they blocked access to Kings Bay, now they're killing what fish are left with their stinking experiments!"

"What kind of experiments are you talking about?" asked Tubbs inquisitively.

"Tubbs, I've lived here all my life, and have trapped and fished all of these parts. I know as much as you do about what's going on. All I'm asking you is to stop it."

The mayor cleared his throat. "Well, Gary, maybe you should contact Kings Bay public relations with your complaint. As you know, the base is out of my jurisdiction."

Gary's face flushed with anger. "I came to you for help, not them. They're the cause of all this. You tell your Navy friends that if they don't stop the fish kills, I will, and that's a promise!"

Gary walked out in disgust, dragging the tail of the slimy fish across the mayor's carpet.

The carnage at North River continued unabated. The numerous complaints reported to the mayor's office fell on deaf ears.

CHAPTER TWENTY-FIVE

Lieutenant Chamberlain returned to his office after a morning jog. He plopped down in his chair and chugged some chilled OJ right out of the bottle. The phone rang.

"Lieutenant Chamberlain, this is Matt Maury."

"Well, what have you been up to?"

"Trying to stay warm. It's cold up here in Massachusetts. The reason I called is to invite you on a cruise."

"Where are we going, to the Bahamas?"

"No, not quite, but you're not far off the mark. My department is scheduled to survey the offshore submarine springs east of Miami Beach, down through the Florida straits to the Dry Tortugas."

"Is that a submarine spring?" asked Tom.

"No, the Dry Tortugas is a partially submerged landmass which is the southernmost point of the United States. There's a fort on the island that once held John Wilkes Booth, the man who assassinated President Lincoln."

"Interesting," replied Tom. "Who's dime?"

"The University of California is funding the project."

"Woah! Big time!"

"They received a grant from the National Science Foundation to investigate the submarine springs that ring southeast Florida."

"Investigate them for what?" inquired Chamberlain.

"There's growing concern among geologists and hydrologists that the saline ocean water may be seeping into the submarine springs, traveling through a system of caverns under the landmass, and contaminating the fresh water in the Biscayne Aquifer. Southern Florida has a population ten times that of Saudi Arabia, yet not one desalinization plant."

"How many plants does Saudi Arabia have?" asked Tom.

"Over a thousand steam-driven plants!"

"I guess that a glass of good scotch will be cheaper than a glass of fresh water."

"Yeah if only we could water crops with scotch."

"What kind of submersible are you going to use?"

"The Navy has been good enough to supply the geological survey with a submarine capable of descending to three thousand feet."

"That must be the NR-1," said Tom.

"Yes, I believe you're right."

"How did I get invited?" asked Chamberlain.

"Well, we had an open slot. I suggested your name to the director. He in turn called Admiral Farragut, who gave the okay."

"Well, thank you for thinking of me."

"I felt that you were the most qualified to identify the various marine life we may encounter down there."

"This sounds like an opportunity not to be missed. When do we begin?"

"I'll get back to you with those details," said Maury. "Goodbye."

No sooner had Chamberlain hung up than a gray car drove up to the lab. Albert went out to greet the driver. He returned with a brown manila envelope, which he handed to Chamberlain.

"What do we have here?

Inside were a set of orders and a letter from Admiral Farragut.

"Let's see. Which one do I open first?"

He picked the letter.

Dear Tom:

Your coastal survey report on submarine springs must have piqued the interest of the submarine brass. Your mission is to write a report on the dimensions of the submarine springs. Identifying the presence of these undersea features may be useful against the prying eyes of the Soviet spy satellites or possibly serve as temporary berthing for our submarine fleet.

I will contact you after you return from your mission.

Very respectfully yours,

Admiral J. Farragut

Tom reached into the envelope and brought out his orders, reading them to himself.

"Well, Albert, looks like I'm on the road again!"

"Where are you headed, sir?"

"I report to Naval Station Mayport next Monday at zero eight hundred."

"Are you being transferred, sir?"

"No, just going on a survey. You'll be in charge while I'm gone. If you have any major problems, call Admiral Farragut at the Navy Surgeon General's Office."

The following Monday morning Chamberlain got up bright and early. He drove down to Mayport Naval Base located in Jacksonville, Florida. He stopped at the main gate and was saluted by a white-gloved marine.

"Morning, sir, how can I assist you?"

Chamberlain handed the Marine his orders. After reading the paperwork, he returned it to Chamberlain.

"Sir, the MV *Carolyn Chouest* arrived last night. She's tied off at berth two."

"How do I get there?" asked Chamberlain.

"Go down this road, sir, stay to the right of the airport and there will be signs directing you to the ship."

Chamberlain drove down to berth two, where he stopped next to a group of sailors taking a smoke break.

"Where's the NR-1 submarine?"

A sailor pointed to a thick rope running from the stern of the MV *Chouest*. "Follow that line down and you'll find the NR-1," he said.

He thanked the men, then drove down the wharf, watching the rope as it angled downward until it disappeared behind the wharf piling. He stopped and got out of the truck, then walked over to the edge and looked down. *There she is,* thought Chamberlain.

A security patrol suddenly pulled up next to him.

"Can I help you, sir?" asked the security officer.

"Yes, I'm scheduled to board the *NR-1.*"

"Sir, the long-term parking is located down near the gangway."

Chamberlain looked down the wharf. "Oh yes, I see it," he said.

After parking the truck, he walked down the gangway. His path was blocked by a sailor standing guard.

"Morning, sir, may I see your papers?"

Chamberlain lowered his bags, then removed his orders from his shirt pocket. The sailor checked the manifest list with Chamberlain's orders.

"You're good to go, sir."

The guard then got on the loudspeaker. "Petty Officer Lindstrom, report to the deck."

After a few minutes, a man appeared from below decks. The guard handed him the manifest list. He looked it over, then glanced at Chamberlain's nametag.

"Good morning, Lieutenant Chamberlain. My name is Petty Officer Lindstrom." He reached out and shook the officer's hand. "Welcome aboard the *NR-1.* I will be the liaison officer for this tour. Let me give you a general rundown on our submarine."

Lindstrom pointed to the heavy mooring line tethered to the bow of the sub.

"The maximum speed of this vessel is only three knots; therefore, we must be towed from location to location by an escort ship. The <u>*NR-1*</u> is powered by a nuclear reactor. We can remain submerged indefinitely or until our food stocks run low.

"The *NR-1* can dive to a depth of three thousand feet. We have an array of features, such as viewing ports, exterior lighting, and both TV and still camera capabilities. We also have at our disposal an object recovery claw fitted with various gripping and cutting tools."

"What about weapons capability?"

"There are no weapons aboard this vessel. It is strictly used for research. Are there any other questions?"

"Not at this time Ensign," replied Chamberlain.

When Lindstrom reached the deck, he moved against the bulkhead to allow Chamberlain room to lower himself.

"Told you it was tight down here, sir."

The sound of laughter could be heard corning from a small cubicle directly across from them.

"The crew must be on lunch break, sir."

Lindstrom stuck his head into the galley. The sub commander, Captain George Crawly, a 20+ year veteran of the silent service, sat at the end of a small table crowded in by other crew members.

"Sir, our last guest has just arrived."

"Show him around, I'll speak to him shortly."

Lindstrom withdrew his head, then stood up.

"Where are the scientists from Woods Hole working?" asked Chamberlain.

"You mean Dr. Maury and his assistant Vince?"

"Yes," replied Chamberlain.

"Follow me."

Lindstrom walked past the control station into the viewing room.

"So, this is where you've been hiding," said Chamberlain in a loud voice.

Dr. Maury looked up from the reports on his desk. "Ah, Tom," he said. "We meet again."

Vince turned from the viewing portal. "Welcome aboard, sir," he said and shook Chamberlain's hand. "Isn't she state of the art? There's enough high-tech equipment on board to keep me interested."

"Have you completed your thesis yet?"

"Not yet, sir, but this survey is the perfect medium for a thesis. How many undergraduate students have had the opportunity to examine these submarine springs?"

"None," replied Chamberlain.

Vince smiled broadly, then turned back to the viewing portal, leaving Maury and Chamberlain alone.

"What are you working on, Matt?" asked Chamberlain.

"I'm reviewing the geological reports on the freshwater outflow to the ocean floor," replied Maury. "My first point of reference is designated JOIDES-1, a test well that lies twenty miles east of Fernandina Beach."

"What does the designation JOIDES-1 refer to?"

"Joint Oceanographic Institutions for Deep Earth Sampling, a one-of-a-kind ship that has the capability of well-drilling in waters five miles deep and can extend approximately six miles of pipeline to obtain core samples."

"She sounds like an amazing ship," said Chamberlain.

"It is. The JOIDES-1 test well was bored to a depth of three-thousand feet below the ocean floor and found large quantities of fresh water off the north Florida coast."

Maury then handed Chamberlain an abstract entitled: *Red Snapper Sink.*

"This may interest you as an ichthyologist."

Maury watched Chamberlain as he reviewed the report.

After finishing the report, Chamberlain shook his head. "Wow, if this submarine spring was discovered by fishermen in 1962, why wasn't it recorded on any charts until 1976?"

Dr. Maury stood up abruptly. "It was a fisherman's goldmine," he said. "Only after extracting a hundred-thousand pounds of red snapper from the shaft, depleting the fish population, did they inform the authorities of the location."

"I wonder what species of sea life exist in those brackish zones where the fresh and the saltwater mingles?" said Chamberlain.

"You may find out on this very survey. Here's another interesting site off the coast of Daytona Beach," said Maury unrolling another chart. "There are many collapsed features indicating some are filled in, but one submarine spring at this site has not breached the ocean floor."

"What if the roof were removed and we discovered to our dismay that the entire shaft was filled with air?"

"What a whirlpool that would create," added Maury as he gathered together several of the charts. "Do me a favor," he said to Vince. "Copy these charts and give them to Lieutenant Chamberlain."

Petty Officer Lindstrom entered the cabin.

"Gentlemen, our escort vessel has reported a low-pressure area developing offshore; the captain of the *Chouest* wants to leave port before it gets rough. I recommend that you be seated during undocking operations."

The *Carolyn Chouest* turned in the ship's basin with *NR-1* in tow. The ship then entered the Saint John's River, traveling easterly into the Atlantic Ocean. The skies began to darken over southeast Georgia as clouds of gnats choked the still air before the storm.

PFC Grace, patrolling the North River, began to feel the presence of the pests. The young Marine had failed to apply bug repellent as instructed by his superior. Soon his neck and hands began to itch as he heard the dreaded buzzing of the gnats in his ears; the cloud had now entirely enveloped him. He tried to dissipate the cloud with his unrolled raincoat, but it was a futile effort. Grace retreated along a marked path that led to a wooden walkway. The retreat offered him some relief, but the gnats had done their worst as welts began to appear on his neck and ears.

He scratched his ears and neck until he drew blood but the itching would not stop. He rested his M-16 against the bridge rail, removed his backpack, and then proceeded to climb down the steep hill. He knelt down on the muddy banks of a small feeder stream. Grace reached into his shirt pocket and withdrew a white handkerchief, which he opened then dipped into the stream. He rinsed it and then placed it against his neck. The saltwater stung at first but eventually relieved the incessant itching. He removed the handkerchief then rinsed it in the stream and began to clean his ears and face. *Thank God, he thought. I've finally got some relief.*

K was busy chasing fish when he suddenly disgorged a gullet full of speckled trout. He swam at full tilt across the lake, his pectoral fin cutting through the lake surface like a knife cutting through butter. He arrived at the far end of the lake with mouth agape. K entered the small feeder stream, then began to slide back and forth in the soft mud bottom. His forward motion was slow, but no force on earth could stop him now.

* * *

Just outside the base, near the hoisting operation stood Caradon. For the last few weeks, the pungent metaphysical odor had increased. Curious, he had to know the source. As darkness fell, he slipped his canoe into the water. The scent led him under the bridge where the North River flowed. He paddled slowly, sniffing the air, and listening intently.

Caradon felt a presence around him, large yellow eyes shone in the reflection of the full moon. He could tell by the body movements the alligator measured twelve feet or more. The man of the marshes slowly bent over then picked up a pike with a sharpened point. As the alligator moved closer to the boat, Caradon jabbed at the belly of the alligator, and the gator dove causing ripples in the water. Caradon could feel he was moving away. He watched as a large head followed by a long body crawled onto the bank on the other side of the river. That's old Charlie, he thought. Bet if I slit his belly, I'd find ten or fifteen dog tags.

Caradon returned to the work at hand, finding the source of that pungent smell.

He drifted to the far end of the river where he could hear men yelling orders. Suddenly he heard a shrill scream, a cry of death, he thought.

He pulled the canoe on shore then tracked through the thickets to a place where the land ended. There before him was a great ship with its crane angled over the side like a great arm. He watched as the wire ropes lifting the load slowly tightened, the great ship seemed to list to one side. Suddenly the load popped out of the water, the ship rocked back and forth, with the load swinging freely in the air. The ship's rocking action stopped. The crane operator swung the load over the waiting barge.

The odor of evil swept over Caradon like a wave and knocked him to the ground. He was paralyzed with fear and began quietly chanting to himself. Caradon wanted to investigate further but the federal judge's admonition to him rang loud and clear. There would be jail time if he was to enter the base again. For a man like him, the loss of freedom would be devastating.

Plus, he'd given his word.

Caradon stood his ground and watched as the entire operation wrapped up. As the ship and barge slowly drifted into Kings Bay the smell also dissipated. Caradon took a breath of fresh air and returned to his camp. Caradon had known about the death of Jube Early and the attacks on the Fernandina shrimp fleet. Caradon knew that he must find the source of the odor and looked through his toolbox.

He took out a large old pair of bolt cutters that he laid on the bottom of the canoe. He then inspected a sharpened pole lying next to the cutters. Caradon paddled hard against the incoming tide of the St Marys River. Suddenly he stopped rowing and began to think. Why has this heavy burden been placed upon my head? What is the source of these foul odors? Was evil itself being created behind these fences? If so,

Launching his canoe he paddled back in the direction of the base. Caradon paddled hard against the incoming tide of the St. Marys River, eventually arriving at the padlocked gate to the North River. Reaching down he touched the bolt cutters in his canoe. No, I will not violate the judge's order. He has my word on that, but I will cut the lock and open this gate. Here I will make my stand against the evil inside.

He picked up the bolt cutters using all of his strength to cut the lock off.

Caradon struggled to open the heavy gate, accidentally cutting his hand on the concertina wire wrapped around it, then slowly he pulled the gate open wide. Drops of blood ran from his hand down the paddle and into the water. He picked up the pointed pole, ready to do battle with the evil that lay within. He uttered strange clicking sounds and his heart began to beat against his chest. He could hear his own blood surging in his ears. His forefathers were giving him the strength to fight the evil within. but suddenly he felt chills go up his spine and his muscles became weak, the pike in his hand fell into the water.

Caradon learned too late that he was a sacrifice to the gods from below. The great jaws crushed through the small boat and bit deeply into his flesh. The sweet taste of blood and flesh caused the shark's head to shake back-and-forth, tossing Caradon's tall body around like a rag doll.

The shark crushed his bones and flesh then swallowed him, moments later, spitting out a husk of crushed bone and tendon. Caradon was no more.

* * *

The Marine relief looked at his watch again. *He's over a half-hour late. I better go look for him.* He put on his rain gear, picked up his rifle and radio, and then walked out into the driving rain. He walked down the boardwalk with his head held low. He nearly tripped over the backpack that lay on the edge of the wooden bridge. *What the hell is this?* He then noticed the M-16 leaning against the railing. *No Marine in his right mind would ever leave his rifle unprotected. I better call the duty officer.*

A massive search of the area ensued. Lieutenant Wilson, after hearing the preliminary report, walked over to the lab and banged on the door.

"Open up, this is the duty officer."

Albert opened the door. The duty officer brushed past him.

"I got a man missing. Where's your tracking device, sir?"

"Over here, Lieutenant."

Albert walked over to a darkened screen. He moved the mouse, lighting it up. The entire lake topography lay before him. He turned the volume up; the returning radio signals were intermittent.

"That's funny. The radio signal is very weak..."

The duty officer looked over Albert's shoulder. "Where's he at in the lake?"

Albert looked at the screen thoroughly. He then expanded the image. "I don't see him anywhere." he said.

"Well, he's got to be there," said the duty officer. "Maybe he beached himself?"

"That could be. Our program only covers the lake itself."

The duty officer stood up and began to rub his forehead. "Let's see," he said. "I have a missing man and a missing killer shark."

Wilson's radio began to beep.

"Unit one to the duty officer."

Wilson pulled the radio out of its holder. "Duty officer here."

Albert's face turned from confusion to total disbelief when he heard the reply.

"The gates are wide open, sir."

Wilson radioed base security to have the gates secured, then looked at the screen again. "Either this equipment is defective or that shark is gone! Mister, I order you to remain at this screen and report to me if he shows up. My call number is one zero one."

The duty officer then walked out the door into the driving rain.

* * *

K drifted down the Saint Marys channel past the jetties and into deep water. Something familiar attracted him. He traveled patiently through a boulder field to an opening in the seafloor. A warm flow of brackish water brought him forward but K was blocked by a series of rods. He remained there until the outflow of warm water ebbed. K then turned from the spring opening and headed for the open sea.

For two days, the *Carolyn Chouest* endured rough seas generated by a winter storm that pounded Florida's northeast coastline. The seas became calm as the escort vessel approached Miami Beach. The coordinates 25 degrees, 42.2 North, 79 degrees 58.6 West were fed into the ship's LORAN.

"We got a match," shouted out the ship's communications officer. "Radio the *NR-1* of our position."

The *Carolyn Chouest* slowed, then stopped its forward motion. The call came from the bridge: "Unlocking crew, report to the main deck."

Captain Crawly crept the sub forward, creating slack in the mooring line. He looked into the viewing screen.

The loudspeaker barked: "This is Captain Crawly. Remove the tether pin."

Lindstrom removed the pin, then stood up and waved at the camera.

"Clear the deck and secure the hatch," came the call from the captain.

Lindstrom looked around the deck for anything not tied down. He then climbed down the ladder, closing, and securing the hatch above him. In a loud voice, he called, "Hatch secured."

When all was ready, the dive signal was given. The NR-1 started its slow descent to the ocean floor. At three hundred feet, the natural light from above began to fade into an eerie otherworldliness. Becoming dimmer, the sub's exterior lighting automatically switched on, illuminating the water within fifty feet of the sub.

Captain Crawly guided by the NR-1's sonar and a narrow beam echo sounder, maneuvered the sub down to the edge of the gaping shaft. There, the crew began collecting sonar readings, seismic, and echo sounder data. Conductivity, water temperature, and depth were logged by a sensor mounted on the sail of the sub.

Dr. Maury walked into the control room, then sat down behind Captain Crawly.

"How we doing, Cap?"

The captain pointed to his instrument panel, "The ship's sonar is picking up an anomaly," he said. "Coming from the bottom of the shaft."

Maury stood up and looked over the captain's shoulder. "Could it be a ship?" asked Maury.

"It's definitely metallic. Let's go down for a closer look."

The captain carefully looked at the sub's instrumentation.

"The diameter is fifteen hundred feet across and the depth of the shaft from rim to bottom is one hundred feet," said the captain. "Turbulence seems manageable; I guess we can drop into the hole and nose around a bit without getting into too much trouble."

The NR-1 moved over the center of the shaft and entered into the submarine spring. Chamberlain watched as a large manta ray slipped out of one of the limestone ledges surrounding the rim of the spring.

"Vince, do you see it?"

"Yeah, there he goes. What a specimen. His wingspan must be fourteen feet."

The sub stopped its descent twenty-five feet from the bottom of the shaft. The powerfully ducted thrusters kept the NR-1 on location and stable.

"Look at that!" exclaimed Vince.

"Where?" asked Chamberlain.

"Directly below us."

Chamberlain moved his head farther into the concave portal and looked down. "I would never have expected to find this," laughed Chamberlain. "They must have had one hell of a party."

"Look at them all, the entire basin is filled with empty beer cans," observed Vince pulling his head out of the portal. "You know, it makes sense."

"How's that?" asked Chamberlain.

"Submarine springs are constructed much like common kitchen sinks," explained Vince, "An example would be a thrown cigarette butt in a sink will eventually wash toward the center, and then down the drain. Miami had been dumping their municipal waste directly into the ocean and it has finally settled down here."

"Ah, so that explains all those beer cans out there," said Chamberlain. "But wouldn't it be wonderful if we discovered a Spanish galleon sitting on one of these limestone outcroppings?"

"Yeah, that'd be cool, especially for the topic of my doctoral thesis," replied Vince.

Maury walked briskly into the viewing room, "Do you see the anomaly?"

"Yeah, Doc, there's a bunch of beverage cans down there. Look for yourself!"

Maury poked his head into the viewing portal. His eyebrows began to twitch.

"Doc, doesn't this beverage discovery debunk your theory on infilling?" asked Vince.

"No, not at all," said Maury. "My theory still stands. The cans at the bottom of the shaft are probably new arrivals. This spring is inactive, meaning the saltwater flowing down the shaft will carry any loose material into the tunnels at the bottom of the shaft back toward the landmass. It's probably nature's way of giving back to man the trash he throws into the ocean."

The *NR-1* took photographs of the seafloor with its digital camera before making its ascent to the surface.

"Dr. Maury, have you collected enough material yet?" asked Captain Crawly.

"Oh yes, it will take us several months to collate all this data," answered Maury. He sorted through some printouts. "Our next survey point is twenty-five degrees fifty-one point five minutes north, eighty degrees zero one point nine seconds west."

Captain Crawly studied the topographical map, and then radioed the escort vessel advising them of the next set of coordinates to be studied.

* * *

The *NR-1* entered the Key Biscayne sinkhole, which lies twenty miles east of Key Biscayne, Florida. The sub skirted the northern flank of the hole down to a depth of twelve hundred feet, at which point the submarine spring narrowed significantly and deeper investigation became impossible.

Dr. Maury noted in his preliminary report that there was no evidence of infilling of sand or other debris. He returned to the viewing room and sat down next to Vince.

"My theory still stands. No infilling of the Key Biscayne sinkhole."

Vince shook his head in agreement. *I should think before opening my big mouth,* thought Vince.

Chamberlain excused himself then walked into the control room.

Captain Crawly turned his head. "Well, if it isn't our ichthyologist," he growled. "Have you identified any interesting species yet?"

"Oh yes, we photographed a huge manta ray inside the Miami submarine spring. Expansive schools of baitfish congregate at these seafloor openings. I think they're attracted to the nutrients in the brackish water column. Captain Crawly, what's your opinion of the stability of these structures?"

Crawly turned in his chair and looked into Chamberlain's face. "Why don't you ask the geologist?"

Chamberlain felt the captain's piercing eyes. Watching every word, he said, "Oh, I'll get a final report from them, sir. My orders are to do a feasibility study on berthing our submarines within these structures. I can show you my orders if you like."

Crawly's gaze softened. "No, that won't be necessary."

"Sir, I would like your opinion. Do you think it's practical?"

"The NR-1 is capable of entering any of these shafts," said Crawly. "The attack boats shouldn't have any difficulty either."

"I should expect not, sir."

"The trident ballistic missile carriers are a different story," noted the captain. "They measure over nine hundred feet long and have a depth capacity of only nine hundred feet but as you know numbers can be deceptive. Personally, I think it's a good idea. Turnbuckles could be drilled into the rock walls; cables could be strung and connected to the subs when they arrive safe from satellites and ocean storms. Does that sound like a plan?" asked Captain Crawly.

"Yes, sir," replied Chamberlain. "Your opinion will be incorporated into my report. Thank you for your viewpoint."

* * *

Maury sat in the viewing room going over his coordinates. "Vince, we are headed to the Pourtalès Terrace. How do you think the area got its name?"

"I don't have a clue," said Vince.

"I knew that, but the name Vince..."

"Har har, doc."

"Well, I'll tell you. In 1850, a Cuban fisherman using only a line attached to a heavy weight surveyed an area about the size of Rhode Island."

"Did he get paid for it?"

"No, I don't think so. An idea probably came into his head and he pursued it to completion. Anyway, his name will remain on all NOAA charts forever."

Maury looked up as Chamberlain entered the viewing room. Maury's eyebrows began to twitch.

"Hey Tom, our next survey site should be of interest to you."

"How so?" asked Tom.

"The Gordon submarine spring lies directly under the gulf stream."

Tom scratched his cheek. "That shaft must be a predator's paradise." Chamberlain sat back in his chair. "Matt, do you know where the Gulf Stream originates?"

"In the Gulf of Mexico, I believe."

"You're partially correct," said Chamberlain, tracing his fingers along the wall as if a map. "Follow the map north to the Canadian Rockies. Freshwater flows from the mountains and washes down bits of rock and sediment. These streams converge, forming the Mississippi River, which in turn enters the Gulf of Mexico. A warm flow of water develops, travels around the southern tip of Florida..." he draws Florida with his finger, "and turns north, attracting many species of Pelagic fish including bluefin tuna, marlin, and many species of whale. The warm river of water continues north, dropping sediments on the beaches of North Carolina."

"A weary traveler," mused Vince.

"The next time you go swimming at Cape Hatteras, just remember that the sand below your feet came from the jagged cliffs of Canada. While we're on the subject, who first charted the Gulf Stream?"

Matt smiled, "Oh, I guess Columbus," he said.

"Nope, way after that."

"Nixon!" said Vince.

"Ha! Well, you are actually warmer, but not that recent."

"Who then?"

"It was none other than Ben Franklin!"

"I thought that he was into electricity and the printing press."

"Ben Franklin was also interested in making money. Representatives of English shipping firms complained to Franklin that their cargo was arriving at the port of America in an untimely manner. Ben Franklin spoke to local Philadelphia fishermen about the problem. They suggested that merchant ships tack the edge of the Gulf Stream, thereby reducing wind and tide resistance. The shipping companies took Franklin's advice. Cargo ships began arriving at their port destinations weeks ahead of schedule. Ben Franklin was rewarded handsomely by the British shipping companies."

"That's a very interesting story," said Maury. "Are you sure that you didn't take geology as your major in college?"

"No, I just like to do a lot of reading."

Maury looked at his watch. "We must be near the next survey site," he said. "Come on, Tom, let's go see what Captain Crawly's up to."

"Okay."

Maury got out of his chair, followed by Chamberlain.

* * *

Up on the bridge, Crawly stood over a map in deep ponder.

"Captain, are we there yet?" asked Maury.

The captain straightened up and pointed to his instrument panel. "The water temperature has risen significantly. I'd say we've entered the Gulf Stream."

A call came from the escort vessel. "Twenty-four degrees, sixteen point five north, eighty-one degrees, zero two point one west." Crawly said, "We're on location, gentlemen." Captain Crawly called on the PA system, "Lindstrom on deck. Prepare to remove the tether."

Captain Crawly guided the NR-1 to a depth of a thousand feet below the ocean's surface. Positioning the NR-1 over the Jordan Spring, the captain scrutinized the sub's instrumentation more carefully.

"I'm getting a very powerful upsurge coming out of the hole," declared Crawly. "The current is running at zero point five knots. I'm afraid we won't be able to enter this spring and all observations will have to be conducted from at least fifty feet above the rim."

The portals in the viewing room were all occupied, as the scientists watched a plethora of baitfish moving in and out of the shaft. Predators were there to greet them. Jackfish ran through the schools, swallowing some and crippling others; tiger sharks raced through the wounded, snatching up the hapless fish.

The sonar pings emitted from the NR-1 into the shaft did not go undetected by a very large predator far below. The strange pinging sound intrigued the hunter fish, and the beast began to swim around the shaft. It rose in the column of water to confront the alien stimuli. The ocean outside Chamberlain's portal suddenly became devoid of sea life. *The fish are all gone,* thought Chamberlain. *I wonder if the sub spooked them.* He moved his head deeper into the globe for a better view. Looking down, he noticed a large fish swimming around the perimeter of the shaft.

Chamberlain's heart began to beat faster as the sea creature rose to the top of the shaft then disappeared. Chamberlain rubbed his forehead, then removed his hand. The sight before him caused Chamberlain to panic. He reared back, falling off the stool.

Maury and Vince popped their heads out of the viewing portals and helped Chamberlain off the floor.

Lindstrom, who was in the control room, heard the commotion. He walked into the viewing room. "What's going on in here?" he asked. "You guys fighting again?"

"I was attacked by a huge fish," said Chamberlain. "His eye was as big as a pie plate. You guys saw it, didn't you?"

Maury smiled, then shook his head in disbelief. "Gentlemen, I'm afraid the intense water pressure has affected Tom's vision."

Lindstrom smiled. "I think that I can resolve this question," he said, leaving the viewing room.

The scientists resumed their positions at the viewing portals. Vince was the first to see the shadow emerge from the darkness. Maury saw it next, and then Chamberlain who said, "See, I knew there was something out there."

The predator circled the NR-1 three times and then vanished into the blue-green vastness.

The scientists sat back in their chairs trying to figure out what they had just observed.

Lindstrom re-entered the compartment with a solemn look on his face. "Our cameras confirm that we were attacked." He handed a photo to Chamberlain. "This look familiar?"

"A marlin..."

"Look at the size of him.

"Must be twenty feet long."

"Here Doc, take a look at this."

Lindstrom passed a second photo to Chamberlain. "What's the difference between the first and second photo?"

"Looks like the same fish," Chamberlain said. "Wait a minute! His bill's missing."

"Yup, it broke off when he attacked the sub," said Lindstrom. "It's not uncommon for the NR-1 to be attacked by billfish. When the wooden-hulled vessels of the 18th century were dry-docked for repair, the first thing the shipwrights did was to remove the broken bills embedded in the hull."

"You think the marlin did any damage to the sub?" inquired Vince.

"Not likely," stated the petty officer. "The most damage we could have sustained would be a scratch in the exterior paint."

The NR-1 continued south, hugging the seamless bottom of the Pourtalès Terrace. Captain Crawly noticed that the sonar signals emitted from the sub were not returning with the usual frequency.

"Hey Doc," the captain said, "you aware of this shaft?"

"What's our position?" asked Maury.

The captain read out the coordinates—24 degrees 14' north, 82 degrees 18.2' west—as Maury sifted through his charts.

Finding no references to the question, Maury declared, "This seems to be a new find. Excuse me, I'll be right back."

"Running off to take credit for it right way?" teased the captain.

"Ha! No... I need to double-check some other charts to be sure..." clarified Maury, "then take credit for it," he added before closing the door behind him.

Captain Crawly hovered over the top of the shaft, taking a series of concentric reflections on the side-scan sonar record.

Dr. Maury returned to the control room.

The captain turned his head. "Well, Doc, what'd you find out?"

"Nothing. Absolutely no reference to this location!"

"Well, my instruments tell me that the diameter of the spring is over three thousand feet wide and a depth of nineteen hundred."

Maury's eyebrows twitched. "We could probably lower a skyscraper in here and never see it again. Can we go in there?" asked Maury.

Captain Crawly emitted a skeptical *Hmmm but* studied the NR-I's instrument panel all the same. All systems were functioning normally and there were no indications of loss of buoyancy that had occurred at one of the previous sites, nor was there any evidence of powerful upsurges coming out of the spring.

"I'm not going into this uncharted spring but will do all the recordings above the shaft."

Maury nodded in agreement, then walked into the viewing room.

"Vince, set your eyes on a new discovery," Maury crowed.

The young assistant looked into the vastness below him and said, "This spring, Dr. Maury, will be the subject of my doctoral thesis."

Upon completion of the survey, the NR-1 slowly rose to the surface and was towed to Naval Station Mayport.

* * *

Upon arrival into Mayport, the crew and their guests said their goodbyes. Chamberlain passed his bags up to Lindstrom.

"Sir, an enlisted man is waiting for you," said the petty officer. "He's driving a big Navy limo."

Chamberlain climbed up the ladder into the bright sunlight. His eyes slowly adjusted to the brightness. He walked down the gangway and was greeted by an enlisted man dressed in white.

"Lieutenant Chamberlain, my name is Seaman Copley. I have been instructed to give you this package and drive you to your quarters."

"You mean Kings Bay?" asked Chamberlain.

"No, sir. Georgetown, Washington D.C."

CHAPTER TWENTY-SIX

A day out of Mayport, Chamberlain reported to the Navy Surgeon General's Office, to find himself once again awaiting a face-to-face with Farragut.

"Admiral, you have a Lieutenant Chamberlain to see you."

"Send him in."

The secretary opened the door. Tom made a formal salute, then walked up to the admiral and shook his hand.

"Sit down, Tom. Tell me about your trip."

"Sir, it was fascinating, just fascinating. The springs surveyed would, I think, be an ideal place to conceal our sub fleet. I will have a completed report on your desk within two weeks."

"Good, Tom. The sub brass will be interested in seeing it."

"So it's back to Kings Bay I guess..."

The admiral pursed his lips, then leaned forward. "Tom, your project at Kings Bay has been terminated, at my request, while you were at sea. A Marine patrolling the north river holding facility was reported missing. A search of the area ensued, but the Marine has not been recovered."

Tom rubbed his throbbing thumb. "Sir, did they examine the shark's gullet for human remains?"

"He's gone."

"Yes, missing sir. I'm suggesting if we examine the shark—"

"The fucking shark's gone, Tom."

"Gone? How'd—"

"Someone cut the lock, then opened the gate."

"K couldn't have done that!" Chamberlain began to rub his forehead.

"Who's K?" asked Farragut.

"The letter K was crimped to the shark's dorsal fin. We nicknamed him K."

Farragut leaned back in his chair. "That tag's the only link between the Navy Department and that shark. Tom, I'm directing you to keep a file on this matter. Being the regional naval EPA director will give you influence with researchers and the press. I suggest that you subscribe to coastal newspapers for possible tips. Any questions?" asked Farragut.

"No sir, not at this time."

The admiral extended his hand and shook Tom's hand.

"It's good having you on board," the admiral said. "I'm sure you'll like working here."

Chamberlain saluted, then left the office. He walked down the long hallway rubbing his hand. Disturbing thoughts began to enter his head. What happened to the Marine? Was it a conspiracy? Did the marine go AWOL? Surely K couldn't bite the lock off. Maybe old Charlie killed the Marine. Visions of the hapless victim clasped between the shark's jaws flooded his mind. *Could this tragedy have been averted if I was there?* These unanswerable questions would gnaw at him for the rest of his life.

* * *

The Earth turned on its axis many times and K had grown to the size of a school bus; his blackened teeth were now as big as a man's hand. K was without question, the dominant predator at the apex of the food chain. Weighing 10 tons, his gullet required large meals to satisfy his primal appetite. K began targeting pods of whales as they migrated from their birthing grounds in the warm Gulf Stream, following them as they moved to their feeding grounds off New England. The whale migration to the feeding grounds was now in full swing, with many pods of whales entering the northerly flow of the Gulf Stream. It was this combination of warm water and concealment that provided ideal hunting conditions; K only needed to wait in the shadows of the submarine springs for schools of fish to pass overhead.

Captain Ed Baker, a charter boat operator from Key West, was known for satisfying his customers. He had chanced upon a set of coordinates that proved to be a real fish producer and he milked his find for all it was worth, guarding this secret spot zealously, even to the point of traveling in the opposite direction as he left port. After losing sight of land, he would reset his coordinates to a destination known only to Captain Baker.

The sun glared bright, and the seas lay calm the morning Tom McKenna and his friend Louie Hart boarded Captain Baker's boat. They were businessmen from Detroit, Michigan, and had waited two years for this day of fishing.

McKenna sat in the fighting chair, eyeing the gold fishing reel before him as the boat headed for the open sea.

"Ya like that reel?" asked Captain Baker while checking his equipment.

"Certainly is the largest reel I've ever seen."

"This is a Penn two speeder, loaded with a hundred-and twenty-pound test line."

"What kind of fish may we expect to find out here?"

Captain Baker scratched his chin. "Let's see," he said. "We may hook up with marlin, sailfish, and large sharks. Any one of these critters can pull you overboard, so I suggest you wear a safety harness when fishing."

"I know what that is," said Louie Hart, who was seated in the other fighting chair.

"So, you know about downriggers?" asked the captain.

"Yes, up north, we use them when fishing bottom for lake trout."

The captain laughed. "You won't have to worry about fishing bottom, 'cause there ain't none out where we're heading."

Captain Baker noticed a shadow form on the transom. He looked up at the sun, then started up the steps.

"What's the matter, Cap?" asked McKenna.

The captain stopped and turned. "The current turned us around," he said. "I'll have to drive the boat manually."

"Anything we can do?"

"Naw, you boys relax, we'll be there shortly."

"Hey, pass me a beer," said Louie.

Tom opened the cooler and brought out two bottles. He passed one to his fishing partner then looked at the label on the bottle.

"You'll never forget your first girl." Tom smiled, twisted off the cap, then took a sip. "Ah, life doesn't get better than this."

The captain traveled at high speed until the reading on his LORAN indicated he had reached his destination. The boat was now within a thousand yards of the target area. He slowed the engine to an idle, then joined his guests.

"You boys ready to catch big fish?"

"Yeah, Captain, lead us to them."

Baker reached into the bait cooler and retrieved two fully rigged ballyhoo. McKenna watched as the captain threaded the fishing line through the swivel. He tied a knot then tested his handiwork by pulling on the line.

"That knot will hold a thousand fish," said the captain smiling.

Baker repeated the process on the other rod, then instructed the fishermen to drop the bait hooks into the water. The captain watched as the bait drifted away from the boat.

"That's far enough. Engage your spools."

The drags were checked, then the captain connected the downrigger clips. He lowered the heavy downrigger ball into the ocean, releasing line until the ball reached a depth of one hundred fifty feet.

"Are we ready to catch fish yet?" asked Louie.

"Yes, I believe we are," replied the captain. "My fish finder marked pods of baitfish at one hundred and fifty feet. Your baits will be trolled through the marked fish. Oh, I left a knife within reach, should you be forced to cut your line free."

Louie's stomach filled with butterflies. "Captain, is there a chance that we could be pulled overboard?"

Baker patted him on the shoulder. "Don't worry," he said. "I haven't lost a client yet."

The captain climbed into the pilothouse and began to troll slowly across his secret location.

K felt the vibrations of a propeller far above. This meant weak and struggling fish would be nearby.

The hair on Captain Baker's neck began to rise. A large fish had entered the viewing screen of his fish finder. He looked down at the stationary rods below him.

Suddenly Louie yelled, "I got one!" His rod was now bent in half. Just as quickly, his rod sprang back to its original position.

"Stand by," yelled the captain who now stood behind the men. "He might be mouthing the bait."

The line began to roll off McKenna's reel, slowly at first, then at a fast clip.

McKenna felt the reassuring hand of Captain Baker on his shoulder.

"You gotta big fish on, Tom. Keep the rod tip high and let him run."

After a few minutes, the line coming off the reel began to slow.

"Now's our chance to work him in. Pull back on your rod, then reel quickly."

Tom followed the captain's advice. The battle between fish and man had changed. Tom glanced down at the spool, which was now half full. The line went slack sending the rod tip backward.

"Reel in the line," commanded the captain. "He's running toward the boat."

McKenna turned the reel handle frantically. "He's still on, Cap," he said.

"Keep reeling," said Baker. "Let's see what you got."

"Look, I can see his bill sticking out of the water!" exclaimed McKenna.

"Yeah, I see him," said Louie, "but where's the rest of his body?"

Captain Baker looked over the rail. "Gone," he said.

"Gone!?"

"Yup," Baker said with a click of his tongue. "Something much bigger than him chopped off his body."

Baker pulled the gaff out of its holder and waited for the carcass to move closer to the boat. *It's a damn shame. All that good meat wasted,* thought Captain Baker.

"Cap, get the gaff ready."

Baker slipped the long pole tipped with a sharp curved spike over the back of the carcass and pulled hard, impaling him.

"Hey, Lou, how do you think he would look hanging from the wall in my office?"

Captain Baker spoke up, "I can just picture this blue beauty crashing through your office wall. I know a taxidermist that can make him come alive." He leaned against the rail. "You boys grab the bill. I'll hoist up the other end.

The three men got into position.

"All together now: one, two, three, hoist" the captain grunted.

The bloodied carcass flopped over the rail and onto the deck. He turned the hose on and began to wash the blood from the once-great fish. The captain expected to find tear marks where the flesh would have been torn from the body, but this was not the case. The predator must have come up from behind and swallowed the marlin up to its gills, shearing off the body. *But how could this be?* Baker thought. The marlin's body must have been twelve feet long. The captain shook his head in disbelief.

"Hey, Tom, get me some burlap bags. They're in the galley. We'll cover your trophy, hose him down to keep him cool." After hosing down the fish, the captain stood up and stretched. "You boys want to catch some eatin' fish?"

"Why, sure," said Louie. "That's what we're here for."

"I'm going to a spot that's loaded with dolphin fish. I guarantee that your coolers will be full when we return to the marina."

Early the following morning, Captain Baker left the marina long before the first light of day. He steered the boat in a southwesterly direction, then entered into his LORAN the coordinates 24 degrees 14' north, 82 degrees 18' west. He stood at the wheel thinking, *That damn fish ain't gonna ruin my livelihood.*

He arrived on location at the crack of dawn, then went to work preparing the fishing rig. He opened the cooler and brought out a large dolphin that had been caught the day before. A treble hook was impaled deep into the dolphin's back. A heavy wire was twisted into the eye of the treble hook. The other end was threaded into the eye of a single hook that was pushed into the tail.

Baker began to laugh out loud. He then yelled out loud, "Let's see if you can break free of this one."

He connected the air hose that supplied power to a winch that was bolted to the deck floor.

"I've pulled many a heavier weight from the seafloor than you, my friend," snickered the captain.

After everything was ready, the captain dropped the bait overboard. He disconnected the foot brake and watched as the wire rope rolled off the drum. He then nodded approval.

Down, down the bait went, deep into the recesses of the Pourtalès Terrace. Baker slowed the drum speed; only eight wraps remained. Seven, six, five. Captain Baker became alarmed at the loss of line. He locked the foot brake.

"Shit, ran out of line. Maybe there is no bottom out here."

Satisfied that all was secure, the captain sat back in the deck chair, lit a cigarette, and began to relax.

K sensed the lifeless fish nearby, but made no effort to seize the bloody morsel, preferring to make his own kills. There was, however, a creature in the shaft that was not as particular about what it ate. This predator climbed the wall of the shaft like a spider on a windowpane. Taking advantage of the limestone outcropping, the giant squid wrapped its tentacles around the natural structures to help support its upward climb. Stopping from time to time to rest; the squid made it to the rim of the spring, wedging itself into a crevice. The bait came within eyesight of the slimy beast. Suctioned tentacles shot out of the crevice, wrapping tightly around the bait, then pulled it to the squid's parrot-like teeth.

Baker felt the strain. He engaged the friction hoist, but it slipped.

"Goddamn, what am I hooked into?"

He tightened the hoist friction brake until there was no more adjustment. *Let's see how we do now,* thought the captain. He engaged the friction hoist. The wire rope began to inch up onto the drum. Down below, the baited end of the wire rope, now wedged under coral rock, began to fray, then parted. Sensing the release of pressure, the giant squid thrust itself free of the crevice and sank into the murky darkness with its tentacles wrapped firmly around his catch.

CHAPTER TWENTY-SEVEN

Five hundred miles north of the unexplored submarine spring, a research vessel, the *Challenger Deep*, was busy tracking the movements of tagged northern right whale cows. The director of the survey, Dr. Cynthia Tynan, was sitting at her desk when a teletype printer in the communications room started printing a new message on its iconic yellow paper. When it stopped typing a seaman tore off the message and dropped it on her desk.

"This just came in, ma'am."

She began reading.

Priority

Captain Thomas Chamberlain, USN EPA Director (202) 379-4000

Dr. Cynthia Tynan

Challenger Deep

Dear Cindy:

Since our last meeting, the Navy Department has reviewed your suggestion and has decided to implement it. All surface ship command centers on the East Coast have been notified regarding the vulnerability of the endangered northern right whale to propeller collision. I have contacted the Coast Guard regarding this matter. They have agreed to follow the Navy's guidelines.

Very respectfully yours,

Thomas Chamberlain

PS: The last time we spoke, you were off the coast of Peru. Hope to talk to you again soon.

"Well, Tom, you're going to get your wish."

Cindy picked up the phone and made the call.

"Navy Environmental Protection Agency, Chamberlain here."

"Tom, this is Cindy."

"Wow, that was fast. I just dropped that message off at the comm center about twenty minutes ago."

"Tom, I'd like to thank you personally for all you have done for my organization."

"Just doing my job," replied Chamberlain. "Did you enjoy your cruise to Peru?"

"Oh, yes, that was a remarkably interesting survey. Tom, have you ever heard of the species *megalodon peruvian*?"

Tom thought for a second. "No," he finally said. "I don't believe so."

"No," said Cindy. "You couldn't have known about this species of whale because it's a new discovery. The first of this species documented was found dead on a Peruvian beach in '74 by a marine researcher. He told me that the dead whale didn't conform to identified beaked whales. He removed the skull, put it in a deep freeze, then forgot about it. A few years went by and our organization starts getting reports of unidentified whales washing up dead on the beaches of Peru and caught in fishing nets offshore. The scientific community was skeptical at first but caved in as the evidence began to mount."

"So, you're saying that the first discovery was made in 1974, but wasn't identified as a species until years later."

"Exactly," said Cindy. "It seems that we scientists are extremely cautious when identifying new species."

"That's an interesting story," said Tom.

"There are many creatures in the ocean yet to be discovered."

"What kind of research are you doing now?"

"We are tracking northern right whale cows. The birthing grounds of this endangered species are exceedingly small. It extends from the Saint Marys River, which divides Georgia from Florida down to Daytona Beach."

"Why would the whales be restricted to such a small area to give birth?" asked Tom.

"We don't know; that's the primary reason for this survey."

"I wonder if the offshore submarine springs are attracting the whales?" asked Tom.

"Submarine springs? I've heard of them, but I don't see the connection."

"Let's see... how can I explain this?" said Tom. "Rainwater falls on the landmass of Florida and travels down into the aquifer, forming huge pools of fresh water. The slightly acidic water breaks down the limestone, forming tunnels that travel up to the land surface, but some of these tunnels travel far out to sea."

"That's amazing, Tom, go on."

"A good example is the manatee, or sea cow, which inhabits the coastal waters of eastern and western Florida. During the winter months, the ocean water cools at night, forcing the manatees into submarine springs that regulate their body temperature range from the mid-seventies to the high nineties. When the sun warms the ocean waters, the manatees leave the springs."

Cindy put her hand up to her chin. "So, you're suggesting that there may be a connection between these springs and the birthing grounds of the right whale?"

"Exactly. I did an environmental impact study of the Saint Marys River system when I was stationed at Kings Bay. We did overflights using Landsat imagery and found numerous hot spots on the water surface. I have U.S. Geological Survey abstracts that cover the entire coastal waters of northeastern Florida."

Cindy's interest was piqued. "Tom, could you send me copies?"

"I'll do better than that," said Tom. "Why don't I drop by and give them to you myself?"

Cindy began to roar with laughter. "You better have a pair of high chest waders to walk all the way out here to me."

"Do you have a heliport?" asked Tom.

"Why, yes we do."

"Then it's settled. I will arrive tomorrow around noon with reports in hand."

Cindy was dumbfounded. "Tom, won't you get in trouble?"

"No, no, my job as EPA director is to check on Naval environmental projects."

"Fine, I'll leave the light on. Oh, Tom, thanks again for all you've done. See you soon."

Cindy hung up and rocked back and forth in her chair. *So, Tom is coming all the way down here to see me,* thought Cindy. *He is pursuing me as I pursue the whales.* Cindy looked down at her hands which were cracked and dry. *Maybe some lotion will soften them up. And these nails—I must do something with them.*

CHAPTER TWENTY-EIGHT

Cindy waved as the helicopter set down. Tom emerged and walked up to Cindy giving her a welcoming hug. He felt her warmth melting against him, then went about his duties.

Tom handed Cindy a manila envelope. "Here are the abstracts I promised you."

"Oh, thanks, Tom. Let's go over them in my office."

The two walked through the vessel to her desk.

"Pull up a chair, Tom."

Cindy sat down at her desk and removed the abstracts, reading through them slowly. After finishing, she placed the paperwork on the desk, then looked up.

"What do you think?" asked Tom.

"This stuff is great." Cindy leaned forward. "These reports may complete the puzzle to the life cycle of these endangered whales."

Tom looked into her eyes, making her uncomfortable.

"Is there something on my face?" Cindy asked.

"Where did you get those blue eyes?"

"I don't know, are they really that blue?"

"As blue as the deepest ocean."

Cindy blushed, revealing large dimples on her cheeks. "My parents brought them over from Iceland," she said. "Now, where was I... Oh yes. We know that the northern right whales feed off the northern coastline of the United States. In late fall, the females travel south within the cool waters of the Labrador Current, which guides them to the birthing grounds off Fernandina Beach, Florida. Tom, your information suggests that pregnant females seek out the warm water outflows, then give birth. The birth mother remains nearby in cooler waters, while the newborn calf bathes in water temperatures averaging eighty degrees. Well, what do you think of my theory?" asked Cindy, with excitement in her voice.

"Sounds like you have all the pieces of the puzzle," said Tom. "Does the birthing mother leave her calf unattended when searching for food?"

"The females don't eat while on the birthing grounds but rely on their fat reserves to see them through the winter months."

"You have all your bases covered."

Cindy reached out and shook Tom's hand. "I thank you again for all your help. If this report is published, I assure you that your name will be included in the credits."

"Cindy, I have a question to ask you."

"What is it, Tom?"

"Would you go out to dinner with me?"

"No, that wouldn't be appropriate!"

Tom was taken aback by her cutting reply.

Cindy began to smile, showing her dimples. "Tom, I have a question to ask you."

"What is it?"

"I'd like to take you out to dinner. The menu tonight includes fresh-caught speckled trout."

Tom reached out and put his hands over Cindy's. "I'd love to," replied Tom.

The touching of hands sent a warm glow coursing through Cindy's body.

"Tom, a marine research group from Brunswick, Georgia has been invited by Kings Bay Submarine Base to go on sea trials."

Tom interrupted her. "Are you asking me to intervene on your behalf?"

"No, I'm not implying that." Cindy thought about her answer. "Well, I guess I'm asking for your assistance."

Tom pressed his hands firmly against Cindy's. "Your wish is my command."

Tom and Cindy talked and laughed about their lives. Two separate lives began to turn on each other. Left over right, right over left, pulling their relationship tight, like a square knot.

Chamberlain returned to Washington that evening. The following afternoon, Cindy received a call from Tom. "We've been invited to a one-day shakedown inspection of the USS *Pennsylvania*."

"What kind of ship is that?" asked Cindy.

"It's not a ship, but a submarine, capable of blowing up all of the Soviet Union."

"That sounds scary and not so environmentally friendly," said Cindy. "Do you think the crew will allow me to listen in on their sonar transmissions?"

"I don't think that would be a problem. I have arranged for you to critique the crew on your propeller safety program."

"Good, when do we leave?" asked Cindy excitedly.

"Let's see. Today is Tuesday. The submarine departs Thursday from Kings Bay at thirteen hundred hours. I'll pick you up at zero nine hundred hours that morning. If there is any change in plans, I'll call you."

* * *

Cindy was up bright and early on the day of their departure. After showering, she dried herself off, then picked up a hairdryer in one hand and a brush in the other. She began to draw the brush through her blond hair, styling it to her liking. A light blush of rouge struck her cheeks. Next was the eyeliner. *Wait a minute!* she thought, *I'm going on board a submarine loaded with young, horny men.* She looked into the mirror one more time. *That's good enough. I only want to please one man.*

Cindy walked over to the closet and removed a beige one-piece jumpsuit and draped it in front of her. *I'll wear this today; professional looking and non-revealing.*

Cindy finished dressing then packed her day bag.

She stood inside the bridge conversing with Captain Tooms when there was a radio call requesting permission to land. Tooms picked up the microphone and pressed the button.

"Permission granted," said the captain. He then got on the loudspeaker: "All personnel, stay clear of the heliport! I repeat, all personnel stay clear of the heliport." The captain turned to Cindy. "Madame, your taxi has arrived."

"Cap, you sound as if I'm being driven around New York City."

"Is that the same officer that showed up here last week?"

"Yes, his name is Tom. Lieutenant Thomas Chamberlain."

"I'd like to meet him."

"Come on down. I'll introduce you." "Be careful Doc," Captain Tooms said, putting his weathered hand on Cindy's sleeve. "You know you can't trust a man."

Cindy looked at him. "Where on earth did you hear that one?"

"I'm not sure," replied Tooms, "but I know that I didn't hear it from a man."

Cindy began to laugh, causing the captain to smile. "Come on, Captain, let's go down and greet Tom."

The Navy chopper landed. An officer dressed in a white uniform disembarked.

"Tom, Tom." Cindy waved with excitement.

Chamberlain waved back, then walked up to Cindy and picked up her bag. She turned to Captain Tooms and winked. "See, I told you that he was an officer and a gentleman. Captain Tooms, I would like to introduce you to Captain Thomas Chamberlain."

The men thrust out their arms and gave each other a strong handshake.

Chamberlain then escorted Cindy into the helicopter.

"Would you like the window seat?" asked Tom.

"Yes," replied Cindy. "Maybe I'll be able to spot some spouting whales."

Cindy became so mesmerized watching the ocean surface that she completely forgot about the man holding her hand.

The chopper slowed, then descended on the helipad. Lieutenant Chamberlain was greeted by a duty driver assigned to Tom and his guest.

"Where to, sir?" asked the driver.

"Ah, yes, our itinerary. First, to the security office. Cindy, are you hungry?"

"Yes, my stomach is starting to growl."

Tom tapped the driver on the shoulder. "The second stop will be the officer's club."

Cindy obtained a civilian security pass, then the couple went for a light lunch. After eating, Cindy glanced down at the photo ID pinned to her jumpsuit.

"Tom," she said, "do you think that this photo looks like me?"

Tom leaned across the table. He scrutinized the ID, then turned his attention to Cindy's face.

"This photo doesn't do you justice. If you want, I will demand that Pass and ID retake your photo."

Cindy smiled, showing her dimples. "No, that won't be necessary, Tom." She then brushed her leg against his.

She's a playful little thing, thought Tom.

Chamberlain looked at his watch. "Cindy, we have some time before departure," he said. "I'd like to show you something that may interest you."

She rubbed his leg again, causing him to blush. "What can you show me that would be of interest to me?" asked Cindy coyly.

"Besides that, I would like to show you some whale bones that are fifty million years old."

Cindy's scientific mind took over. "Did you say fifty million?"

"Yes. They are on display at the base library."

"Where'd they come from?"

"Right here on base. They were dredged up from a depth of eighty feet."

"Those fossils may show a timeline for the birthing of whales! Are they northern right whale bones?" asked Cindy.

"I'm not sure," replied Tom.

Cindy got up and grabbed Tom's hand. "Come on," she said. "Show me your fossil collection."

The pair walked through a tree-lined path that had a reflecting pool at its center. They sat down momentarily on a bench facing the pool.

"This is a beautiful place. It seems so far from the workaday world."

Tom put his arm around Cindy's shoulder, bringing her closer to him. The pair sat there for long moments enjoying the solitude. They got up and walked down the path to the library entrance. Tom opened the door for Cindy. Once she was inside, she was instantly attracted to the glass case filled with ancient artifacts.

"Tom, look at all the whale bones."

"Everything in this case was dredged up when this base was being built. The arrowheads, pipe stems, and all the pieces of bone and teeth were collected by our archaeological team and students from the University of Florida."

The librarian happened to be walking by. Chamberlain asked her permission to examine the artifacts.

She thought for a moment. "Oh, I guess it would be alright." She unlocked the door, then stepped back.

Tom opened the doors, then reached into the case and picked up a hand-sized shark's tooth, then placed it in Cindy's hand.

"Wow, heavy," she said. "It must weigh two pounds. How old do you estimate it to be?"

"Oh, about ten years old."

Cindy smiled. "Did you say ten million?"

"Nope! I said ten years. This tooth was extracted from a King Carcharodon female that was entombed in a limestone mound."

"Tom, I've never heard of such a species."

"You and the rest of the world have not heard about the discovery because it can't be revealed at this time," Tom said. "Do you remember the story you told me about the scientist that discovered a new species of whale? He threw the skull in the freezer. For years his find remained a secret from the world. I'm in worse shape. I would lose my commission if I told this story."

Cindy looked him in the eyes. "Why would you reveal this to me?"

"I had to tell someone—someone I could trust."

Chamberlain returned the tooth, then thanked the librarian. The couple returned to the waiting duty driver.

Upon arrival at wharf one, Chamberlain and his guest climbed up to the top of the gangway where they were stopped by a rifle-toting sentry. Cindy became aware of the fact she was now boarding a sophisticated war machine.

"Sir, I'll need to review your identification and that of your civilian guest," demanded the sentry.

Lieutenant Chamberlain passed the appropriate documents over to the security officer who, in turn, passed them to the deck officer. The deck officer checked the documentation against the ship's manifest.

"Welcome aboard, Lieutenant Chamberlain and Doctor Tynan," the sentry said, after satisfying final clearance. "I'll bring Seaman Collins topside to act as your escort."

After a few minutes, a thin man popped out of a hatch and the deck officer waved him over. "Collins, you're assigned as tour guide for our guests."

The seaman saluted and said, "I'll first show you to your berths and then we can review the rest of the sub."

They descended a spiral stairway and proceeded through a series of open hatches. The last compartment had large tubes on both sides of the passage; the ominous-looking tubes extended up through the bulkhead.

Collins suddenly stopped and read the number printed on the tube. "Ah, here we are, number eleven. These are your sleeping quarters."

Tom pushed the curtain aside that was fastened between the tubes. Inside the cramped enclosure was a desk and chair alongside a simple cot.

"Looks pretty claustrophobic in there, seaman," Tom said, "Where're Doctor Tynan's quarters?"

"The communications officer has given up his berth for the doctor," stated Collins.

"Well, I'll be. The civilian gets first-class accommodations, and the officer gets pigeonholed."

Further inspecting the compartment, Cindy's curiosity about the ominous tubes overcame her. "Are these part of the nuclear reactor?"

"No, ma'am," said Collins, slapping one of the cylinders with his hand. "These here are the D-5 missile silos. Each silo contains five warheads."

"How fast do they travel?" she asked.

"Well, let's put it this way," the escort replied, "if we launched from Miami Beach, the missile would impact New York in about a minute."

Cindy looked at Tom. "I hope you can sleep soundly tonight."

"Oh, don't worry about me, I'll sleep like a baby."

Seaman Collins led Cindy to her room and then gave the visitors a guided tour of the sub. They climbed up on deck and walked to the rear of the USS Pennsylvania.

Collins pointed to the glistening propeller; the fins extending from the hub of the screw were spinning in artistic rhythm. "How much does one of those babies weigh?" asked Chamberlain.

"They're equal to about ninety full-sized cars," said Collins.

"Seems like those props have the potential to be real whale killers," added Cindy with concern.

"I don't know, ma'am. You might want to speak to the sonar man about that."

"We intend to do just that," replied Chamberlain.

A call came from the conning tower informing everyone on board that the USS Pennsylvania would be leaving the pier side in ten minutes. The crew began casting off the mooring lines and prepared to remove the gangway.

"Do we have to go inside?"

"No, ma'am, we won't submerge until we clear Saint Marys channel," said Collins.

The submarine, assisted by two orange tugboats, left wharf one then moved slowly out of Kings Bay into the Saint Marys River. The Pennsylvania was greeted by hundreds of flag-waving Boy Scouts, who lined the walls of Fort Clinch. The crew stood on the deck at parade rest. When the signal was given, the crew saluted the scouts, sending them into a frenzy of flag-waving.

The *Pennsylvania* passed between the jetties, entering the Atlantic Ocean. When the ocean depth reached 300 feet, the captain ordered all personnel to get below deck and the hatches were secured. The *Pennsylvania* slipped beneath the ocean's waves and the crew began the shakedown exercise.

Seaman Collins introduced the guests to Captain Glasgow.

"Glad to have you aboard," the captain said. "So, you're the Navy EPA director! Are you looking for leaks on my boat?"

Chamberlain smiled. "No, not at all. The Navy has embarked on a program to reduce propeller-whale collisions at sea."

"I've heard about that program," said the sub captain.

"Sir, Dr. Tynan is the director of the Save the Whales Foundation. I was wondering if she could critique the crew on the Navy's new program."

"That's an excellent idea," replied Glasgow. "Anything else?"

"Yes," replied Chamberlain. "I was wondering if Dr. Tynan could be permitted in the sonar room as an observer. Her interest is the calling of the whales."

"That sounds like a valid reason, but let me check with the communications officer first."

"I don't want to be a bother, if—" Cindy said.

"No no, ma'am," said the captain. "It is just sometimes the teams run drills and I don't want them in your way."

Chamberlain shook the captain's hand and thanked him. Cindy and Tom followed Seaman Collins through the tube-like passageway.

Cindy squeezed Tom's hand, then whispered in his ear, "You're a real salesman."

Collins walked up to a man who was standing in front of an open hatch. He smiled, then said, "Dr. Cynthia Tynan, the captain has given you permission to enter the communications room." He stepped aside, allowing her to pass, then closed the hatch.

She was given a notepad and a set of headphones.

"Write down the times of anything that may interest you," said the communications officer.

Cindy spent the afternoon listening to the mysterious clicks, pulses, and groans recorded by the sub's sophisticated side-scan sonar system.

At eighteen hundred hours, the sub rolled violently from port to starboard. Captain Glasgow called from the bridge asking for a clarification report. The sonar officer looked at his chart coordinates.

"Sir, we just passed over the J-1 test borehole."

Suddenly, Cindy began to hear the sounds of whales calling. The sounds faded as the submarine moved away from the area. Cindy removed her headset. She then waved at the sonar man, who in turn removed his headset.

"May I help you, ma'am?"

"Yes. I picked up the calling of whales shortly after the submarine rocked."

"Ma'am, we frequently pick up on whales at the J-1 site."

"What is that?" asked Cindy.

"The oil companies drilled a test bore deep into the ocean floor. The only thing that came up was huge amounts of freshwater. When the sub passed over the site, we lost buoyancy due to the freshwater intrusion."

"That's a very interesting phenomenon. I'll have to look that up on my charts."

Cindy put her headset back on, absorbing sounds from the ocean until she could not keep her eyes open.

CHAPTER TWENTY-NINE

D r. Tynan was awakened by a soft knock on her compartment door.

"Who is it?"

"The fellow who sleeps with ballistic missiles, that's who."

"Oh, the tenant residing in silo number eleven."

"Yes, I just wanted to let you know they are serving breakfast," said Tom. "Would you like to eat something now?" he asked.

"Ah, yeah. Give me a few minutes to freshen up."

"I will wait at the end of the passage for you."

Moments later, Cindy emerged from her berth, but her mind was not on breakfast.

"Where's the J-1 borehole?" she asked pointedly.

"It lies about twenty-six miles east of Fernandina Beach. I believe they drilled through the ocean floor to a depth of forty-five hundred feet below the seabed. They found huge amounts of warm freshwater that became of particular interest to the geologists, but not to the oilmen. Why do you ask?"

"We heard the whale calls in the vicinity of the JOIDES. I wonder if there is a connection between the warm water outflows and the whale's birthing process."

"Yeah, could be," said Tom. "Certainly sounds like you could be on to something."

"Coming through, coming through, make way for hungry sailors!" shouted a man leading a group of sailors through a passage.

Chamberlain brushed his body up against Cindy to allow the men to pass behind him.

She looked up at him. "Why, Tom, you've put me in a compromising position."

"It couldn't be helped."

"Oh, the seaman was at fault?"

Tom didn't know what to say.

Cindy and Tom, their hands occasionally bumping the other's, waited in the breakfast line.

"Tom, I greatly appreciate everything you have done for me."

"If I did anything, it's entirely my pleasure," said Tom. "Say, would you like to finish this tour with a visit to Saint Augustine, which is the oldest city in America? They have a fort down there that was built entirely of seashells."

"I'd love to go."

"We can have dinner in Jacksonville." Tom paused momentarily. "I took the liberty and made dinner reservations at the Holiday Inn."

Cindy looked at Tom with a glow on her face. "Are we going to be doing um research?"

Tom smiled. "Yes, research. Heavy research."

* * *

The following day, Cindy waved goodbye as the chopper lifted off the Challenger Deep.

She climbed up to the bridge.

"How was your trip?" asked Captain Tooms.

"The submarine trip was very informative. We heard whales calling from an area called the *JOIDES-1*. See if you can find it on your charts."

"Where do you want me to start?" asked the captain.

"Let's see. Start at Fernandina Beach, then go east about twenty-six miles."

They walked to the Captain's quarters.

Tooms paged through his NOOA charts finding nothing. He opened up a large book entitled *U.S. Geological Survey Abstracts*.

"Let's see—southeast. Here we are. Blake's Plateau Abstract. Your information was correct, Doc. The JOIDES is twenty-six miles east of Fernandina. We're presently southeast of that location. It will take us about two hours to get there."

"Captain Tooms, I want you to transverse the JOIDES location until you pick up whale marking on your sonar. I'm going to get some sleep. Don't hesitate to call me if something develops."

The skipper got on the loudspeaker: "Weigh anchors, I repeat, weigh anchors!"

The research vessel traveled to the JOIDES site and began to crisscross the area.

Late that night, Captain Tooms called Cindy. "Doc, sonar has picked up some large blips on the screen. They're rising to the surface."

Have the crew ready the workboat. I'll be there in a few minutes."

She dressed quickly, then draped a camera around her neck. Picking up her tagging equipment, Cindy opened the door and was blinded by the ship's floodlights, which were trained on the ocean surface.

A crewman ran up to her. "Doc, look out there."

Cindy's vision slowly returned. She stared in amazement at the large numbers of black forms drifting slowly before her. The crewman pointed out to a pair of whales swimming closer together.

"The small one must be her calf."

Dr. Tynan shook her head in amazement. "This is an incredibly encouraging sign to researchers. No northern right whale births have been recorded in recent years, until now. That female is the one we want to tag."

Cindy walked briskly to the waiting workboat, climbed on board, then down into the roiling waves. The workboat made its way into the pod of right whales.

Cindy prepared a satellite probe on the end of an extendable pole.

"Do you want me to do the sticking?" asked one of the crewmen.

"Mister," said Cindy sternly, "the term is tagging!"

"My apologies, ma'am."

"We are not here to stick the whales, but to preserve the species."

"Yes, ma'am. Do you want me to tag that nursing whale?"

"Yes, please insert the tag just behind her head."

Cindy handed him the pole. He then walked up to the bow, steadying himself. The pilot motored slowly into the pod.

"Here she comes. The calf is with her."

Cindy began taking snapshots as the sailor thrust the probe deep into the whale's blubber. Immediately, the birthing mother sounded, followed by her calf and the other members of the pod.

"Our work is finished for the night," said Cindy.

The workboat returned to the *Challenger Deep* and was hoisted on board.

Cindy hurried up to the bridge. Captain Tooms opened the door for her.

"What ya do, Doc, scare all the whales away?"

"Yes, but we managed to tag the birth mother."

"What's the camera for?"

"I have a catalog of all identified northern right whales. I'm hoping that the birthing mother will be amongst them, or that I can add her to my list."

"How can you tell the difference?" asked Captain Tooms. "They all look alike to me."

"We know them by the calcite formations that grow on maturing whales, giving a distinctive look to each whale."

"That's very interesting, Doc. Say, what are you going to call the little one?"

"Little one? Oh, you mean the calf."

"Yes, you can't let him or her swim the oceans with no name."

"You're right," Cindy said, putting her hand to her chin. "The calf must have a name. I got it. We'll call him Joides."

The captain walked over to the sonar screen. "Doc, do you want to see your baby Joides?"

Cindy smiled, then walked over to the screen. "I can see the probe blinking, but I can't identify the female."

The captain put his index finger on the screen. "Always look for the oversized blip. The female and calf are always close to each other, forming a larger blip."

Cindy watched for long moments. A fondness for Joides filled Cindy's being.

The pod began to move off the screen.

"Doc, do you want me to follow them?"

"Yes, until further notice. Keep a safe distance. I don't want to disturb them."

"The Friends of Whales sure must have deep pockets."

Cindy turned and looked directly into the skipper's eyes. "Captain Tooms, my organization is funded entirely by private donations. Have you ever seen any of the documentaries about captured orcas?

"Why, yes, I have seen one or two," replied the captain.

"The theme parks had us believe that the orcas depicted in the documentaries were released unharmed into the ocean. The truth is they sold them all to an aquarium in Mexico where they lived in a cesspool. Their bodies were loaded with sea lice and scabs. Had it not been for our organization's concern, they would all be dead."

"What happened to them?" asked the captain.

Cindy smiled. "Monies were donated to build a twenty-million-dollar aquarium complete with a waterproof TV screen and a full-time staff, who nursed them back to health."

CHAPTER THIRTY

K was hungry. The huge schools of migrating fish that passed over the shaft had thinned. K's senses detected a strong steady beat coming from above. The largest creature to have ever lived on the Earth was now undulating through the ocean's surface, its ten-ton heart sending a pulsating signal to K's brain. He began to snap his jaws uncontrollably.

The predator rose to the surface to attack his prey, unconcerned that the creature above him was six times his size or that it weighed as much as ninety times his weight. Nevertheless, K's genetic make-up ordained him to be at the pinnacle of the ocean's food chain. K's extended jaws wrapped around the creature's tail as black, serrated teeth seven inches long pierced the tough skin, slicing their way through layers of blubber, his jaws frantically seeking to sever the creature's spinal cord, thus inflicting instant paralysis.

The creature, a blue whale, felt the attack and thrust its mighty tail upward, throwing K into the air. He landed with a huge splash.

K, stunned at first, slowly regained his bearing and began to seek out his quarry. The blue whale had sounded and was now long gone. K snapped his jaws in protest, for this predator was not accustomed to losing a meal.

* * *

K had not made a kill in days and he was hungry. High above him on the surface of the Atlantic Ocean sat the *Harbor Branch II*, a marine research ship. Jake Rhodes and his assistant, Manuel, were seated at the captain's table reviewing the instructions for the impending dive.

Jake picked up the abstract that lay on the table, "Let's see what we have here. As per request from Captain Mike Sherman's office to the US House of Representatives, NOAA has approved a survey of opportunity of the NR-1 Hole located at eight-two, eighteen west, twenty-four point fourteen North."

Jake dropped the paper on the table and looked at Manuel.

"I guess that's us," he said.

The co-pilot nodded in agreement. But his mind was troubled. *This is the deepest dive we have ever attempted,* he thought to himself.

The loss of the original *Johnson Sea Link I* still troubled him, and a lump began to form in his throat.

Jake slammed his hands on the desk, "Well, let's get going, time's a-wastin'."

The crane operator waved and hollered to Jake and Manuel, "You boys be safe down there."

The divers waved then entered the submersible.

The ship's captain gave the signal to hoist the load. The sub swung away from the ship, then gently lowered onto the ocean surface. The captain signaled a mate who pulled the pin from the shackle releasing the sub into the sea.

The light above began to fade as the sub descended underwater. The sub's lighting system turned on illuminating the ocean for some distance into the darkness.

As the sub entered the *NR-1 Hole*, Jake turned on the recording machine.

Speaking into the microphone he said, "*Johnson Sea Link II* at nineteen hundred sixty-eight feet below surface, stop."

The machine recorded as the submersible continued its descent. After what seemed like hours in the fishbowl of light that surrounded the vessel, the sub's lighting showed that they were approaching the bottom of the hole.

"Slowing descent, stop."

There was a muffled sound of the vessel's propellers reversing as the vessel made a soft landing in sand.

"On the bottom of Submarine Spring NR-1, stop," he spoke into the microphone.

"Bottom stable, sandy, stop. Observe large cable running down the west wall, stop. The cable is estimated to be two feet in circumference, stop."

Jake thought for a second. "I suggest that the cable may have been a connection between Key West, Florida, and Cuba, stop," he recited.

The submersible lifted off the bottom and began to slowly take in its surroundings. As the vessel rotated, Jake saw what appeared to be a large lower jawbone.

"Observe mandible of large sea creature, unknown, stop."

"Attempting to take a sample, stop."

Jake manipulated the arm of the *Johnson Sea Link II* and broke off some bone material that was instantly sucked up by a vacuum hose attached to the arm.

The sub continued exploring, when suddenly everything went black and the sub shook violently from side-to-side, then the phenomenon ended as quickly as it had begun.

"What the hell was that?" Jake asked.

After regaining their composure, the crew checked gauges and safety controls.

"Everything within normal range," said Jake.

Manuel felt something dripping on his head. "Jake, we got a leak."

"Can you locate it?"

Manuel slid his hand across the smooth interior of the plexiglass shield. "I think I found it. I think something sharp has penetrated the bubble."

"How can that be?" asked Jake. "This shield is over three-inches thick! Let's get out of here."

Slowly the vessel began to rise and after what seemed like an eternity, the vessel and crew returned to the safety of the mother ship without further incident.

* * *

K entered the northerly flow of ocean water referred to as the Gulf Stream. The current running three knots faster than surrounding waters propelled the darkened form forward. Day and night, he traveled, never slowing, or speeding up. K began swimming in ever-widening circles.

The taste of whale waste entered his senses, minute at first, but stronger as he moved forward. The taste moved out of the warm waters of the Gulf Stream into the cool, surrounding waters. K picked up speed. The whale pod being tracked by the *Challenger Deep* research vessel rose to the surface to rest off Cape Hatteras, North Carolina.

K rose from the ocean floor, intent on taking the smallest target. The birthing mother, sensing imminent danger, rolled in front of her offspring. Plumes of blood sprayed from the gaping wound. K was now in full frenzy, tearing and spinning off huge chunks of blubber and flesh from the dying whale. K ignored the calf that continued to circle its mother.

The *Challenger* floated a thousand yards from the whale pod.

Captain Tooms relieved the third shift pilot, then sat down and began to sip on his morning coffee. *Something is missing*, he thought. He turned his head toward the sonar screen.

"Holy shit, where's the probe light?" He checked the instruments, which were in working order. He immediately called Dr. Tynan, then turned on the floodlights. "Attention, attention, all personnel assigned to whale watch report to the deck immediately."

Cindy burst onto the bridge. "What happened?"

"We lost the GPS signal."

"How'd that happen?" asked Cindy.

"I don't know, and without that tag, we can't track the movements of the whale pod properly."

Cindy began to rub her hands together.

"What do we do now, Mr. Tooms?"

"Let's wait for daylight, then we'll begin the search."

Captain Tooms heard the familiar cries of gulls. He and Cindy walked outside to the guardrail and watched as the gulls circled overhead.

"You know what that means?" asked the captain.

Cindy stared into the darkness. She put her hands on her head then over her ears. She uttered the word: "Death."

* * *

The tide had shifted and new sensations from the direction of the beach were now rippling through the outlying ocean waters. K suddenly disgorged the whale meat and began to swim hard toward the beach. K came out of the depths, brushing past horrified swimmers.

A newlywed couple was holding hands in the waist-deep surf. The man slipped his hand underneath the breakers and ran it along his bride's silk-smooth leg.

"Ooh, don't," she squealed, kicking her legs in the water as another breaker washed over them.

"But I like them so," said the husband with a grin.

"I shaved them just this morning. Be gentle, they're still sensitive."

The micro-abrasions on the woman's freshly shaven legs released human blood products that were hard-wired to the predator's very being. The woman was ripped from her husband's arm and dragged through the surf, leaving behind a scene of panic and mayhem in the wake.

* * *

The *Challenger Deep* had hoisted anchors at first light and followed the bloodline to its source. Cindy stood at the rail with a photograph in her hand. The carcass rolled slightly, giving the researcher a good view of its head.

"That's the birthing mother! But where the hell is Joides?"

Captain Tooms, who was standing nearby, walked up and down the rail telling the crew to be on the lookout for the calf. He returned to Cindy, who was staring out into the ocean and tapped her on the shoulder. Gloom and loss were written all over her face.

"What happened, Mr. Tooms?"

"I'm not sure, but I suspect the whale was struck by a ship's propeller."

"No, that's not it," replied Cindy. "A propeller would have made slice marks. This whale had huge plugs of blubber and meat torn from its body."

"What's our next move?" asked the captain.

"Move. Yes, we must move forward. Ready the workboat. Make sure the crew has life jackets and radios. Captain, where is the whale pod located?"

The captain scratched his whiskered chin. "Last time I looked, they were on the edge of the sonar screen."

Cindy grabbed his forearm. "Captain Tooms, it's imperative that we track the pod to their feeding grounds. Make a heading for the whale pod after we lower the workboat. Make sure the whale pod remains on the sonar screen at all times."

* * *

After all was readied, the workboat was lowered into the crimson ocean, then headed for the carcass. A flock of gulls rose from the whale, screaming in protest as the intruders approached. Two crewmen positioned themselves, one at the bow, the other at the stern. When the workboat drifted against the carcass, sharp hooks were thrust into the blubber, then quickly tied off with ropes.

Cindy took a couple of photographs, then stood up with her workbag draped over her shoulder. She unexpectedly climbed on the railing, then jumped into one of the gaping wounds.

"Where's she going?" asked one of the crew members.

"Hey, Doc," said another.

Cindy just waved back. Immediately she felt something warm flow into her boots. It must be blood, she thought, without looking down. She began to bounce up and down, as on a trampoline.

"Hey, Doc," yelled one of the crewmen, "you're standing on the whale's guts." He then threw her a rope. "Tie yourself off. We don't want to lose you in the whale's stomach."

Cindy dutifully tied the rope around her waist. She removed a measuring tape from her bag, then stretched it to the far side of the bite mark. *What the hell could have caused such carnage?* she thought. The bloodied tape was retrieved and dropped into the bag. She then removed a plastic bag with a scalpel inside. Cindy began removing samples, then stopped momentarily.

She slipped her hand into one of the slash marks that lined the perimeter of the incision. She withdrew her bloodied hand and looked at it. *Where did I see a tooth mark like this before?* she thought.

A yell came from the workboat, "Hey, Doc, something is swimming around the whale's head!"

Cindy's heart began to pound. "Is it the attacker?" she asked.

"Not sure," came the reply. "You better come out of there."

Crew members tightened up on the rope as Cindy bounced across the whale's bladder to the safety of the boat. The tie-down hooks were removed from the blubber. The crewmen rowed the boat around the other side of the whale.

Cindy was the first to see him. Her heart leapt for joy.

"Joides is alive!" she shouted.

There before her was the calf, nuzzling its dead mother.

"Do you want the whale tagged, Doc?"

"No, he is attached to his mother. Row away from the whale, then start your engine.

Head for the *Challenger*. We'll tag one of the whales it's been tracking."

After the tagging operation was complete, the workboat returned to the *Challenger Deep*.

* * *

Dr. Tynan sat at her desk, staring at her bloodstained hands. She picked up the phone and called Tom.

"EPA Chamberlain here."

"Tom, we've had a whale kill!"

"Was a Naval ship involved?"

"No, no, it wasn't anything like that. The whale was killed by a shark." Tears began to well up in Cindy's eyes. "The bite marks were ten feet across."

Tom's stomach muscles began to tighten up. Memories of the lost Marine under his command entered his mind. "How big did you say the bite was?"

"It was bigger!" replied Cindy.

"Than what?"

"Than anything," Cindy said, sniffling. "Than anything known."

Tom's head began to pound. "The only shark species with a jaw spread like that would be King Carcharodon. That begs the question: could the attacker be K?"

"I don't know, but one thing's certain. If the attacks continue, the whale pod we are tracking will be decimated."

"What are you going to do with the dead whale?"

"Oh, that's only half the problem. The dead whale has given birth to a calf who won't

leave her side."

"What is your present location?"

"We are off Cape Hatteras. I can see the beach."

"You're not far from Norfolk Naval Base. I'll send a tug down there to retrieve the whale. Do you think the calf will remain with its birth mother?"

"I don't know," said Cindy. "But we'll have to take that chance. Tom, I have contacts with the Boston Aquarium. They would need permission to enter the base."

"Not a problem."

"Oh, one more thing. I'm going to accompany the tug to the base."

"Fine," replied Tom. "I'll be waiting for you there. Look, I gotta get moving on this. See you soon."

Cindy leaned back in her chair and began to rock. *Tom would do anything for me. He must love me.*

* * *

Chamberlain made a few calls, then he walked down the hall to Admiral Farragut's office.

"Good morning, Mary, is the admiral busy?"

"Let me check." Mary tapped on the adjoining door. Hearing nothing, she poked her head inside. She then motioned for Tom to enter.

The admiral sat at his desk, waving his arms. "Come on in, Tom, and have a seat. What can I do for you today?"

"Well, sir, I would like to update you on an old problem that has resurfaced. It appears that our tagged shark, which escaped from Kings Bay, has killed a whale off Hatteras Sound."

"What do you propose to do?" asked Farragut.

"I'm sending a Navy tug to retrieve the whale and tow it back for analysis."

The admiral picked up a pencil and began to tap the eraser on the desktop. "Tom, I'm concerned."

"About what, Admiral?"

"That tag. It must be retrieved at all costs. Our relationship with most of the environmental groups is very good at this time. I don't want that relationship soured by some creature from the past."

"I'm on it, sir."

The admiral reached out and shook Tom's hand. "Good luck with your mission."

* * *

Chamberlain returned to his office and called Cindy. "The tug is on the way."

"Good. The whale pod hasn't moved and we're still in view of the dead whale. Tom, could you have the tug pick me up at the research ship? I want to keep an eye on Joides. Oh, and before I forget, we received a pan-pan call from the Coast Guard station at New Bern. They advised to be on the lookout for a girl that was attacked in the surf by a large shark, then dragged out to sea."

"I'll have to check that out," said Tom.

"Do you think that this species of shark poses a major threat to coastal communities?"

"The tenacity of K and his kind for human blood cells is likened to our love for sugar. It is my theory that the intrusion of human waste and blood products into the Florida aquifer made this species what it is today. K has no fear of humans. He enjoys our taste."

Cindy shook her head. "It figures that we humans had something to do with this carnage that has visited us," she opined. "Keep in touch, and stay safe."

They slowly hung up.

Chamberlain sat at his desk and thought, *No other species could have caused such huge bite marks.* Tom picked up the phone and called Information.

"Yes, I'd like the number for the New Bern Sheriff's Department, North Carolina."

He copied the number on a piece of scratch paper, then dialed New Bern.

"Sheriff's Department, Corporal Hunt here."

"My name is Chad Rumsfeld, a reporter for the Washington Post. I would like an update on the attack on the beach."

"Not another one!"

"What do you mean, sir?"

"You're the fifth reporter to call here on that case."

"Were there any eyewitnesses to the attack?" asked Chamberlain.

"A few," replied the corporal. "One of the local surf fishermen told me that the shark had a head the size of a Volkswagen. Swallowed her whole, he said. You know, fishermen tend to stretch the truth a little."

"Has the victim been found?"

"Nope, seems like she was swept clear off the earth."

"Thank you for the update."

Tom hung up the phone. He was now convinced that K was the attacker.

Tom picked up the Pentagon directory. Paging through it, he found the man he was looking for: Captain John Dewey; a man who knew how to keep his mouth shut.

Dewey was looking out the window when the phone rang. He slowly walked over to the phone and picked up the receiver. "Dewey here."

"My name is Captain Thomas Chamberlain. I work for Admiral Farragut. You and I worked together on the Kings Bay recovery operation. You were the skipper of the *Glomar Explorer*."

"Yes, sir," said Dewey. "Go on."

"I need you as a team leader. Your mission will be to retrieve a tag from a rogue shark that had escaped Kings Bay."

"What kind of ship are you gonna give me?" asked Dewey.

"Sir, this will be a mobile operation. No need for a large ship. You will have the authority to use a wide range of equipment and manpower for this operation."

"Well, it will do me good to get out of this stuffy office and back to sea. Say, how big is that shark?"

"About the size of a whale," said Chamberlain.

"That big? I guess at the top of my shopping list will be a harpoon with an exploding head."

* * *

Late that evening, Chamberlain stood pier side at Norfolk Naval Base with Mrs. Van Horn, a representative of Friends of Whales.

"Sir, our organization is eternally grateful for your help in this rescue operation."

"All the credit should go to Dr. Cindy Tynan," replied Chamberlain.

"Yes, I don't know what we'd do without her." Mrs. Van Horn began to rub her shoulders. "My, it gets chilly down here at night."

"Why don't you warm up in the car until the tugboat arrives?" Chamberlain motioned to the duty driver to open the door.

Chamberlain then walked over to the foreman, who was directing the rigging gang.

"How's everything going?"

The foreman turned. "Just fine, sir. How many whales are we gonna hoist out of here?"

"Just one. It weighs about five tons."

The foreman bent down and fingered and shook the netting. "This hemp will hold twenty tons."

"Good," replied Chamberlain. "Oh, we have a large dead whale coming in also. Tie it off to the piling and cover it with tarps."

The foreman's radio began to crackle. He pulled it out of the holster. "Repeat the last transmission."

"The tug has entered the base."

The foreman looked skyward. "Hey you!" he yelled, getting the crane operator's attention. The foreman raised his arm, then turned his hand in a circular motion. The net slowly lifted off the deck and away from the pier.

"If I may ask, sir, where's that live whale headed?" asked the foreman.

"The whale's headed for the New England Aquarium. If anybody can save him, they can."

The foreman pointed to the tractor-trailer sitting under the crane. "Sir, I ain't never seen a tank truck like that."

"You'll probably never see one like it again. It was specifically designed to transport large sea animals. The tank is filled with temperature-controlled seawater. Aerators ensure an adequate supply of oxygen."

A toot from an air horn alerted everyone to the oncoming tug. Chamberlain and the rigger foreman walked to the edge of the pier.

"I suggest you make the rescue away from the pier," said Chamberlain. "I don't want the calf crushed against the piling."

"Yes, sir," replied the foreman.

Chamberlain's eyes locked on the tug, trying to get a glimpse of Cindy. He didn't notice the crane swinging the precious cargo over his head. His thoughts were only of Cindy. The tugboat drifted toward the pier. Tom spotted Cindy standing at the rail. He waved frantically, getting her attention.

The mooring lines were cast onto the pier, but before the tug touched the pier, Tom jumped onto the deck. He slid, but Cindy caught his fall.

"Hey, fella, where you going in such a hurry?"

Tom straightened himself up, grabbed Cindy, and hugged her, then quickly regained his demeanor.

"Sir, we're all tied off," said the foreman.

Cindy put her hand on Tom's chest. "Oh, let me say goodbye to Joides."

They climbed onto the pier. Tom followed her to the tanker truck waiting below as she said her goodbyes. She watched as large amounts of air bubbles floated to the surface. Cindy gently placed her hand on Joides' back. Tears streamed down her face.

"You'll be safe now, baby," she said. "Nothing can harm you."

After a few minutes, she climbed down and joined Tom. "I guess Joides will be alright."

Tom put his arm around her. "You did all you could do," he said. "I've made arrangements for the tug to take you back to your ship. I must return to Washington to augment the next phase of the operation."

* * *

That afternoon, the Navy tug caught up with the *Challenger Deep*. A rope ladder was dropped over the side and Cindy climbed up. When she reached the top rail, a strong hand grabbed her forearm.

"I got you, Doc."

"Well, thank you, Captain Tooms."

"How's the whale calf doin'?"

"Fine. Joides is headed for the New England Aquarium. Captain, are we still in contact with the whale pod?"

"Yes, we continue to track the newly tagged whale, which is traveling in a pod of three. We were tracking four, but one of the whales disappeared from the screen."

"You think that another attack has occurred?"

"Can't say, Doc, but I haven't spotted any birds scavenging or blood trails on the ocean."

Cindy began to rub her forehead. "Mr. Tooms, did I ask you about firearms?"

"Yes, we have a rifle and a couple of shotguns on board."

"Bring them up to the deck, please. I want security guards to patrol around the clock. If anyone spots a large shark with dirty teeth, shoot it dead!"

"Yes, ma'am, will do. Oh, before I forget, Lieutenant Chamberlain sent you a message."

Cindy's demeanor lightened.

"He wanted to know if you made it back safely?"

"That's sweet of him. I'll write a reply to him when I get back to my quarters."

CHAPTER THIRTY-ONE

Summer and early fall are the times of the year when tourists flock to the New England coastline to whale watch. Large numbers of humpback, finback, and northern right whales arrive here to partake in the rich harvest of krill, a small shrimp-like creature that numbers in the billions of tons in the world's oceans.

A pod of killer whales that had migrated from the Arctic Circle arrived at the feeding grounds hungry and exhausted. The taste of whale blood excited the pod, drawing them to the whale carcass. The killers fed heavily, filling their gullets. They drifted away with the current, waiting for their strength to return.

The *Challenger Deep* came upon the stripped carcass shortly thereafter. Dr. Tynan measured the bite marks. Some were identical to those of the first kill, but she also found many peg-like holes throughout the body. Cindy returned to the ship, then made a call.

"EPA, Chamberlain..."

"Tom, my whales are being decimated!" Cindy launched right in. "My research project is coming to a sad end, and I don't have the power to stop it. What's worse, killer whales have joined in the attacks."

"What makes you think killer whales had anything to do with it?"

"The whale's tongue was ripped from its mouth. You know, Tom, I never thought that I would hate predators, but that's what's happening to me. I'm full of hatred."

"What's your present position?"

"North of Montauk, Long Island."

"Cindy, you must trust that I will put an end to this carnage."

"I do," replied Cindy.

* * *

A meeting was held the following morning at Norfolk Naval Base. Chamberlain introduced himself and the operations officer, Captain John Dewey, to the seven-member Navy SEAL team, led by Petty Officer Townsend.

"Gentlemen, let me start by saying that this mission is classified. Only those with a need to know will be informed of our movements. The goal of this mission is to retrieve a Navy tag much like this one." Chamberlain passed the tag to Dewey, who passed it to the SEAL leader. Chamberlain then picked up a photo from the desk, then passed it on. When all in the room had looked at the photo, Chamberlain said, "This is the rogue shark we seek."

After moments of silence, the SEAL leader raised his hand.

"Yes, you have a question?"

"Sir, this shark has black teeth. Did he bite into an offshore electric cable?"

Chamberlain smiled. "No, the tooth shading is genetic," he said. You may note that the size of this shark is nearly forty feet. That's nearly twice the size of the largest known white tip shark. If you have no other questions of me, I will refer you to Captain Dewey."

Townsend raised his hand. "Sir, are we bringing the carcass back with us?"

"Yes," said Dewey. "We will be outfitted with an oceangoing tug and barge. Bolted to the deck will be a harpoon gun with exploding heads. If the carcass begins to sink, we will haul it in with the tethered rope."

That afternoon, a helicopter left Norfolk Naval Base and arrived early that evening at the Navy's fast attack submarine squadron located at Groton, Connecticut. Captain Dewey was first to disembark and was met by an old-time friend.

"How are you doing, John?" asked the base commander, John Sigenthooli.

"Not good, Sig. I've been trapped inside the office for too long. Ah! It'll feel good to get back out to sea."

"Yeah, well, what are you doing up here?" inquired the base commander.

"Training exercises," replied Dewey with a wink.

Chamberlain joined the officers and was introduced.

Captain Sigenthooli watched as men with close-cropped hair and wearing full field packs disembarked from the chopper and were escorted to the enlisted men's mess hall. Captain Sigenthooli reached into his shirt pocket, opened up a folded document, and began to read the requisition orders for the mission: *Sea Link Alfa Operation.*

"Let's see. The Pentagon requested that my command provide you with the following: a one-hundred-foot barge with electric hoist, one seagoing tug, and crew—here's a good one, John—one deck-mounted harpoon, one fifty-caliber machine gun, and one crate of intermediate-depth charges."

The base commander began to refold the orders.

"Sig, before you put that list away, write down one fast attack submarine."

The base commander smiled and then said, " Now you're dreaming. Come on, let's discuss this operation over dinner."

"Fine idea," replied Dewey. "What's the special tonight?"

"Shark!" replied the base commander with a hearty laugh. He then patted Dewey on the back. "Do you think that anything escapes my attention on this base?"

* * *

While eating dinner, the base commander's curiosity got the best of him.

"John, what really happened during that retrieval operation out in the Pacific when you skippered the *Glomar Explorer?*"

John's eyes narrowed slightly. "You know, all information on that subject is classified."

"Yes," said the base commander. "The best kind of gossip is the top secret kind."

"That though is on a need—"

"I have a need to know, John,"

Captain Dewey smiled and said, "I can give you a brief overview of the operation, but no more."

Sigenthooli nodded in agreement, which is all he could do.

Dewey took a sip of coffee and then leaned back in his chair. "We arrived on location northwest of Hawaii on June 25, 1974. We could have started the operation on that date, but the CIA operative wanted to wait until the 4th of July. He reasoned that if we were successful, the event would be cause for celebration someday. On July 4th, we cast a clam bucket more than sixteen thousand feet down to the bottom of the Pacific Ocean and latched onto the K-129 Soviet submarine that went down March of '68. We hoisted her into the belly of the *Glomar Explorer* and steamed the hell out of there."

"Did you recover any bodies?" asked Chamberlain.

"We recovered most of them but kept only six."

"Why only six?" asked Dewey.

"Protocol, pure and simple. We filmed the funeral inside the *Glomar Explorer*, placed the bodies in Conex boxes, and dropped them into the sea just off Hawaii."

"That's an amazing story, John. Now, Mr. Chamberlain, what light can you shed on the *Sea Link Alpha Operation*?"

"Well, sir, information on this subject is on a need-to-know basis."

Chamberlain noticed the base commander's aggravation. "But you, sir, have a need to know," Chamberlain said.

"Lieutenant Chamberlain, why are you targeting a specific shark?"

"Sir, when the base at Kings Bay was first excavated, we retrieved a species of shark that was thought to have been extinct. The problem with this shark is that it is a documented man-killer. So we tagged him to track him. My job is to retrieve that tag if possible."

"I see," said the base commander. "The Navy has a potential public relations problem."

"Yes, that's it, in a nutshell," replied Chamberlain.

"How are you going to locate him?"

"He's been targeting a pod of migrating whales. I hope to be there when he makes his next kill."

CHAPTER THIRTY-TWO

Captain Dewey stood on the deck of the seagoing tug whittling a piece of wood. He watched as Chamberlain walked up the bow towards him.

"How're things going?" hollered Chamberlain as he approached. "We ready to shove off?"

"Yes, sir. We're just doing some last-minute maintenance checks."

"Good!" replied Chamberlain. "I just received a call from the *Challenger Deep*, and there's been another kill."

Dewey stopped whittling and pointed his knife to the east. "See those clouds forming? We're in for a nor'easter. Do you want to wait it out here, or head into the storm?"

"We sail today," replied Chamberlain.

* * *

Gale force winds and crashing waves enveloped the *Challenger Deep* like a cork in a bathtub. All hopes of tracking the whale pod were put on hold. K drifted with a recent kill, unconcerned with the roiling waves crashing down on him.

The following morning, the seas began to calm. The sun began to warm the ocean's surface. A seagull appeared over the carcass and began to circle slowly, much like a vulture over roadkill. Soon gulls from all directions arrived at the kill site. Their cries of delight disturbed the early morning silence.

K rose to the ocean surface and watched as the ravenous birds fed. K's nervous system became agitated. He swam around the carcass, looking for a would-be intruder. The ocean current alerted him to the presence of an ancient antagonist. K waited with jaws agape. His senses centered on the many squeals and chirps of the incoming sea creatures. K had time to drift off, but retreat was not in his makeup. His kind was ordained to reign over all other denizens of the deep.

Many black dorsal fins cut through the ocean surface, headed toward the whale carcass. A large male orca, weighing eight tons, led the pod. He intended to charge in and disperse any scavengers, giving freedom to the rest of the pod members to safely feast. The alpha male paused, unsure of the creature before him. K interpreted this wariness as a sign of weakness and thrust his body forward, encasing the orca's head within his jaws. Black stone-like teeth pierced the skull, killing the orca instantly.

K's large yellow eyes watched as black and white forms rapidly passed his view. Pain surged through K's body. A large tear was made in K's stomach, exposing his guts. The orca's peg-like teeth had done their job. Suddenly, a small female came towards K at lightning-fast speed, slashing him on the face, taking out his left eye. The rogue propelled himself through the circle of death and disappeared into a cloud of blood and entrails. The orca pod did not pursue but began to tear at the whale carcass.

K circled the kill site, watching with his remaining eye. Small fish and crabs began to pick and snap at his exposed guts. He turned on the interlopers, smashing broadside into a feeding orca. The orcas resumed their attack in deadly earnest. Multiple black and white forms flashed past K's remaining eye as K was attacked in quick succession. His powerful jaws began to weaken; his hand-sized serrated teeth now failed to penetrate much beyond the killer whales' thick skins. K's time had come, and with a final rush of fury, K swallowed the head of an attacking orca, his teeth holding onto his final victim, still wedged into his gaping jaws, shaking and thrashing from side to side. The attack on K continued mercilessly until the orca pod sensed their adversary had succumbed. The most fearless sea creature on Earth now floated on the ocean surface, its jaws locked in death with its ancient adversary. The remaining orcas, sensing their losses, slowly drifted away from the kill site.

A Navy search plane spotted a dark stain coursing across the ocean surface and reported the coordinates to the operations tug. Captain Dewey directed the pilot to increase speed to full throttle. All personnel were ordered to their duty stations.

Chamberlain walked up behind the harpoon man, who was busy aligning the crosshairs on the ocean before him.

"I see him, I see him! Permission to fire harpoon?"

The SEAL team leader, who was standing nearby, raised his hand, signaling the pilot to reverse the tug's engines. "Lock and load your weapons." A series of metallic clicks could be heard around the tug.

The harpoon man released the safety. "Sir, I'm on target. Request permission to fire."

"Request denied," said Townsend.

Chamberlain raised a pair of binoculars to his eyes. He then adjusted the lens. "There's a pair of humps out there," he said., "One of them is a shark. They're not swimming, just drifting with the tide."

"Can I fire on them?" asked the harpoon man.

"No," said Chamberlain. "You may destroy too much flesh."

What a bummer, thought the harpoon man.

"Officer Townsend, have your men clear their weapons. We're going to concentrate on hoisting the carcasses onto the barge."

"Clear all weapons. Man the grappling hooks."

Chamberlain, with a canvas bag draped over his shoulder, joined Dewey on board the barge.

Dewey shook his head. "I'll tell you one thing, Tom, in all my years at sea, I ain't never seen anything like this before. A giant shark and killer whale locked in a dance of death."

The men watched as the winch operator released heavy wire from the drum. The crew members dragged the end across the deck, then looped the shackled end around K's skull. The signal was given to hoist. The carcasses slowly came up on sets of rollers that extended to the other side of the barge.

Chamberlain walked over to Townsend, who was busy securing the sea gate. "Townsend, I'll need a ladder over here. When my work is completed, cover the carcasses with tarps." He pointed skyward. "We don't want anyone taking photos."

"Yes, sir, will do."

Chamberlain and Dewey stood in silence as K rolled past them. His large yellow eye seemed to be watching them.

A crew member arrived with a ladder. "Where to, sir?"

"Lean it against the shark," said Chamberlain.

"I'll hold the bottom for you," said Dewey.

Chamberlain put on a pair of surgical gloves then climbed up the ladder. He ran his hand back and forth across the sandpaper-like skin. "Ouch, you son of a bitch."

Dewey began to laugh. "I thought he was dead."

Chamberlain ignored the remark and the blood seeping into his glove. He gently ran his finger over the skin surface. Feeling something sharp, he probed the object with his fingernail. *That's it*, he thought. *The flesh must have grown over the tag.* He retrieved a pointed scalpel from his bag, then poked a hole into the skin, making a circular cut. Subsequent cuts loosened a plug of flesh from the shark's back. He climbed down the ladder with the prize in his hand.

"So that's what we've been looking for?"

"I sure hope so," replied Chamberlain. "John, clear the cooks from the mess hall, I gotta clean this up."

Chamberlain then went to work. He washed the blood from the flesh, then laid it on the drainboard. He then picked up a large butcher knife. Successive passes of the blade released the tag from its entombment. The only letter visible was the letter *K*.

"John, John, this is it." He walked briskly over to Dewey, who was guarding the door. He placed the tag into his hand. "John, make sure Admiral Farragut gets this tag. I'm going to get cleaned up."

The tugboat headed northwest. After an hour's travel, she came alongside the *Challenger Deep*. A rope ladder was cast over. Its end landed on the tug's deck. Chamberlain grabbed the rungs and began to climb. When he reached the top, a strong hand grabbed his wrist, helping him onto the deck.

"So we meet again," said Cindy with a smile on her face.

"I hope it's forever," replied Tom.

Captain Tooms, who was standing nearby, pointed to the tug, which was now steaming away. "Hey, Tom, you missed the boat."

"Oh well, Tom, I guess that you'll have to sleep in my berth tonight."

Cindy raised her hands to her heart, flashing a beaming smile. Tooms nodded in agreement and watched as the couple walked hand in hand towards her quarters.

Darkness fell as the seagoing tug and barge headed south towards Norfolk Naval Base. Captain Dewey fell asleep at his desk while finishing a report. A rolling wave smashed against the port side of the tug, sending Dewey to the floor.

Dewey woke up in a daze. "Holy shit, the barge must have broken free."

He got up and ran out the door. To his relief, the tie-downs connecting the tug to the barge were secure. Dewey returned to his bunk. He began to laugh. "This is one story that will never be told." He reached over and turned out the light.

A thousand miles south of Dewey's position, a desk light was switched on in Snoop's room. He took a sip of corn liquor, then adjusted his headset. While waiting for police and fire reports, he reached into his desk drawer and brought out his ledger book, and began to underline his most memorable reports.

EPILOGUE

The submarine spring located at coordinates 82 degrees 18.2' west by 24 degrees 14.0' north were discovered by the research vessel NR-1 in October 1994. In 1998, the author, John Lahm, contacted the US Advisory Committee of Undersea Features requesting that the submarine spring discovered by the NR-1 be named the NR-1 Hole. In April of 2002, approval was given to include the NR-1 Hole on all NOAA ocean charts.

This story is dedicated to Dr. Fran Kohut, a member of Woods Hole Geological Survey, and Dr. Lewis Land, who was aboard the NR-1 submarine during its 1994 survey of submarine springs off the east coast of Florida.

To
Madison
Yours Truly
John J. Lahm

Made in the USA
Middletown, DE
29 April 2021

37978352R00156